To Pam –
Hope you
enjoy!
You are a ray
of Sunshine!
Love
Marie Hillegas

The Canine Handler

PAYBACK

M.C.
HILLEGAS

Cover art by Garrett Hillegas
Topographical map courtesy of SARTopo.com

ISBN 13: 978-1-942430-36-0
ISBN 10: 1-942430-36-1

Year of the Book
135 Glen Avenue
Glen Rock, Pennsylvania

This book is dedicated to all First Responders.
For all you do "So That Others May Live."

In Memory of Maci
Beloved partner and family member (1999-2012)

You always made me look like a rock star.

Certified in Wilderness: Search and Rescue Dogs of Maryland / American Rescue Dog Association

Certified in Human Remains Detection: National Narcotic Detection Dog Association

Beneath the Fray

Underneath thin layers that bind our soul,
Creep malicious judgments dreadful yet bold.
Unwarned targets stand naively at bay,
Unaware of what might slither their way.

Murderous thoughts, malevolent not mild,
Without reins, silently galloping wild.
Among dark shadows where they lay,
Vengeance planned for another day.

Dispatch, disposal, death now is at hand.
Brutal, disastrous, from this tortured band.
Discreet, hovering, like a bird of prey,
Watching, admiring departed decay.

Satisfied with the finished piece,
Woeful mind can finally cease.
Hides away, never can she stay,
Finally content, the debt is paid.

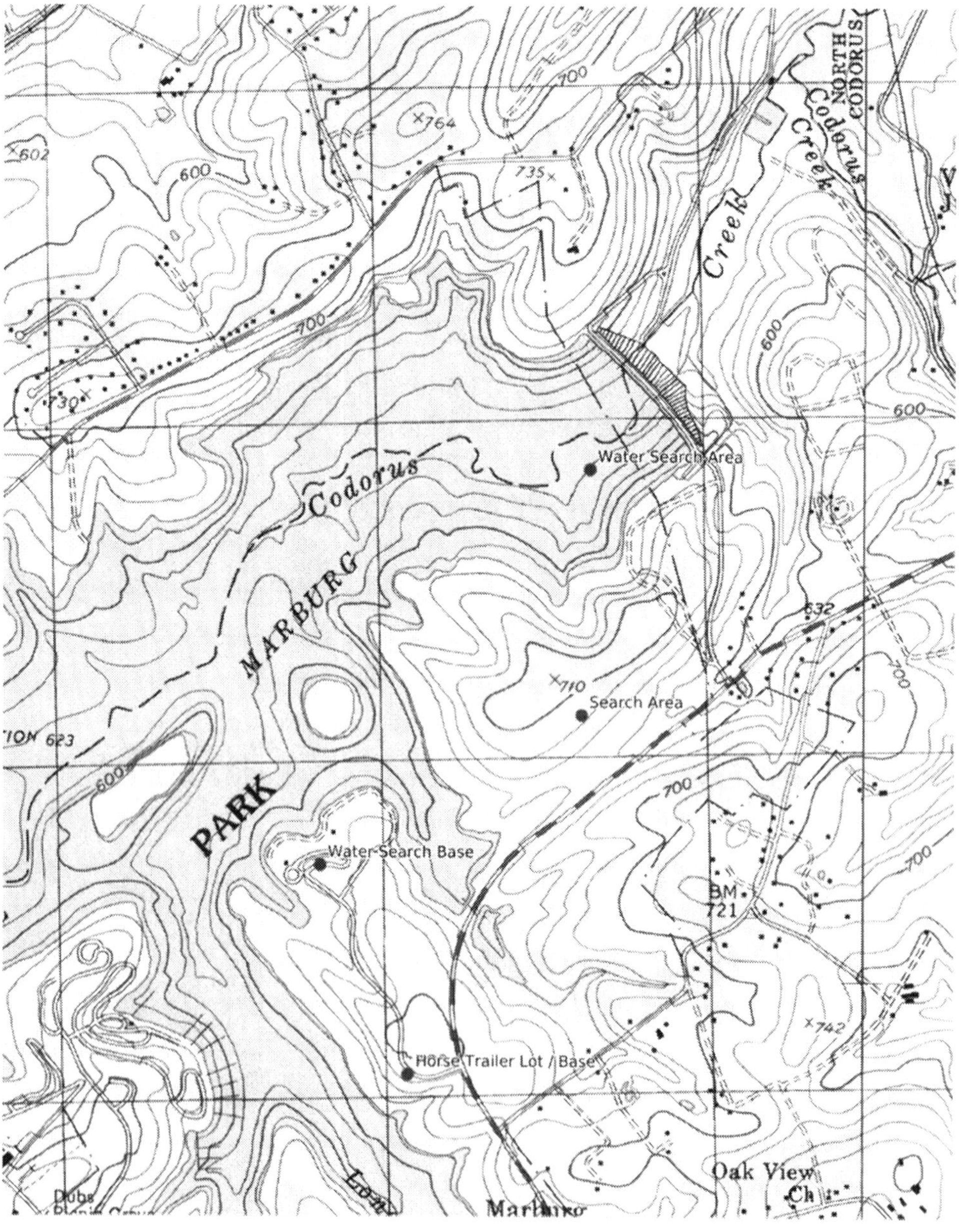

Water Search Area
Search Area
Water Search Base
Horse Trailer Lot / Base
Codorus
Creek
MARBURG
PARK
NORTH CODORUS
Codorus Creek
Oak View
BM 721

Prologue

The vacant fishing skiff floated gracefully on the quiet waters of Lake Marburg. Slowly, it made headway toward the earth-filled dam that blocked Codorus Creek. The small motor sputtered as it sustained its neutral position. A fishing pole lay limp and unused in the hull. Birds hidden among the brightly colored leaves of trees lining the shore called as the late autumn sun peeked over the lengthy concrete barrier. A peaceful calm radiated despite what may have transpired during the early morning hours.

A lone hiker made his way from the soggy trail to the edge of the shore; a sharp reflection caught his attention. The intense eastern rays stung his eyes as he peered out across the lake. He spotted a boat that bumped and bounced softly along the dam's wall. Squinting, he wanted to make sure the small boat was unmanned before alerting authorities. Convinced there wasn't anyone operating the vessel, he decided to report it. *Hopefully, the boat just got away and the owner was along the shore somewhere*, he thought optimistically. If they had fallen into the spring-fed waters of the lake, there'd be little chance for survival before hypothermia set in...

CHAPTER 1

Sarah

Sarah jogged along the damp trail that embraced the lake. Overcast skies cast a gloomy gray setting. She swore under her breath as she trudged through the misty air. Her scalp was wet from the humidity and perspiration. Sweat ran down her forehead and into her eyes. They burned from the salty mix. She swiped her hand across a damp brow. It alleviated the sweat from her vision momentarily.

"Son of a bitch," she murmured under her breath. She wiped her hand on her shorts as she moved along. *Lovely weather,* she contemplated with sarcasm and continued to push forward. *At least the wet weather is supposed to move out soon. The forecaster promised an autumn change for the better,* she remembered. The thought gave her a little inspiration as she sprinted up the last hill.

Topping the peak, she noticed a sole figure perched on the concrete bench overlooking the lake. It appeared to be a man. *Great!* Her thoughts automatically turned to protection mode. His hoody was pulled tight over his forehead, throwing his face into shadow. It gave him an ominous look.

Sarah wasn't startled though. She would often see hikers sitting at the bench taking a break and enjoying the view. A hitching post stood beside the bench where horseback riders could tie horses, or cyclists might rest their bikes. This was a normal stopping point, halfway on the main trail which wound through the forest and around the lake. *But a man with a hoody in this weather, at this time a day? What's he hiding?* It didn't feel right.

Something seemed remotely familiar about the man when she moved past him. Her heart skipped a beat as she peered at him peripherally. She had a sinking feeling in her stomach. Several hairs rose up on the back of her neck. *Breathe deep,* she told herself, trying to calm her body's reaction. Sarah pushed on harder to put distance between her and the seated figure. She thought it was someone she used to know.

Convinced it couldn't be who she thought it was, that it wasn't possible, Sarah dialed back her tempo and continued on at a jog. She headed toward a meadow that would drop her back onto the asphalt a few miles away from home.

Sarah liked to run. It kept her physically fit, but it also helped her decompress, relieving built-up tension that accumulated in her life.

The stresses of her daily situation were catching up to her. She had been working diligently for the last several years between a full-time position with the county and going to school. Finally, all the hard work was paying off. Graduating near the top of her class with a B.S. in criminal science, her dream of entering the FBI Academy might actually become a reality. Sarah had done well on the examinations so far and hoped to be one of the 900 accepted out of nearly 50,000 who applied each year.

In the next few weeks, she would take the last two tests required by the academy. Sarah thought they were the toughest out of all of them: the physical fitness assessment and the psychological evaluation. The first one she knew how to prepare for, but not so much the latter. *I've seen more in my 24 years than most people will ever see in their lifetime. I think that qualifies me more than anything.* Her mind raced as she thought back to her upbringing in the foster care system. *Nothing will stand in my way.* Sarah was determined that no matter what, she was going to make this work.

Thankful her workout was almost done, she began her cool down and pondered plans for what was left of the day. Her dogs still needed to be worked and fed. Obedience training was on the schedule. *They ought to be brushed and have their nails trimmed as well,* she realized as she remembered how their summer coats were starting to shed and be replaced by a denser winter coat. These were responsibilities she deeply enjoyed. She started a mental checklist as she walked the last quarter-mile home. Time management was always a challenge and there was much to do before she had to return to work later that night.

CHAPTER 2

Eva

Cracking and yawning, the old house reacted to the changing season. Autumn whispered lightly on the gentle breeze that wound its way through a stand of trees surrounding the old structure. The house had settled years ago and though solidly built, still creaked and grumbled with flexing temperatures. As evening drew closer, a chill and recent heavy rainfall took effect on the integrity of the foundation. It was as though nature and the house were having a private conversation. The dwelling radiated a character all its own.

Eva listened to the old house's responses to the creeping of the cooler wet weather. Thoughts, schemes skirted through her determined head. She sat un-moving, transparent, as though she was just another piece of furniture. Blending in to her surroundings and not drawing attention was important to Eva; she was just part of the graying background. Calculating that the timing was right, she contemplated her next move.

Now that the occasion had finally arrived, allowing her to put her conceived strategy in motion, it was time to take action. It had been what she considered an eternity of waiting, but in fact, was only a handful of years. Remaining in the shadows fully aware that someday there would be a perfect opportunity, Eva had bid her time. Keeping patient and maintaining her silence were crucial. She knew her moment was coming. The mere thought allowed her to stay quiet and under complete control while she waited mutely. Nothing would get in her way now that the occasion had come. She wasn't about to let anything—or anyone—block her.

Conniving, she formed a flawless plan in her mind, a deserving plan. But still she couldn't force it. Timing was everything. She had to move forward cautiously with considered actions. Finally, she could repay debts long overdue.

Eva treaded lightly in stocking feet. Moving with careful and deliberate steps, she made sure to avoid loose hardwood floorboards to keep them from squeaking with dreaded opinion, revealing her location. She wanted to stay un-evident, anonymous and not disturb her roommate. Although it was already into the late evening, Sarah was still soundly asleep before her nightshift job and Eva tried to keep it that way.

Quietly she crept past her roommate's slightly ajar bedroom door. As she tiptoed past the opening, she peered in just enough to see two large German Shepherds curled up in their sheepskin dog beds against the far wall. Both canines raised their substantial heads and turned to look to the hall where she stood, unmoving and rigid just outside the shadow of the door jam. Sam and Gunner emitted low guttural tones of dislike and uneasiness. She stood frozen and stared at them, lying there in the obscure light of late day which streamed in from a large window above their dog beds. Impressed with their size and regality, she also felt disdain and apprehension for the dogs. She cautiously retreated, stepping back down the hall.

The dogs always seemed to know exactly where she was in the house, regardless of her anticipated movements. The dogs didn't care for Eva. And they made it known. Sometimes they growled and raised a lip at her, exposing large white canines. But mostly they just tried to avoid her at all costs. The dogs seemed perplexed and confused about her, always apprehensive and uneasy in her presence. Eva's feelings were mutual. She was also a little frightened of them. Generally fearful of all dogs, she avoided interacting with them no matter what she had to do to keep her distance.

The end of the short, narrow hallway spilled into a proportionately small kitchen. The diminutive two-bedroom home sat back off the quiet and less traveled Pine Tree Road. A small lawn area at the rear of the house was surrounded by tall, mature trees that backed up to the local state park. There were insignificant trails forged by deer through the park that dropped into the rear yard. On occasion, a handful of deer could be found in the backyard eating acorns from one of the old established oak trees or raiding the bird feeders that hung on shepherd's hooks near the edge of the deck.

Partially opening the side door from the kitchen to the breezeway, she continued to keep her movements slow and contained. She wanted to make sure the old hinges of the heavy wooden door wouldn't groan as she pushed it the rest of the way open. Still trying to be cautious about drawing attention, she kept her actions deliberate and measured. She pushed the screen door gently and leaned out into the breezeway, visually scanning the concrete flooring of the covered space, searching for just the right pair of athletic shoes.

Her eyes finally settled on the pair she was looking for. They were an older, well broken-in pair of Merrill hiking shoes that belonged to her roommate. Both women wore close to the same size and the shoes wouldn't be missed for the short time she intended to borrow them. They were well worn and dirty from hard years of hiking the park's trails. It would be difficult to tell when they were last used.

Walking over to fetch them, Eva took note of the cool air coming through the passageway and inhaled deeply. As she breathed the freshness, she accepted the change of weather as a positive sign of readiness. The earlier thunderstorm had cleared the humidity and left behind clean, crisp, drier air in its place.

She sat down on a well-worn wooden bench placed by the kitchen door just for the sole purpose of putting on and taking off shoes. As she pulled the faded tan hiking shoes on, and tied them precisely, she paid close attention to the time of day and estimated how long before complete darkness settled in. The sun was slowly descending in the western sky. Long shadows already stretched and cast themselves among trees which would make the forested park dimmer and more difficult to navigate. It would also mean the park would soon be empty of most of the daytime hikers, bikers and horseback riders. Park hours were from dawn to dusk; the park was a day-use facility. But that didn't mean the entire daytime park-goers made it out by dusk. Sometimes there were stragglers. She did a few leg stretches to flex her calves and thigh muscles before standing back up.

In the breezeway, she made one more quick check of the contents in the little fanny pack she wore around her waist. She felt satisfied she had exactly what she needed. A quick, wicked smile escaped as deep, dark inner thoughts raced across her increasingly malicious mind. It was time to get moving, daylight was getting short. Eva patted her cropped black hair with the palms of her hands and strode down the breezeway steps from the back of the house.

She crossed over the rear deck and headed across the lawn toward the nearly hidden deer trails leading directly into the park. Starting into the woods, she took one last glance over her shoulder at the back of the house. She was alarmed when she saw their eyes tracking her. The dogs stood rigid, staring intently through the bedroom window. They continued to observe her as she disappeared into the greenery and slipped into the covered forest. As she took off at a slow jog and headed deeper into the park's forest, her thoughts shifted to what may lay ahead. She hoped her opportunity was waiting.

CHAPTER 3

Sarah

A soft hum interrupted the solitude. It was Thursday morning and Sarah was caught somewhere between dreams and reality. She had left the communication center around 0800 hours after finishing third shift. Once arriving home and taking care of Gunner and Sam, she fell into a deep sleep on the living room couch.

Something was pulling her from her slumber. It interrupted her fitful dreams. She was tired, fatigued. It felt like she had just drifted off. Lately, nightmares of the past had reawakened in her dreams. Things she hadn't thought of in years resurfaced and she didn't understand exactly why. Horrible things. Things she wanted to forget.

Could it be her job and some of the awful situations she handled? Many dealt with domestics, abuse, and violence—high pressure situations. Could one of her more stressful calls have triggered the deep, dark memories to come beckoning? Sarah had tried to push her past behind her, but it was always just a breath away. Sometimes a physical scar brought back memories like dirty open wounds, savage and raw.

She didn't want to dwell on it at the moment, and pushed it from her mind. There were other more pressing matters to contend with.

She shifted slightly, and her two faithful German Shepherds heard her stir. They were soon up from where they had been sleeping near her on the cool, hardwood floor. The dogs were by Sarah's side in an instant.

They whined and stretched, looking to Sarah with great anticipation. Gunner, the larger of the two, laid his bulky sable head on the edge of the couch, close enough to let his cold, wet nose rest against the back of her bare arm.

"Gunner!" she spat out, reacting to the surprise of his chilly nose against her bare skin. Gunner sat back on his haunches and looked at her with his best impression of "What'd I do?" She was used to her dogs *pushing* her to move or play, to do anything with them. Both dogs were always on and ready to go.

The annoying humming continued. Finally, Sarah pulled herself from the comfortable confines of the worn sofa and realized her phone was vibrating on the table. She had switched the ringtone off when she had gotten home from work.

Without getting up, she grabbed the phone. Glancing at the screen, she didn't recognize the number as she tapped the talk button.

"Hello," she answered in a groggy, irritated voice.

In response, the caller stated, "Oh hey, Sarah, this is Trooper Dave Graves." She knew right away who it was. He was with the Pennsylvania State Police, liaison for the York County Communication Center.

For hell's sake, Sarah thought to herself. She had only been home from work a few hours. *Was there already something wrong at the communication center?*

Sarah bolted upright to a sitting position, "Oh, hey Trooper Graves, is there something I can help you with?"

"I'm hoping you, or at least your dogs can help."

She knew the trooper professionally. They had attended a few emergency preparedness classes together and chatted, but they were really only acquaintances until a few weeks ago.

Dave had recently been accepted into the canine division. The state outfitted him with a black and tan bloodhound to use for tracking suspects. He had come from a non-dog background, though. He had a lot to learn—not only about scenting, but about dog behavior as well.

He had always been friendly, asking her questions about her German Shepherds, the scent work they did and how her job was going at the 911 center. Dave had made her work station a daily stop on his way out each evening as she headed in for third shift. He peppered her with questions concerning scent training and working canines. He seemed to hold her opinions in more regard than others who also showed interest. Sarah looked forward to their conversations.

Still trying to clear her sluggish head, Sarah apologetically asked him to repeat himself. She grabbed a notepad and pen from the coffee table drawer.

"Sure, we're available. What do you need?"

"Well, we're not quite sure yet. Possible missing person's case."

"Possible? Either you're missing or you're not," Sarah grinned to herself.

"Well, yeah, I know," Dave slowly replied. It was as if he was trying to concentrate on his wording. "A hiker spotted an empty boat early this morning out at Lake Marburg. Boat was caught up along the dam, halfway across the lake with the electric motor still running."

I wonder how long one of those motors will run, Sarah thought. *Maybe something to inquire into.* Her boat experience was limited and she didn't have a great deal of knowledge when it came to their mechanics.

"Do you know who the boat belongs to? Has a cursory inland search been done?" Sarah continued.

"Park rangers are still trying to identify the vehicles in the parking lot with empty boat trailers and are working on finding out who owns the boat. Rangers have also visually checked along the shorelines without success. It's been a few hours since it was found and no one has come to claim it. Right now we have a few agencies responding… local dive team and a small ground-pounder unit. We'd like to get your team out there as well. They're certified for water search, right?"

Sarah cringed at the mention of the local dive team. She recalled that they had been difficult to network with from earlier experience. *Pretentious bastard,* Sarah thought as she remembered her encounter with the dive team's commander. Not a thought she wanted to convey to Dave at the moment.

"Oh yeah, both of my dogs are certified for water recovery as well as a few other handlers and canines on my team." She watched her dogs stretch and yawn continuously as though trying to defuse a tense situation. They watched her from the corners of their eyes. Their behavior perplexed her, but she put it off, thinking they were feeding off her energy. "What's base camp's coordinates?" Sarah asked.

Dave read off the coordinates and Sarah copied them down along with a few additional notes in her waterproof notepad.

"Can I also get a contact number for you and base camp? Once I find out how many team members are available and their ETA, I'll call you back." Dave gave her his cell number as well as that of the lieutenant managing the search.

"Great, Sarah, really appreciate it. Looking forward to hearing back from you soon."

Sarah ended the call. Her mind raced with thoughts of all that needed to be done. Her pulse quickened and her anxiety level pushed higher.

Stop it. Just chill out, she told herself. One deep breath, and Sarah began to make mental notes. First off, she texted her teammates to see who was available. She typed in the code for the deployment, and the search type.

Once Sarah sent the call-out, she began to get herself and her dogs, Gunner and Sam ready. Most of her equipment was already loaded in the truck, so there wouldn't be much to prepare. Most first responders kept their supplies ready and waiting in their vehicles. Right now, she needed to wait on responses from her team.

The reality of it all started to dawn on her. This was the first time she had personally responded to an agency request for the team. Although she had been on numerous past searches in a supporting role, she had never actually deployed with her own dogs. Newly certified, they had only recently passed all of their evaluations.

But we train like we'd been deployed, she thought. She took a deep breath trying to control her excitement and nerves. A lot will be riding on this call-out.

First things first, she thought. She'd only had a couple hours of sleep. *Coffee. Strong coffee.* She filled the brewer to the top with water, doubled up on the grounds and flipped the switch.

The dogs picked up on her heightened anxiety. You could see the energy radiate from Gunner and Sam. The more boisterous of the two German Shepherds, Gunner ran laps between Sarah and the front door. Sliding to a stop, he almost knocked her over. Sam pretty much glued himself to Sarah's side and wouldn't take his attention off her.

"Settle!" she yelled. They both looked at her numbly. "How do you guys even know what's going on?" It was like they could read her mind.

Both Gunner and Sam were search and rescue canines skilled in the art of air-scenting to locate lost people. The public normally referred to them as sniffer dogs. They were certified in wilderness and urban settings to search for live humans. Both dogs were also certified in recovery, or as some handlers classified it, human remains detection. And this past summer they had passed their evaluations in water recovery.

The dogs were obsessed with their noses and scenting. Anything and everything was fair game, even when they were not training or working. At times, it could be embarrassing where they would stick their noses. No place, no area, nothing was off-limits or private that didn't deserve a good sniff.

Sarah thought it might be best to load the dogs in the truck prior to changing into her search uniform. She herded both dogs out the front door.

"Truck," she commanded and they ran to the vehicle and stopped at the tailgate. "Wait." The dogs stood and watched Sarah as she made her way to the back of the truck. Dropping the tailgate, she told both dogs to "hup" and they responded by jumping into the bed of the truck. Two extra-large dog traveling crates were secured just inside the truck bed. The dogs patiently waited while Sarah opened the crate doors. Giving the cue, "Crate," each dog went into his respective crate. She locked and secured the doors behind them.

"You guys are awesome," she lavished them with praise. Leaving the tailgate and hatch of the truck cap open to allow cool air to circulate, Sarah turned and headed back inside the house.

"Okay, my turn," she said out loud, and headed down the short hallway. No pictures or decorations of any sort hung on the walls. The dark wood paneling dated her home. The lack of décor expressed the frugal minimalist in her. No reminders, no pictures of the past, no sentiment of days gone by. The only item that hung on any wall was an unframed mirror above a small table at the end of the hall.

Sarah went to the closet where her team uniform hung. Her phone started to ping with responses from teammates as she pulled her official issued team shirt and BDUs—military type trousers—off the hangers. She would wait to hear from everyone before she called Dave back.

It was the responsibility of each team member to send a return text stating whether they were available or not. They were all civilian volunteers. Never expected to show up to every search or call-out, they still needed to respond regardless. It wouldn't be much longer since most of the team had already sent their reply. As in the past, when she had acted as the dispatcher for her commander for a call-out, it was only a matter of minutes.

The smell of coffee circulated throughout the house. Sarah pulled two travel mugs from her cabinet, and filled one for now and one for later. She liked to be prepared and preferred her own stout homebrew over the usual watered-down crap that was normally offered at a search.

Stepping outside her kitchen door into the breezeway, Sarah covered herself with bug repellent. She stood for a moment to let the spray dry. Gunner and Sam excitedly barked in their crates. She laughed thinking how eager they were to be going out to work.

"Chill out, guys! We'll be heading out soon!" she yelled to the two impatient dogs.

They didn't know the difference between training and actually being deployed on a real search, she contemplated. To them it was all the same. It was a game. They used their noses to locate humans and in return, they got to play enthusiastically with their favorite toy and their handler. What could be better to a couple of extremely high play-driven dogs?

Checking her phone again, she went through the responses on the screen. Texts had come in from everyone. The team commander, as well as two other canine handlers were available and could respond to the search within half an hour. She sent all three a text with an ETA of 1100 hours and the base camp address.

Finding Dave's number, she dialed. He picked up on the first ring.

"Hey Dave, Sarah here." She could hear the commotion of base camp in the background ratcheting up her anxiety another notch.

"What can you provide for us?" Dave asked.

"We can supply five dogs. They can provide shoreline search as well as work off boats. ETA of 1100 hours for all handlers except me—I can be there in 15 minutes."

"Great, we really appreciate it, Sarah. See you soon."

Sarah tied a red bandana around her head in a tri-fold and secured it in the back. It helped to keep her feral curls in place. Next she pulled on her team-issued ball cap with logo and unit number embroidered across the front. She checked herself in the hall mirror. Her hat helped hold her hair in place. Copper-colored curls pulled back, name tag in place, shirt tucked in, she headed out the door.

The reality and excitement of the search hit her. *This is really happening*, she thought. *I hope I'm prepared and ready for this. I know the dogs are.* And then the intense adrenaline kicked in.

Chapter 4

Sarah

With the sun shining in the cloudless sky, Sarah sped down the road toward the state park. After several days of massive thunderstorms, cooler, drier air had replaced the humid, sticky wet weather. A trail of broken branches, downed trees and small flashflood gullies passed by as Sarah made her way toward the entrance. In her rearview mirror, she could see Gunner and Sam looking through the truck's back window. Their eyes were glued to the back of her head. She laughed. They knew they were heading somewhere to run scent problems and they weren't going to take their focus from their handler.

Sarah arrived onto an already hustling and active scene as base camp continued to grow. Other first responder search teams were arriving. Missing person searches seemed to bring everyone out. Even though the state police had jurisdiction over the park area, there looked to be police agencies onsite from every local podunk agency. *Must be a slow morning,* she thought, *nothing else going on in the area.*

As she entered the public marine parking lot, she was stopped by a state trooper managing the traffic congestion. She rolled down the window of her pickup truck and came to a halt. Gunner and Sam instantly broke into a barking frenzy as the officer approached the vehicle.

"You here for the search, I assume?" the trooper asked. "Your guys seem a little excited," he smiled.

"Sorry," Sarah said with a sheepish grin. "Always on the edge of out of control," she laughed. "I'm with the local county search and rescue dog team. There should be three other handlers and their dogs from my organization arriving shortly."

The trooper asked for her identification and contact information, and noted all the details on a clipboard. "Okay, Ms. Gavin, you can head toward the back of the lot if you want to park the dogs furthest away from all the commotion." He pointed in the direction he wanted her to go.

"Sounds perfect, thanks." Sarah pulled her truck forward and headed to the back of the lot. Driving slowly due to all the foot traffic, it gave her time to scan the area and pick out a spot where she could back in near the trees. After she put her truck in park and killed the engine, she sent a text message to her teammates to let them know where she was situated within base camp.

She secretly hoped Kellee would arrive soon. Sarah had always followed Kellee's lead at a search. Thinking back to when they had first met several years ago, she felt it must have been fate. Although Sarah was not religiously dedicated, she did feel grateful and lucky to powers beyond herself and her control. That chance meeting guided her onto a better path in life and gave her hope there were better things in this world... and people who were actually good and kind.

Sarah had been eighteen and fresh out of foster care. Aged out on her birthday, she was put to the curb with her few belongings. Not knowing where to go or who to turn to, she had contacted a woman from a shelter who was a social worker. The woman put her in touch with a few other social workers she thought could help her situation. Although social workers weren't always helpful, one had eventually helped Sarah find cheap housing. She also gave her the information on an open-house and job fair at a county firehouse in which Sarah ended up attending.

From that event, Sarah enrolled in a program for the county's emergency services system and landed a job as an emergency management technician and 911 dispatcher. But most important of all, she met Kellee at the job fair. Kellee was the president of the local canine search and rescue organization that specialized in training German Shepherds for air-scenting to locate missing persons. Kellee had a booth at the job fair for her search team and two of her dogs were there. She had been looking for volunteers to join the team. Sarah, instantly smitten with the dogs, had let her guard down with Kellee.

Sarah joined the team and had spent hours hiding for her other teammates' canines, reveling in the training. She'd become a dedicated and skilled canine handler. She also took the many necessary classes required by NIMS, the National Incident Management System. When she was ready to become a handler herself, Kellee helped Sarah find suitable dogs to train for air-scenting to become her partners in search work.

Gunner and Sam came into her life. Both dogs had a background that mirrored Sarah's turbulent past. They had both been through several homes. Due to their high energy level and excessive play and prey drives, they had been difficult to place in a regular family home environment. Becoming frustrated in their situations, they had become destructive as well. The dogs were still young, and both proved to be perfect candidates for search work. The search training and level of activity kept the dogs satisfied mentally and physically. This kept them happy and balanced. They developed a deep bond with their handler, more than the average dog owner experienced. Sam and Gunner would do anything for Sarah.

Over the past several years, Sarah had opened up to Kellee. Insight into her emotionally and abusive fractured past. Kellee was one of the few people who understood the sins of the foster care system and what Sarah endured. She had come into her life at the right time and helped guide Sarah toward a better path, a better life. Sarah had been a little rough around the edges, but with Kellee's consistent help, support and guidance, Sarah ended up blossoming into a successful adult. With Kellee's assistance and persuasion, she enrolled in a state college program for women and worked toward a degree. She had only needed someone to care about her.

Sarah's jumbled nerves were beginning to expose themselves again. She had never been the first to arrive or the one to speak with the agency running the search. This part was all new to her. Their team had never been called out by this county or agency and there would be much riding on how her team behaved professionally and how their dog teams performed in the field. This search would make or break whether they'd ever get called back as a resource in the future. There was no fixing a wounded relationship with an agency. *Cowgirl up!* she told herself and grabbed the handle to open the truck door.

Stepping out, Sarah quickly surveyed her surroundings. She had backed her truck into a spot near the trees with the nose pointing out toward the lake. She not only wanted her dogs shaded and their vision away from all of the activity, but she wanted a spot that gave her a vantage point to view that activity. It would keep the dogs cooler, calmer and let Sarah keep up with base camp goings on.

There were several vehicles between her and the shoreline. The state police had brought their older, smaller command unit and had situated it near the edge of the lot along the shoreline and tarmac. Beyond the command unit, Sarah could see a small, white fiberglass skiff grounded with a couple state troopers standing nearby. The sun was almost at its peak and the wind was blowing in from the water directly toward Sarah.

She walked to the back of the truck to drop the tailgate and lift the cap. She slid the side windows of the cap open as well to allow air to blow through the dog's crates. Sam and Gunner were still barking. "Hey, guys," Sarah spoke softly to them. The dogs stopped barking for a moment and tilted their dark sable heads at her. She couldn't help smiling at their silly antics. "Just chill out, guys, I'll be right back," she told them and started toward the command center.

The local search and recovery dive team was already on scene gearing up to go out. She had run into this particular team at past searches she'd attended when still a trainee. She remembered them well. This dive team was not fond of the use of canines in water searches. They had new technology. Expensive equipment they believed infallible. They also needed to justify the expense of the unit. Side Scan Sonar (SSR) was finally making it into the hands of smaller run resources. Sarah agreed it was a great resource, but it still didn't take the place—or could compete with a canine's scenting ability—as far as she and her teammates were concerned.

As she approached the command unit she could see a small table set up in front. Dave who had called her earlier was seated there running the sign-in sheet for the first responders.

"Oh hey there, Dave" Sarah said as she drew near. Dave smiled when he saw her.

"Glad you could make it, Sarah. Is the rest of your team here yet?" he asked.

"Not just yet, but they should be pulling in any minute, especially the way some of my teammates drive when they're enroute to a search," she laughed.

"Well, let's get you signed in." Dave handed her a sheet with areas to fill in for herself and the team's information. "You need to talk to the lieutenant coordinating the search when you're finished here. Lieutenant Janet Langenberg is the incident commander and she can brief you on the event so far and talk to you about what kind of assignments work best for you and your dogs."

"Great. Thanks." Sarah finished with the paperwork and handed it back to Dave. She turned around to look at her truck for a quick check. "Hey, can you just keep an eye on my truck and the dogs please? Just while I'm in the command center? I'd really appreciate it."

"No problem. I can watch the truck from here. I won't let anyone go near the dogs."

"Great! Thanks."

Sarah left Dave and the sign-in table behind as she entered the command unit. She had previous brief encounters with the lieutenant through work. Lt. Langenberg had occasionally asked her about the work she did with her dogs and what air-scenting was all about. The lieutenant seemed a little skeptical but she had never seen dogs work. She also didn't understand much about how air-scenting canines performed so she had given Sarah and her dogs the benefit of the doubt.

"Good morning, Sarah. Come in and have a seat," the lieutenant directed when she saw Sarah enter the unit. The lieutenant stood close to six foot, physically fit with small cannons for arms. She was a fair person, but resembled someone you would not want to tangle with if you happened to cross her. Sarah had heard stories from the past of male subordinates trying to pull a fast one on her and getting caught. She had developed a no-nonsense reputation. The lieutenant pointed to an open seat at the table where several maps were laid open.

"Morning," Sarah replied with a nervous smile. "Trooper Graves advised me to check-in with you ASAP," she spat out quickly.

"Great, glad you could make it. What about the rest of your team?" asked the lieutenant.

"Our team's commander and two other handlers with canines certified in water search are on their way. They should be here any moment. We will have five dogs in all and four handlers available to work the search today," Sarah responded.

"Sounds great. Can you describe to me how the dogs can be best utilized in searching for bodies underwater and the most efficient way to task your team today?" the lieutenant continued. "How do they actually locate a drowned subject?" she asked with a hint of skepticism in her voice.

"Sure." Sarah took a deep breath and gathered her thoughts. She hoped her team wasn't on trial today, put under the microscope and having the stress of proving canines were great at this type of job.

Sarah continued, "As with air-scenting on land, canines are scenting rafts or follicles from a human body. People lose millions of these skins rafts every minute of every day. These rafts float on the air currents. In water, the rafts carrying the scent of the human rise to the water's surface and float on the air flow as well. The dogs catch these follicles on the breeze and can follow them to the source. There are also other components such as decomp gases that a body will give off. These vapors float up to the surface and dispense on the wind. The dogs can help pinpoint a drowned victim's location."

Arms crossed and lips pursed, the lieutenant leaned up against the command center's wall as she tried to digest the information. She looked like a formidable creature. Sarah tensed as she watched the lieutenant go through this mental process. Sarah wanted her on board with the use of canines in this type of search situation. Sarah could tell she had reservations regarding canines being able to locate a human body under water.

"They can really follow human scent blowing on the surface of a body of water all the way to where it is emerging from the source underneath?" The lieutenant asked. Sarah could hear a hint of sarcasm in her voice.

"Yes, you'd be amazed at what scents a canine can isolate, identify, and locate with its nose. Dogs have been used successfully to locate specific items such as humans underground as well as underwater for several years. Our dogs have to certify by testing and passing a stringent water evaluation before we are allowed to deploy."

"Explain how this helps in a water recovery search? Once you locate where the drowned subject might possibly be? What next?" The lieutenant continued to pepper Sarah with valuable questions.

"The canines help to make it easier and safer for the recovery divers, so they won't have to be submerged as long. The dogs can narrow down the area which gives a smaller investigation site for the divers to search. Or if a drag is used, they help determine where it should be put in and run. Our dogs can work the shoreline as well as go out in boats to grid areas of the lake," Sarah explained.

"Sounds good in theory. Work with me now. Let's look at the maps of the lake and surrounding areas." Sarah and the lieutenant turned their attention to all of the maps spread out on the small table. Sarah let out a sigh of relief. It seemed like the lieutenant was on board with the canine team. *A small victory.*

"The boat was found here," the lieutenant pointed to an area along the dam on the eastern edge of Lake Marburg. "The park rangers did a quick check along the shores and the parking lots and didn't find anyone missing their boat. The boat registration does not belong to the boat we found so we are still in the process of trying to locate the owner's identity." She pointed to the areas on the map where rangers had checked with the tip of her pencil.

"So in actuality, we have a very large area to cover. How do you want to deploy your team on this type of search?" The lieutenant continued, "What would be the most efficient and effective way to utilize your dog teams?"

Sarah thought about it for a moment. She knew each of her teammates well and how their canines worked. Kellee's partner Meika had just been put back into service after impaling herself on a branch while working a wilderness search a few months ago. That would cut Meika's endurance back so a smaller, inland problem seemed right for her. But Joe and Garrett's dogs were both up to working off search boats for long periods of time. Boat work included less running, but the work itself could be tougher. It required more intense sniffing and keeping their bodies steady. The dogs always seemed to be on the muscle.

"What I would like to do if there are boats and drivers available, is to send two boats out with dogs to grid the water starting from this west point," Sarah pointed to Round Island on the map, "and have them grid east to west from the island to the dam and back. The breeze is currently strong and steady coming from the north. Perhaps have the dogs start from the north shoreline and work their way back to here on the south shoreline."

"Kellee Durham, our team's commander, and I can work the sandy area of the south shoreline. I'll have Kellee and her canine start here working from west to east." Once again Sarah pointed to a cove on the map where there was a public boat ramp, just west of the parking lot. "And I'll work the shoreline as well but from just east of the cove toward the dam heading east. Will this work for you?"

The lieutenant made a quick check to see if there were available boats and drivers. The park rangers confirmed and offered to drive as well. "Okay, sounds like a good plan and we have boats and drivers. How soon can you and your team be ready?"

Sarah had received texts from her teammates while she was involved in the conversation with the lieutenant. "It looks like all the dog teams are here. We can be ready to go in 15 minutes. I just need to brief the team and get my dog's vest on him."

"Sounds great. See you back here in fifteen minutes—1130 hours," the lieutenant stated.

Sarah was out the door and stepped down onto the tarmac. She had found the small confines of the command unit repressive. Taking a deep breath, she congratulated herself on keeping her cool while under pressure. She looked toward her truck and could see her teammates' vehicles parked near hers. She smiled. *Thank god,* she thought.

Taking another deep breath, she slowly exhaled to try to tame the adrenaline which was now sky-rocketing. *We don't have much time*, she realized and quickened her steps. Fifteen minutes wasn't much to brief them on the search, their assignments, get the dogs together and get to the staging area. *I hope everyone is ready to go,* she thought nervously.

CHAPTER 5

Sarah

Sarah gave the team a quick brief of what was known of the search subject so far. *Which isn't much, s*he thought. She made sure everyone had all the information surrounding the event and gave each canine handler their assignment. "We need to be in the staging area in just a few minutes, 1130 hours," she continued, "so get the dogs ready and head over there ASAP."

"Joe, make sure you and Garrett have your PFDs for you and your dogs," Kellee reminded them, "extra water, notepads, pens and GPS in a Ziploc baggie. I'll have my FRS radio on channel 9 if you need to contact me."

Quickly grabbing her smaller pack from the back of the truck, Sarah hiked it up over her shoulder. Since this was a water search and not a wilderness search, she wasn't heading too far from base camp, so she wouldn't need her heavier pack which included all of the survival gear. She checked Sam's water to make sure he had plenty. Sarah would be working Gunner first, leaving Sam confined to his crate. The search assignment was a smaller area that was open and easy to traverse. One dog could cover the area in a quick, efficient manner.

She reached in to unlock Gunner's crate. She held the door closed as he spun around with excitement. "Settle, Gunner," she shouted at him. He stopped for a moment, enough time for Sarah to get his complete attention. "Wait," Sarah said as she opened the crate door. Gunner started to exit his crate but responded to the command and stood just outside it in the back of the pickup truck's bed. Sarah grabbed a leash with collar and snapped it around Gunner's thick neck. Snatching his canvas vest from where it hung along the inside of the truck cap, she slid it over the dog's head and secured Velcro fasteners around the front of his chest and under his belly.

Sam whined in his crate, not accepting the fact he was being left behind. "We'll be back soon," Sarah spoke soothingly, trying to console and calm the dog.

"Off," she commanded Gunner and watched as he jumped down from the bed of the truck. The nervous vibes Sarah projected were not lost on the dogs. Both were having a hard time keeping their energy in check because they were feeding off their handler.

Sarah took Gunner to the edge of the tree line and gave him the command, "Potty." The dog spun around her as far as the length of the leash would allow. She tried to get him to do his business so she could move to the staging area. She was running out of time. She could see the rest of her team already heading that way. "Come on, Gunner! Do your business," she pleaded with him.

As Gunner circled Sarah once again, a strong breeze hit them from the direction of the shoreline rolling in from the lake. Gunner stopped suddenly, closed his mouth and stuck his snout up toward the sky. Sarah studied him for a moment. The dog continued to focus intensely on a scent. *Wonder what's caught his interest?* He was showing body language normally presented when he caught human scent on a search task. The frame of his body rose up taller and his tail flagged. She watched as he stood on hind legs and tried to zone in on the particular scent that had caught his attention. Sarah was puzzled. The parking lot was full of people, but he didn't seem interested in any of them.

"Whatcha got?" Sarah asked Gunner, trying to provoke him to work it out. He whined and strained at the end of the leash. Torn between getting over to the staging area on time or trusting her dog's judgment, she made the quick decision to let him try and work it out. She let Gunner pull her across the parking lot through the stationary vehicles and first responders. He paused fleetingly to check the breeze with his nose to the air, then continued heading toward the shoreline. Her teammates saw her zig-zag through the lot as Gunner dragged her forward. Kellee shot her a questioning gesture but Sarah just shrugged and pointed at Gunner while she continued to let him work it out.

The thought, "Trust your dog," ran through her mind. More than words within the canine working world, it was an aphorism. Some canine handlers have a difficult time allowing their dogs to call the shots. They constantly question their dog when working a scent problem. Sarah learned through all of her and her dogs' training to believe in them and let them do their job.

Sarah looked up and could see Gunner was pulling her in the direction of the shoreline, toward the officers chatting beside the grounded boat. Her team looked on from the staging area beside the command unit. The lieutenant had entered the staging area as well and watched Gunner drag Sarah to the boat area.

Sarah was still in conflict about causing a scene with her dog. This was not part of the plan today, but she felt it was right to let her dog follow up the source of a scent he felt so strong about finding. Reaching the officers next to the boat, Gunner inhaled quickly at each man and started to proceed to the boat.

One officer stepped in front of the dog. "Are you supposed to be working this area?" he asked Sarah.

"No, it wasn't an assigned task, but Gunner picked up an odor he really wanted to find the source of," Sarah explained. "He dragged me from my truck across the lot to here," Sarah pointed back to where her truck was parked.

"Well, I think we had better get permission before you proceed," the officer stated.

Sarah was having a difficult time trying to hold Gunner back. She took hold of his collar in one hand and shortened the leash in her other. Jumping and whining, he wanted to move forward and search the boat. Gunner squirmed and tried to wiggle from Sarah's hold on his collar. The lieutenant saw the scene unfolding and made her way over to the party.

"Sarah, what's going on?" Lieutenant Langenberg voiced in a serious tone.

"I'm not quite sure, Lieutenant. When I pulled Gunner out of the truck, he caught scent of a distinct odor. He was so focused and intent on finding the source, I decided to let him follow it up and he led me to the boat. He would really like to check the boat out if it's okay."

"The troopers and park rangers have already gone over the boat. They couldn't find anything of significance—other than an illegal registration tag, a tackle box, fishing rod, and a cooler full of beer."

"I know. It may be nothing," Sarah spoke haltingly as she tried to maintain control of Gunner. "But Gunner really believes there's something more here and I'd like to let him work it out if I can have permission."

The lieutenant looked at the officers who shrugged their shoulders. "I hope we're not wasting time here. Don't make me regret this, Sarah." She looked to both officers, "Go ahead, let her work her dog on the boat." The two officers and the lieutenant stepped back to give Sarah and Gunner room.

Kellee handed Meika off to Joe in the staging area and came over to watch Sarah work Gunner.

"I've never seen him quite like this, Kellee," Sarah whispered low to her commander. She dropped her hold on Gunner's collar and let the leash feed out so he had more line and freedom to work. Gunner seized the opportunity, wasting no time dragging Sarah directly to the boat.

"Let's hope he's really onto something tangible," Kellee responded.

The lieutenant, Kellee and the two officers backed further away from the small fishing vessel as Gunner started a thorough check of the outside of the boat. He took a full turn sniffing along from the bow to the stern and then put his front paws up on the gunwale and looked back at Sarah. A small group of responders had gathered at the edge of the parking lot where it met the sandy point of the shoreline to watch the dog work. They looked on with curiosity to see what the handler and dog were doing.

Please be right. Sarah's insides were in knots. She didn't discount her dog or his abilities, but there was much riding on his immediate actions. She saw the gathering crowd which added more tension to the unfolding scene.

"Hup," Sarah gave the command to Gunner to jump up on. From a standstill, the dog gracefully leaped from the sandy ground to the boat's deck. It was obvious to Sarah and Kellee the dog was following a strong human odor. With his convincing body language and focus on scenting, there was no doubt in Sarah's mind. Gunner was working human scent without reservation.

Gunner targeted the tackle box and tried to lay down beside it. Excited, the dog found it difficult to lie down and decided to scratch the box intensely—one of his trained cadaver indications. With a quick pop-up to look over the boat's edge for Sarah, he made eye contact and tried to "do a down" again. Frustrated, the dog stood and continued to scratch at the tackle box aggressively and bark. He was making a scene—Sarah was in a mild panic as she pulled a ball on a string from her pants pocket to reward him.

"There has to be something in the tackle box," Sarah told the lieutenant. "Gunner is positive." Gunner still had the ball in his grip as Sarah told him, "Hup," once more. He jumped out of the boat with some hesitation. The solid foundation of his human remains training was shining through, making it difficult for him to give up the scent item and go with his handler. The dog preferred to be rewarded at the point of the source as he was trained, but Sarah wanted to remove the dog from the boat as soon as she could. She didn't want him to disturb anything within the confines of the craft.

"Can we get the tackle box out of the boat and check it again?" the lieutenant asked the same two officers near the boat. She stood with her hands on her hips with an exasperated look on her face.

"Sure thing," the one officer responded as he pulled nitrile gloves from his BDUs. He reached into the boat and pulled out the tackle box, setting it in the sand. Standing over the officer, the lieutenant watched as he opened the box. The first layer consisted mainly of fishing lures that he sifted through. At the bottom of the box was a small Ziploc baggy with something which appeared soft and full of a dark sticky substance.

"What's that?" the lieutenant asked as she pointed to the baggy.

"We thought it was just some kind of bait or leftover food that was forgotten and left in the bottom of the box," the officer stated who had originally gone through the container. "There was no reason to believe otherwise."

Kellee and Sarah looked at each other. Apparently there was something out of the ordinary in the tackle box. Although a little relieved, Sarah was still in a slight panic hoping they could figure out what was actually in the package.

The officer lifted the baggy up higher with his gloved hands so the lieutenant could see it better. The sun illuminated its contents while the lieutenant and the two officers studied the small baggy.

"Is that what I think it is?" asked the lieutenant.

"Umm, I believe so," one officer said as he continued to turn the baggy and examine it from every angle.

"Call the medical examiner right away," she instructed, pretty sure what was in the bag. "We need to confirm this now. Secure the boat with tape, cordon off the area," she said and gave an approximate area with her hands. "Don't let anyone else near it. We'll need the crime scene technicians here to photograph and pull fingerprints as well."

Looking back to where Sarah, Gunner and Kellee stood, the lieutenant spoke to the officers. Her demeanor had gone from calm and cool to harsh and unforgiving. "It took a goddamn civilian and her dog to find something you two should have found when you first arrived on scene. Great. Makes all of us look really competent." She was livid. "This changes everything."

The gloved officer dropped the baggy with what appeared to be the remains of a man's penis into an evidence bag and sealed the container.

CHAPTER 6

Sarah

Silently Sarah thanked the search gods Gunner had been correct. She had been right to let him follow up on scent when he had shown intense interest. *This will sure add an element of concern and curiosity to the search! Wonder where the rest of him is?* Sarcastic and morbid were two thoughts that crossed her mind.

The state medical examiner swung by base camp on her way from another appointment near the park. Under close inspection, she confirmed it was indeed a penis and most certainly appeared to be human as opposed to animal. She intended to take it to the lab in Harrisburg immediately. The M.E. wanted to begin running tests on the dismembered part straightaway. Her plans were to run DNA testing and then enter it through the combined DNA index system (CODIS) with the FBI to see if they got any hits to help identify who it belonged to. She wanted to "age" it as well and see if she could tell how long it had been separated from its owner.

The water search was now considered a crime scene versus a routine missing person's case. This meant being more observant of where one tread and what was observed while on the search. It added a certain level of elevated professionalism, and complete confidentiality was expected. How Sarah's dog team performed and behaved on this search would determine if the agency running the case would call them back in the future. A lot was riding on how everything went today.

Re-grouping, the lieutenant planned to continue with the original strategies for the water search by boat and a full check of the lake's shoreline. Dive teams were already working several areas of the lake with side scan sonar by boat but had not yet found any clues that would lead them to believe there was a body.

A side scan sonar unit was set into the water and dragged behind a slow moving boat. The scanner sent out sonar signals which bounced and reflected images from the bottom of the lake. Depending on the strength of each returned "echo," the images on the scanner were more or less definitive. An item such as a boulder or human body would reflect a stronger image than the softer, muddier lake bed. Although not the easiest machine to read to the untrained eye, the rescue dive team was well versed and believed it was the only resource necessary for a water recovery. The dive team was convinced dogs were only a nuisance and a complete waste of time on the water. The commander of the dive team was clearly not a dog person.

The canine team re-organized and prepared for the next stage of the search. The only change of plans was that the lieutenant paired the dogs going out in boats with a park ranger and a diver, not just a ranger. Joe and Garrett had gone out on the water with their canines. It was difficult to keep up a good face when working with people who believed you truly didn't belong. It was plain to see the divers thought the dogs were useless but obeyed the lieutenant, who was the incident commander with full authority over the event.

Kellee and Sarah were preparing to run their dogs along the sandy shoreline. Sticking to their original task assignments, Kellee left the parking lot in her van with Meika and an officer escort. They headed toward another lot several hundred meters west where she would start her dog and end at a nearby cove. Sarah and her dog would begin from the cove, two hundred meters west of the command unit and head east along the shoreline toward the dam where her task would end—approximately 600 meters total.

Both of the dog handlers had been paired with a police escort to walk along with them for support—and also on the chance that another clue was found. Dave volunteered to go with Sarah. It was a chance for him to learn more about air-scenting canines and how they work.

"Secret admirer?" Kellee teased regarding how Dave had jumped at the chance to escort Sarah. Sarah's face flushed, illuminating her splash of freckles.

"No, he, I, uhm, just work together on occasion." She floundered for words. Kellee just smiled and shook her head. "Well, it's about time."

The divers had already covered some of the lake area just out from the shoreline where the dogs would be working. It was common to overlap search tasks when looking for a possible drowned subject. As Sarah and Kellee worked the shoreline, they were looking for more than just the missing person. They were also seeking clues that might lead to unraveling the mystery of where the missing boater could be: tracks in the sand, a piece of clothing, any sign that the boater may have made it to land. The dogs would also catch any human scent blowing in from the water itself.

Sarah decided to let Sam work this task since Gunner had already gotten a chance to work—and actually made a find. The ever boisterous Gunner was not tired in the least from his earlier task though, so he barked and bounced in his confines as Sarah opened Sam's crate. "Gunner, settle!" Sarah tried directing him without success.

"Everything under control?" Dave asked as he made his way over to the back of Sarah's truck. A devilish grin spread across his face in a teasing manner.

"Oh, just trying to tame one of the beasts!" Sarah shot back with a bit of feigned irritation. She turned to Dave. For the first time, she really looked at him. Having compartmentalized him from a professional standpoint as someone she worked with, she never thought of him in any other way. Although tall and muscular, his dark hair in the traditional military cut portrayed a quiet, humble demeanor. She believed he was someone she could trust. *But that was close enough for now,* she thought. *Not ready to open that door yet. Not sure if I'll ever be able to.* A flash of her dark and eventful past swept through her thoughts and she looked away. *Yeah, it will be a long, long time before I open that door, never mind let a man walk through it.*

Turning her full attention back to Gunner, she decided to give him a dog toy filled with peanut butter to keep him busy. She worried he might hurt himself tearing the crate apart while she worked Sam. Not wanting to reward him for outlandish behavior, she decided she had to do something so she wouldn't be worried. She hoped it would help re-direct his excitement. Gunner accepted the gift, but continued to stare at Sarah through the slates in the crate. "Thanks, buddy. You know I feel real bad about leaving you here but it's Sam's turn."

Sarah continued to get Sam outfitted in his working attire. He wore an open-sided vest that was more like a harness with orange and white embroidered patches attached to each side that declared SEARCH DOG. At the top of the yoke, right behind the dog's shoulder blades, Sarah attached a long line to the carabiner that connected to the harness. Connecting the line to the harness instead of the collar would allow the dog to work much more freely. She would only keep him on a long line when he worked near base camp. Once they hit the quiet and more open shoreline, she would cut the dog loose.

Much more tolerant than Gunner, Sam stood on the tailgate of the truck patiently waiting while his handler adjusted the nylon straps. "What a good boy," Sarah bestowed on Sam. Using the same commands as she used for Gunner, she instructed Sam to jump down from the truck and take a bathroom break along the tree line. Once Sam had obliged, the trio headed down the road to the marine lot, toward the cove where they would begin their task.

Although Sam was not as boisterous as Gunner, he still exhibited intense excitement but on a slightly smaller scale. He pulled Sarah along as they walked to the starting point of their task. Sam was animated and lively as he trotted along. He slung his large, dark head from side to side and covered the edge of

Sarah's leg with slobber. "Gee thanks, Sam," she laughed as she looked down the side of her BDUs. "Ready to do this, boy?" She continued to speak to the dog as she and Dave walked toward their destination.

Arriving at the point of the cove where their task began, Sarah put Sam "in a down" on the sandy area along the water's edge. Gentle waves lapped along the shore's threshold. The lake appeared calm and quiet at the moment. From her position, she could see her teammates and their dogs on the divers' boats making their way across the lake in a slow-moving grid pattern.

Sam lifted his nose to test the air. Sarah could tell he had picked up human scent—familiar human scent which didn't concern him. He knew the difference. Sam knew they were hunting for another human, one that had not appeared in his scent picture yet. Sarah would know when Sam caught scent of a different subject. She understood her dog's body language intimately.

She pulled the radio mic from where it hung on the front of her uniform shirt. Pressing the call button, she radioed into base. "Base, this is Canine 3," she spoke into the microphone.

"Go ahead, Canine 3," base answered.

"Canine 3 is beginning task at 1300 hours."

"Base copies, Canine 3 beginning task at 1300 hours."

"Canine 3 out," Sarah ended the exchange.

Sam kept his eyes glued to his handler. Sarah quickly observed her area, checking her coordinates and map before shoving her paperwork back in the pocket of her BDUs. She explained her strategy to Dave and asked him to stay behind the dog as he worked.

Sarah knelt beside Sam, his body shaking with anticipation. He could barely hold his pose. She waited until the dog took a quick glance in the direction they were to head. "Go Find!" she commanded when the dog was looking east. With that, Sam leapt up and started a fast, extended trot along the beach line. Coming back once he circled Sarah and Dave before beginning to work a zig-zag pattern from the edge of the lake across the sandy, rocky terrain to the wood line and back to the water's edge.

Sarah hesitated a moment, allowing the dog to put a little space between them. She didn't like to get in his way. The prevailing wind continued to come from the north which made it a perfect scenario to do scenting work along the southern shore. *They make it so easy for me,* she thought, referring to her dogs. Although her job was far from over, they were extremely thorough and had such good work ethics. They absolutely loved to do scent work. *Hell, if they could drive, they wouldn't need me,* she laughed.

Dave, Sarah and Sam had progressed along the shoreline without discovering anything of interest. They made their way past base camp toward the southern intersection with the dam. This would be the ending point of their task. It had taken the team a little over an hour. Just under 100 meters left to traverse, Sarah noticed Sam's body language change. "Dave," Sarah whispered, "look." She pointed toward Sam.

Dave glanced at the dog. He stood stationary, tail raised high as in a flagged stance. Tipping his closed snout toward the air, the dog inhaled deeply. It appeared as though he was reading the wind. Moving a few meters east along the water's edge, Sam took a few bites of the water. The hair along his spine rose up. "He's got something," Sarah announced to Dave.

"The dive team has already worked this area as a first priority. They've been all through it from the dam west since the boat was found in this proximity." Dave continued, "They even used their side scan sonar."

Sarah looked at Dave through her peripheral vision as she continued to watch Sam work out the scent picture. "I'm telling you Sam has something," she retorted. "I want to give him time to work it out before we call base."

"Sounds like a plan," Dave responded.

Sarah could tell he still wasn't convinced. She really didn't care what Dave thought at the moment.

They continued to observe and slowly follow Sam as he worked back and forth along the sand and rocks, trying to work the exact location of the odor and the width of its scent cone. The wind began to pick up, gusting and changing direction, making it difficult for the dog to identify an exact location.

"Work it out," Sarah encouraged the dog. Sam ran toward the dam, stopped and ran back approximately 30 meters. He repeated the process. "Dave, can you find some large rocks to mark the areas where Sam is stopping and turning? This is the area he has human odor coming in from the lake."

Dave nodded. He laid two large rocks on the dog's tracks where they turned in the sand.

Sam was becoming increasingly frustrated. He jumped in the air trying to follow scent. His body language became more pronounced. Although not originally convinced, Dave was becoming a believer. He watched in awe as Sam ran into the water, bit at the surface and started barking. He looked at Sarah. Her face was engulfed by a huge smile. Dave returned her smile.

"Good boy! What a smart boy!" Sarah lavished enthusiastically on the dog. She pulled a soft Frisbee from her pack. Sam saw the Frisbee. He hesitated for a second, reluctant to give up on the scent flowing in from the lake. It was almost hypnotic to him. He lived to marry scent to its source. "Come on, Sam," Sarah called. She had decided to reward him before he tried to swim to where the source of the odor emanated. A tentative dog left the water in a slow gradual pace. Once on land, he bounded to Sarah to retrieve his reward. She gave the dog a few short tosses, some rough tugs and allowed him to win his toy.

Putting Sam in a down under a shady tree along the forested border, she slowly turned to observe the immediate area. Although Dave was a state trooper, he waited for Sarah to call the shots. This was her show, her deal. "Can you find our coordinates on the GPS? And also for the rocks you placed?" Sarah asked.

"Got it," Dave replied. He pulled out his Garmin Rino, a notepad and pencil.

While Dave worked on the coordinates, Sarah remembered her FRS radio, knowing Kellee had said to contact her if needed. Sarah thought better of using the small personal radio in case someone else had their ears on. She decided to text Kellee on her phone instead. She typed: "Sam has indicated on strong human odor coming off the lake close to the dam." She hit send. Without waiting for a reply, Sarah decided she should radio the information to base. They needed to get a dog on a boat and into the area right away.

Sarah hesitated for a moment, reflecting on the events that took place earlier that morning when Gunner made a hit on the boat. It put her in an internal conflict. *Would they take her seriously this time?* She was running a different dog. *Would they believe him? How would the dive team react to running a dog over an area they had already declared as cleared?* Her anxiety level rose as she deliberated.

Sarah closed her eyes for a moment to gather her thoughts. Taking a deep breath, she refocused. Strongly believing in her dog, she picked up the radio mic to make the call to base camp and the lieutenant.

CHAPTER 7

Dave

Dave watched as Sarah stood among the boulders and rocky terrain on the beach. The sun tracked westward, giving way to a beautiful backdrop that made her copper hair shine. He studied her as she digested the setting, the moment. Sarah looked like she belonged where she was, doing what she was doing—in the outdoors working her dogs.

She was in her element, but he could see she was at odds about making the call to base camp. He could also tell how passionate she was about her dogs and how well she understood them. Even to his novice eyes, it was now black and white when her dogs detected human scent, working to find the source as opposed to hunting or just not working at all.

As he continued to observe her, Sarah sighed with slight exasperation and pulled the mic from where it hung on her vest.

"Base, this is Canine 3," Sarah called.

Dave could hear the radio crackle and come to life where he stood near the tree line with Sam. He felt for Sarah as he watched her, tense holding the mic, readying to deliver the information. He could see her brow knotted, teeth clenched and jaw jutted.

"Go ahead, Canine 3," base responded.

With a slight hesitation, Sarah replied, "I have new information. Dog indicated along shoreline near dam."

Communication and management on the other end of the radio knew the area Canine 3 team had been assigned. They would know the dive team had covered it earlier in the day. But it was not their job to make a determination. They were there to take down radio traffic information, decipher it and use it for planning purposes. In the end, it would be the incident commander's decision how to use the material.

"Canine 3, please respond with coordinates."

Sarah drew in a deep breath and read off the GPS coordinates Dave had written down. She explained in short detail where the scent cone coordinates were and where the dog had stood barking and biting at the water's edge.

At first, she had been met with dead air. Dave could see by her tense stance that she'd anticipated as much. She stood staring at the ground around her feet. As Sarah and base continued to go over details, a member of the dive team broke protocol, busting in on the transmission.

"Dive team with side scan sonar already ran that area. Twice in fact," the diver stated. "We've had two teams grid there several hours this morning. There's not enough current there for the body to have moved yet. Water this cold, the body wouldn't pop for several days," he stated testily.

A fresh or recent drowning subject in cold water usually sinks to the bottom of the body of water immediately. The sticky silt of the base of the lake would, in normal circumstances, help contain a body until it started to decompose and gases built up within the body's core. Cold temperatures would slow the process and contribute to it staying on the lake's floor. Once decomposition ramped up—either by the passing of time, or flesh-eating animal activity—the gases building in the body would cause it to slowly rise toward the lake's surface. It could take anywhere from a few days to several weeks, even months in the cold. Other components could come into play, but this was the usual progression in a cold water drowning.

Dave continued to hold his position between the dog and Sarah. He stood with his arms crossed, but faced Sarah to let her know he was there if she needed him. His police mentality wanted to see more of what Sarah was made of. *Reserved and serious,* crossed his mind, *but seems like she can hold her own. Tougher than she lets on.*

"Canine 3, this is base," squawked across the radio channel. No doubt base needed to reassert control to complete the transmission with Sarah.

"Canine 3 copies," she replied.

Search management read back the coordinates Sarah had provided and she re-confirmed. She gave an ETA for their return to base camp and ended the transmission.

Since it seemed that everything was now under control, Dave turned all of his attention to Sam who was still in a down command along the tree's edge.

Dave pulled a soft bowl and bottle of water from Sarah's pack that sat beside the dog. Not paying attention to his surroundings, he softly spoke gibberish to Sam as he placed the bowl between the dog's front paws and poured water into it. The dog tilted his head at Dave as he listened and waited for him to finish filling the bowl.

"Cute."

Still crouched in front of Sam, Dave turned his head to see Sarah watching him.

"You don't care if I help out with the dogs, do you?" Dave felt his cheeks flush with embarrassment. He knew Sarah had caught him in mid-conversation with Sam.

"No, not at all. Appreciate the help after dealing with these assholes." Sarah smiled. "It would be nice to be somewhat appreciated. If not me, at least Sam and Gunner." She shot Dave an exasperated look with a hint of sarcasm he couldn't help but laugh at.

At least she feels like she can trust me, Dave thought. Standing up, he repacked the water bottle in the backpack. "If you're looking for recognition or approval from the dive team, you may be waiting a long time. What else can I do to help?"

"Not looking for either, but it would be nice to be acknowledged as a competent resource," Sarah sighed. "I want to tie three stands of flagging tape to the trees along there," Sarah pointed to an area near where Dave was standing with Sam. "Do you need a roll?"

Dave reached out an empty hand in answer and she tossed him a few rolls. He watched her pull out her notebook and pen. "What notes are you taking and why?" Dave asked. He wanted to know not only what she was doing, but the reasoning behind it.

"We keep a training log and a search record log for everything we do with the dogs—as I'm sure you do with your new canine. Wind direction, wind speed, temperature, where the dog worked, length of time it took us, where we marked the scent cone, where Sam showed us a full indication by barking. I also add where we walked by drawing a map of our search pattern, time and date." She finished her explanation and pushed the pad and pen back into her deep pants pockets.

"Are we ready?" Dave looked around to make sure Sarah had everything.

She nodded with some hesitation. "Not sure about this next round, though." Sarah looked out to the lake and back toward base camp.

"Anything else you need?" he asked one more time as Sarah headed to the dog and picked up the pack. He wanted to offer more, to make things easier for her. He watched as she bent down and leashed up Sam.

Sarah just shook her head indicating she didn't need any further help.

This was Sarah's deal. Even though Dave was a state trooper, he also thought of himself as a friend. He felt helpless. He couldn't intervene on a professional or friendly support level. She had to figure this out herself.

So far she had fared well in proving herself and her dogs' abilities. He could tell she was built with tenacity and resolve and knew she would come through on the prevailing side. Sarah always proved to be very sharp and forward in her position with the county. She had street sense and book smarts. He respected her.

"I think I have everything." She turned to Sam, "Free," she commanded. Sam jumped up and went to the end of the leash, heading back toward the water's edge. "That'll do," she told the dog. He stopped in his tracks and looked back at her. "Stubborn," she commented, "but in a good way."

She called to Sam and turned to the direction of base camp. Sam got the idea and followed with enthusiasm. Dave watched the pair. It was like they could read each other's thoughts, he mused. *Hopefully I'll have that mutual bond and understanding with my Bella one day.*

Lost in thought, Dave followed Sarah as they made their way back to the search hub. Sarah was quiet. He knew she was contemplating the situation and he didn't want to prod her with questions. He was curious though how she was going to convince the agency and dive team that they needed to recheck the area—and recheck it with a canine.

Dave knew she would have to be careful how she treaded there, how she presented the information and how she would persuade management to follow up on Sam's indication. *Either the body moved or god forbid, they missed it somehow when they ran side scan sonar and gridded the area. Boy, does she have her work cut out for her.*

CHAPTER 8

Sarah

Arriving back in base camp, Dave headed directly toward the command unit. Sarah split off and started to make her way to her truck with Sam in tow.

"Hey, Sarah," Dave called to her, "we need to check in and let search management know we made it safely back to base camp. I'm sure they're waiting for us to debrief as well."

"Can you check in for me, please? I need to take care of Sam first and give him a thorough going-over," Sarah replied, continuing in the direction of her truck without waiting for an answer. She wasn't ready to face the lieutenant and the dive team commander just yet. *Sam is my first priority at the moment anyway,* she thought, *but I also need some time to figure out how to deal with the whole situation.*

Sarah reached her truck and set her pack down on the edge of the tailgate. Gunner started to whine, excited that his handler and playmate had returned. "Hey there, Gunner. Did ya miss us?" *At least he's glad to see me,* crossed her mind as she thought of the dive team. Sam's ears pricked up and he listened to the exchange between Sarah and the other dog. Sarah peeked into the crated dog's confines to check his water. Satisfied he still had plenty, she turned back to Sam. "Okay, boy, your turn."

She had Sam lay down on the tarmac in the parking lot. He sparingly obliged. Sarah kneeled down beside him. It was standard protocol for a handler to give a complete once over of their canine partner to make sure they were physically fine once completing an assignment.

Starting with his mouth, head and ears, Sarah closely examined the dog. She continued down each leg, inspected each paw, the pads and his nails. She finished with his head and limbs and checked his under-belly and tail. Convinced there were no splinters or thorns stuck in his pads or minute cuts or bruising, she allowed the dog to right himself and stand back up. Sam stood and shook himself vigorously. Dog hair flew in all directions. She took a slicker brush along his broad sides and back, and pulled out the last few remaining briers that had hitchhiked back to camp in his thick double coat. Cupping Sam's dark sable head in her hands, she nuzzled him close to her face. Taking in a deep breath she heartily whispered to the dog, "You did a great job!"

Sarah was stalling. She couldn't help feeling like she would be going up against a wall for trying to follow up on her dog's indications. *Time to get a move on and head over to the command unit.*

"Truck," she commanded. Sam jumped up on the tailgate with ease. She directed him into his crate, checked his water and gave him a cookie. Gunner continued to whine faintly. "Oh hey there, boy," she spoke to Gunner in a soft tone trying to appease and quiet him. He was still excited to see them both. Sarah slipped a cookie through the crate slats to him. "I'll be back shortly," she promised and turned toward the command unit. Both dogs stared at Sarah from within their crates. They felt the distracted tension emanate from her, causing them worried concern for their handler.

Sarah pulled her cell phone from her pocket and dialed Kellee. "Hey, Kellee, I'm heading over to the command unit now to meet with the lieutenant and the rest of the search management team including the dive team commander. How do you think I should handle this?"

Kellee and the other canine handlers were slowly making their way back to base from their search tasks.

"How strongly do you feel about Sam's indication being accurate?" Kellee asked.

"It was pretty black and white. Per his body language and strong indication, I'm positive there's a body out there. I'm just not sure how far across the lake." *It was more than just the dog,* she thought. *Weird, it's also a feeling.*

"Well you need to get over to the lieutenant ASAP and explain how strongly you feel that your dog is correct. No matter what the dive team members interject. As you know, they won't support having that area searched a second time, especially by canine teams."

Kellee and Sarah quickly went over what the water search strategy should be once a dog was assigned to grid the area by boat.

"When will you and the guys be back in base camp?" Sarah asked Kellee.

"ETA about 15 minutes. I'll get to the command unit as soon as I get Meika taken care of. You'll be fine, Sarah. Just try and be as professional as you can. It's important that we handle this well if we ever want to be called back for a future search by this agency." Kellee ended the call.

Sweat marks showed through Sarah's long-sleeve uniform shirt. Beads of perspiration appeared along her brow. Her anxieties returned in full force. She wiped her forehead with the sleeve of her shirt and tucked her long curls behind her ears. Completely stepping out of her comfort zone, she stood up tall and left the security of her truck.

Sarah gathered her courage, her moxie, and headed through the lot to the command unit. Collecting her thoughts, she deliberated how to portray her case to convince the lieutenant and dive team to reconsider. They had to run the canine teams on boats in the area in question. Sarah needed to get dogs on the water. There was no uncertainty in her mind. *But how am I going to make the dive team, park rangers and the state police understand that?*

As Sarah approached the unit, she noticed the policeman who replaced Dave earlier at the sign-in table. He was the trooper who had lifted the tackle box out of the boat. She tipped her head in acknowledgment and smiled as she passed by. He never turned his head from the table; he only looked up fleetingly over silver-rimmed sunglasses. He didn't respond to her in the least. She felt a pit in her stomach. *Asshole.*

She watched as ground-pound teams continued to come and go, checking in and out. They turned in their assignments, debriefed and received new search tasks that would take them back out on the trails of the park.

As Sarah reached the steps to the command unit, she could hear a heated discussion in progress. She thought she heard Dave's voice intertwined in the conversation. She could distinctly hear the commander of the dive team. "She's an inexperienced dog handler. She has no idea what she's talking about! We've covered that area thoroughly." The dive team was used to being in control and running water searches in this county. The pit in her stomach grew.

Park rangers and the local police agencies would oversee land searches but generally would concede water search management to the dive team. The lieutenant was the incident commander for this event due to it being both land and water without eyewitnesses. Although the lieutenant had deferred the majority of the management of the water coverage to the dive team, she was still running the show. The dive team was not used to having management involved. Personalities, egos and strategies were clashing.

Sarah surprised herself. She smiled as she entered the unit. *All of this is because of my team and my dogs,* she thought. She was beginning to find the day's events almost humorous. If the situation wasn't such a serious setting, she would have laughed out loud. Normally she didn't like to draw attention. When Sarah stepped into the hallway of the unit, all conversation abruptly halted and everyone turned to look at her.

"It's about time you made your way over here," the lieutenant stated.

Sarah looked from the lieutenant's face to Dave and then to the two dive team members. She had wanted to keep control of this whole situation in the hands of the dive team commander and try and persuade him to take her and one of her dogs out on the lake, but he had already anticipated the dog team's next move and faced the lieutenant, demanding it was not necessary. They knew Sarah would go above their head. She had already proven early in the day that she didn't follow search protocol when she'd let her dog lead her to the boat.

Sarah couldn't help thinking the dive team commander had an ulterior agenda. *Did they view her as a threat? Was he thinking it might make the dive team look bad if a dog located the body in an area they had already searched?* She almost felt like she was playing a game of Risk, and instead of being first-responder resources that should work together toward a common goal, it seemed as if they were fighting for turf.

Sarah pulled the paperwork which included her map, notes and task assignment out of her BDU pants pocket. Unfolding the pieces of paper, she handed them to the lieutenant. "This is the area we covered," she began and pointed to the tattered map. The rest of the occupants stood back with their arms crossed in a defensive manner except Dave. They remained quiet for the moment. Sarah continued giving details of her search task and how her dog behaved. Where and when Sam had first gotten scent, his body language right up to where he entered the water and started barking. She was nervous. Flashes of her childhood and dealing with authorities crept into her thoughts. *Stop it,* she forced herself, *this is different.*

The lieutenant began to question Sarah. "Are you positive your dog had human scent? Can you guarantee the dogs can pinpoint where the body is? The dive team doesn't believe we should be wasting time or any resources covering that area again."

"Yes, I am positive that Sam hit on human scent. No, I can't guarantee anything. But I do feel strongly that we should follow up on this lead." Sarah answered with an air of certainty. The dive team commander rolled his eyes and turned away from the conversation with a huff.

"So what would be your next step if this was up to you? How would you run your search strategy if you wanted to follow-up on the information from the task you ran with your dog?" the lieutenant asked.

Sarah thought back to her recent conversation with Kellee. She tried to choose her words wisely as she thought of the dive team standing there. *Is this some kind of test?* She had never been in a position before where management asked for her input. "If the wind is still predominately from the north as it's been all day, I would put two canines on the water with a boat driver and a spotter. Start one canine team here," Sarah pointed to the north shore on the other side of the dam. "Start that team gridding east to west from the northern shoreline heading south." Pointing to the southern side, she added, "And I would put a second team here gridding west to east heading north. Each team should grid approximately 400-500 meters each way."

Kellee entered the command unit as Sarah was deep in discussion with the lieutenant. Sarah wasn't sure how long Kellee had been standing there. The lieutenant looked up at Kellee and asked, "Do you agree with her strategy?"

Before answering, Sarah watched Kellee collect her thoughts. "Yes, the strategy is correct regarding how we work the dogs once one has indicated human scent coming off the water from the shoreline. I would use the ranger's boats to run the dogs. Their Boston Whalers have a shorter gunwale and will make it easier for the dog to lean over and be closer to the water's surface. If the rangers are available to drive their boats, we can send two of our team members and a canine per boat." She finished by adding the diver team should be on standby so they can be ready to assist should the dogs hit on something while out on the lake.

If the canines were successful in isolating a vicinity, the divers could come into that area to try to locate and actually recover the body.

The dive team commander threw his hands in the air and looked toward the ceiling of the command unit again a second time when he heard Kellee speak of his team serving as standby for the dog team.

Sarah watched as his face went from a tan color to shades of purple. His salt and pepper hair appeared grayer and one could almost see the steam gush from his ears. *What a major asshole. He's gonna give himself a cardiac.*

It didn't go unnoticed on the rest of the responders. They edged further away from where he stood.

"This is a complete waste of time and resources," the dive team commander declared, slamming open the door. He stormed out of the command unit.

Unaffected by the drama, the lieutenant turned toward her communication officer. "Can you raise the park rangers and see if we can get two rangers and two of their boats to meet us over here to run the dogs and their handlers?"

The communication officer immediately put in the transmission. Rangers responded quickly. They could supply two men and two boats at the dock closet to the command unit in twenty minutes.

"Sarah, get Gunner and yourself ready to go," Kellee directed. "I want you two in the first boat starting on the southern shore. I'll ride with you. We'll give Joe and Garrett the other task starting from the northern shore." Kellee picked up her FRS radio to contact the other canine team members and let them know what their next assignment would be.

Tentatively, Sarah stepped outside the command unit and headed back to her truck. She was trying to control her anxieties. Scenarios played out in her head of what the outcome might be. She tried to stay optimistic that this would all work out. Positive her dog was right, she felt like she was being put to the fire.

Water searches could be a long, drawn-out process; it can be stressful work in itself. Adding in all of the negative attitudes from the dive team only made the stress rise to a higher level. She knew if they failed this task, it was pretty much over for her team as far as getting called out from this agency in the future. Resources clashing didn't go unnoticed to those running the incident. Much would be riding on this search assignment. *God, I hope this goes well.*

Taking a deep breath, she tried to focus on the task at hand. She needed to find her PFD—personal flotation device—as well as the dogs, a plastic baggy to store her paperwork and GPS, and change into her water shoes. She would need to check for any changes in the air movement while on the boat.

Don't forget the baby powder, she thought.

CHAPTER 9

Sarah

The radio Sarah had pocketed in her chest halter buzzed with transmission traffic. She listened to the exchanges as she pulled Gunner from his crate and readied him for the water search task. The dog had settled down a notch since first arriving on scene, but he still exhibited boundless energy. He bounced and jumped along the tailgate making it difficult for Sarah.

"Gunner! Settle!" she directed exasperatedly. The dog stopped for a moment and stared at Sarah. He gave her a look that expressed she was ruining his fun. It gave Sarah enough time to pull his vest over his head and latch the hard plastic fasteners along the side. She clipped a long line to the carabineer on the back of his vest and a leash to his prong collar. "Okay, good boy. Off," she commanded and moved back to allow Gunner to jump from the tailgate of the truck.

Afternoon was beginning to wane, which concerned Sarah. Actually, it was getting late in the day to perform a search on the water by boat. Although there were still a few hours of daylight left, gridding a mass of water took a slow and methodical approach if you planned to do it correctly. It was a process you couldn't rush. The lowering sun created shadows on the water which made it more difficult to see into any depth as well. Luck would have to be on the team's side to find a body within the timeframe they were hoping for.

Keep calm and don't rush, she told herself on one hand, *but we need to get a move on to get started!* She felt like she was always in conflict, if not with whatever situation she was dealing with at the time, she was in conflict with herself.

Sarah took Gunner to the edge of the woods so he could take care of his business. She stood a few feet away from him as he sniffed about the tree line, picking out the perfect spot. Eyeing Kellee as she waited for him, Sarah gave her a thumb's up sign to let her know she was ready. Kellee leaned against her van, watching and waiting.

Sarah had begun to tire. She felt the effects of the long day, with just a few hours of sleep between work and the call-out. *At least I will be pretty much stationary while on the boat. Gunner will be doing most of the work.*

Suddenly, she remembered she had brought a second coffee from home. *Jackpot!* She leaned in and grabbed it from her truck cab on the way past. *Cold and old is better than nothing at all,* she laughed to herself. She tried to sip from the travel mug and negotiate walking the large boisterous German Shepherd across the lot to the dock and boat ramp.

"Good to go?" Kellee asked as they continued to the meeting area.

"Yeah, believe so," Sarah said and subconsciously touched the trial-size baby power in her BDU pocket. She knew she had remembered it, but was beginning to feel excited and anxious about the water search. Touching the object made her reel in a degree. The same as she would touch the many scars on her body acquired from foster upbringing. Battle wounds made her, just, feel. *Push it out of your mind, Sarah!*

As Sarah, Kellee and Gunner rounded the bend to the ramp and dock, they could see the rangers already waiting with two boats. Sarah spied the dive team who were on standby. They sat on the dock with their feet dangling over the edge. Their conversation quieted as the women and the dog walked past. Not all of the members of the dive team had an issue with working dogs on the water, but since it worked its way from the top down, there wasn't much chance of changing the team's attitude toward the canine handlers. They followed their superior's attitude and orders. Especially when he was standing right there with them.

As the lieutenant had dictated, the dive team had been given other tasks. They would serve as the safety team while the rangers and dog teams were on the water. Responsible for watching the boats, keeping notes of how long the teams were out and when they made radio contact and checks. They would serve as emergency back-up to the dog teams and rangers if needed and be ready for a recovery dive if a canine team were to pinpoint the body.

Not all divers have issues with dogs, Sarah thought. Sarah's canine team trained with dive organizations from other counties that helped prepare them for water evaluations. It wasn't the type of resource; it was who was in charge of the resource that set the attitude.

Sarah sized up the round-faced ranger with thinning hair who would command their boat. She had met him in the past and welcomed his warm reception. "Hey, Ranger Owen," Sarah said with a tired smile, "we appreciate you allowing us to work our dogs from your boats."

"Oh, no problem. We're here to help." He returned the smile. "We would really like to locate the owner of this boat and conclude the search," the ranger replied warily. "This sure turned into more of a mess than we bargained for," he grunted.

Kellee boarded the boat first so Sarah could hand Gunner's leash off to her. The ranger steadied the boat as Sarah stepped from the dock. Gunner effortlessly followed her lead and leapt from the dock onto the boat's deck. Sarah was more than proud of him. She also worried and fawned over him. She reveled in his agility, ability and beauty; she was emotionally tied to her dogs.

Sarah kept a tight grip on Gunner's leash. "Easy, buddy." The dog was excited to be on the boat. Any chance to scent and work for his reward was reason enough. Gunner pulled Sarah from the stern to the bow as he checked the entire vessel out. The boat had a center console where the driver was stationed. There was room between the console, deck and gunwale. This could prove beneficial because it allowed the dog to have full access to the water from any area of the boat.

As the ranger started the engine, it whined for a moment, and sputtered water when the engine turned over. It purred as he put it in neutral. "All ready?" he called pulling the line from the dock. The women nodded in unison. Once the ranger pointed the bow toward the opening of the small cove to head out to the open waters of the lake, Kellee set about describing to him a loosely laid-out plan of how to maneuver the boat once they reached their search area. She wanted to make sure he understood how the dog worked, and exactly the way to follow the dog's nose and body language.

As Kellee described the strategy and what canine body alerts looked like, she kept an eye on Sarah and Gunner. He was a big, strong-willed animal. "Hang on to him, Sarah. We don't want him jumping over," Kellee warned.

The dog was straining against his long line and harness. They both knew how much the dog enjoyed the water. Although Gunner looked to his handler for guidance, he also had his own ideas of where and when he should start searching and how it should be handled.

Aside from keeping an eye on her dog in the boat, Sarah strained to keep her hat on her head and her hair in place as the boat steered out onto the lake. The small motor wasn't that strong and couldn't go very fast, but fast enough to blow her hat off. The thought made her want to pull the cuffs down on her long-sleeve uniform shirt as well. *One dirty secret leads to another.* At the moment she had one hand looped around her dog's long line and the other holding her hat down, trying to steady herself on the seat near the boat's bow.

Gunner continued to strain at the line attached to his back. He balanced his forepaws on the gunwale near the starboard side of the boat with his hind end standing erect on the seat near his handler. With his nose already searching the air, he alternated between scenting low to the surface of the lake and stretching and testing the air above him. Sarah could tell he was working. He was hunting for an unknown human scent—a scent that didn't belong to the humans who were already in his scent picture.

As they rounded the cove and came to the start of their work area, Kellee pulled out her GPS and marked the start location coordinates. She radioed in to base to let them know they were starting their task and jotted down a few notes on her waterproof pad. The ranger slowed the motor and positioned the boat to grid east toward the dam and parallel to the shoreline where base camp was set up. Starting from the center of the lake, they would work their grid lines east to west, slowly making their way south toward the shoreline. Sarah stood up and reeled out more of Gunner's long line to allow him added freedom within the boat.

"Okay, buddy. All up to you now," she told the dog. It distracted him and he wagged his tail heartily looking at her for a moment before returning to sniff the water and air. Sarah really hadn't needed to bother. Gunner had already begun to work. He didn't need a boost from her to do his job.

Sarah pulled the baby powder from her BDU pants pocket. She stayed downwind of everyone in the boat and squeezed off a few puffs. The talcum powder formed a small cloud at first. She watched as it wafted on the wind, the direction it went and how it dissipated. It lifted up slightly, widened and shot toward the southern shore in the prevailing northerly wind. *Perfect,* she thought, *the wind is still pretty much blowing toward the southern shoreline. This will put Gunner in a great position to follow up on Sam's indication from earlier.*

Even though Sarah had complete trust in both her dogs, her stomach was in a knot. This search had turned into a much tougher situation than anticipated. Feeling as though she was carrying the whole weight of her team and their reputation on her and Gunner's shoulders, she knew they couldn't fail at this task. *Why is everything such a struggle! Always having to prove myself,* she thought. She felt a small spark of anger rise up. As if reading her emotions, Gunner turned back to look at Sarah, locking eyes with her. "Get to work," she said in a high-pitched voice. *Be positive or I'm going to blow this whole assignment.*

"Everything good?" Kellee asked. She stood beside the ranger at the console. The two had been discussing water levels, temperatures and increased vegetation that had grown so well this year in the lake due to how clear the water was and how much sun had been able to penetrate deeper into the lake's waters. Sarah's mood hadn't gone unnoticed.

"Just tired, it's been a long day with only a few hours of sleep. I'll be fine." Sarah mustered up a smile with her reply as she looked up. She knew Kellee was reprimanding her. Sarah turned away to concentrate on her dog and the surroundings. Day was turning into early evening, giving way to longer shadows falling across the glistening water. The sun's rays bounced and reflected off the casual rising and falling drifts the boat forged in its wake. The wind had dropped down in strength, but still had a nice steady breeze flowing south. Sarah spied her teammates working across the lake nearer the northern shore. Gunner caught their scent, identified and cataloged it and went back to his task at hand.

The ranger finished the fourth long grid from west to east. He throttled back on the motor preparing to turn around near the dam and head west toward Round Island. Suddenly, Gunner's head snapped like he had slammed into a solid wall. Jumping from the bow of the boat, he leaned over the side with a closed snout forcefully sucking in the air over his more than 220 million olfactory receptors. The ranger looked up to the women for guidance; the dog's actions were not lost on him either. Gunner started to move along the inside of the boat, trying to keep in contact with this new human's scent.

"Watch where his nose leads him and try and follow," Kellee instructed the ranger and pointed to where the dog wanted to go. "Gunner is trying to work out where the scent is coming from. Once he can really lock on, it will be easier to pursue where he wants to go." The ranger responded by keeping a watchful eye as Gunner moved along the deck.

Pulling the GPS out once more, Kellee hit the Mark Waypoints button on the front panel, and noted the coordinates on her waterproof pad with "Dog's first alert." She pulled out her radio to call in the dog's alert to base camp. She watched Sarah follow behind Gunner giving him the support he needed to help work out where the scent was rising off the water. Water search work took serious focus and stamina for the dog. Between keeping his body steady in the boat and continually staying motivated to search for scent, it could prove very fatiguing.

"Keep us posted," base camp replied. "We'll keep eyes on you from the shore. Dive team has been notified and is on standby ready to go in."

"Copy that," Kellee replied, releasing her thumb off the receiver and pocketing her radio.

They had gone several meters back toward the west when Gunner turned in the boat and headed back to the stern. Sarah looked back at the ranger. "On it," he said and swung the boat sharply back east and in the direction of the dam.

The dog's body movements became more intense, showing frustration. He snapped at the air and hung himself over the gunwale trying to bite at the water. A few short woofs escaped his throat. Sarah painted a serious face, concentrating on where her dog wanted to go. She knew they were closing in. The thought he had actually found the body excited Sarah, but it also caused her a ping of sadness. It meant her dog had located someone deceased. She had to push those thoughts from her mind and believe that she and her team were actually helping someone with closure. Piecing together the other item Gunner had found earlier left several wild thoughts running through her head as well.

The ranger made smaller and shorter grids as he watched Gunner and followed the direction the dog's nose led. The dog stood still and studied the air for a moment. Gunner's decision process could be seen by everyone in the boat as he calculated the situation. He sucked back into a secured position along the gunwale then broke loose. He vigorously began to bark. A deep, full bark spilled out, filled with spittle which sprayed Sarah and Kellee. The dog was locked on. Close enough to where the scent was coming up through the water and leaving the surface.

Appearing almost possessed, Gunner tried to jump over the edge. Kellee took up some of the dog's long line and helped to hold him in the boat. Sarah peered over into the water beside Gunner, pulling a Kong on a rope from her pocket. She swooped the toy down below the barking dog and brought it up to him as a reward for pinpointing the scent. Sarah tried to make it appear as if the toy had come up from the water, but Gunner knew it had been in her pocket the whole ride. There was no fooling him; he knew how the game worked. He latched onto the toy with a forceful bite and gnashed the rubber Kong between his powerful jaws. He continued to bark and mash the toy as he hung over the boat.

"Good boy, Gunner!" Sarah heaped on him as she gave him a few swift, hard pats along his rib cage.

Sarah looked back at Kellee. She couldn't contain the excitement, her grin stretched wide across her face. Kellee returned a quick smile. Picking up the GPS and radio once more, Kellee noted the coordinates and called in a confirmed indication and location. Their boat rested about 50 meters off the dam and 200 meters from the southern shoreline where base camp stood.

"Is anything visible?" base camp called back.

"That would be a negative," Kellee responded to base, "but it seems very dark and thick here. It's hard to see more than a few feet into the water, especially in this fading light. There's not enough direct sunlight to see to any depth."

"Maintain your location until we can get a diver out there."

"Copy." Kellee replaced her radio. She pulled out her smartphone and took a few quick pictures to help triangulate their position. She also snapped a few shots of Gunner and Sarah. They would be pictures she would eventually send to the lieutenant as well for their files if needed.

Sarah knew her dog had located a body. She wouldn't breathe easy until she actually laid her eyes on the cadaver. The area

Gunner indicated was deep, dark and possibly full of vegetation. The visibility sucked. It would make it tough going for a diver as well. Sending one into such a deep area with vegetation and limited light was seriously putting someone's life on the line.

Turning to Kellee and the ranger, Sarah spoke. "Maybe we should wait until morning when there is better light for the dive team to go down." She knew the divers would be hard-headed. They were skilled in rescue and recovery operations and had certain protocol to follow. But she also knew they were out to prove her wrong and would not wait until the morning.

She sat down with Gunner in the stern of the boat. Sarah spoke to him in a soft voice as she petted him with long, slow sweeping gestures to get him to relax. She watched as the ranger poked through the water with a pole that had a hook at the end.

Kellee pulled out water bottles and passed them around. Sarah sucked down a few gulps and watched the dive team's boat round the cove and head their way. Pulling out a soft bowl, she watered her dog.

Nerves raw from lack of sleep and being revved up all day, she hoped she could find the energy to deal with the divers. Leaning back against the cushion of the seat, she pressed her eyes shut. She hoped it would be a quick dive and the team would be able to locate the body without any issues.

CHAPTER 10

Eva

Eva curiously eyed the search events as they unfolded. She appeared calm on the outside as she sat visible, perched and resting during a few minutes of downtime. Inside, her excitement mounted. It was a game. Kellee might have noticed her earlier. She appeared annoyed; alarmed for *some unknown reason?* It was just for an instant, a flash of recognition, perchance?

Eva just smiled in return. Things couldn't have gone better; her timing was perfect. She couldn't have planned such excellent results. It had gone so well. *Who would have guessed? It was like a well-choreographed production. Camera! Lights! Action!* She was satisfied with herself. More like smug, actually.

She continued to observe, contemplating what would happen when the final results were in. She hoped it would conclude by day's end. Thoughts turned to incident management and what came next; and to what had also already transpired earlier in the day. Management would continue to move forward as planned, following protocol regarding search tasks, that was a given.

There was nothing tangible for her to do at the moment but to stay fixed, not draw attention. Inwardly she laughed as thoughts of the morning's activities played back in her mind. Authorities could be so fucking easy to manipulate and make fools of. The expression on the lieutenant's face when the drone had pulled the baggy from the bottom of the tackle box made her stifle a gag. Did anyone know where Lorena Bobbitt was lately? *Priceless!* A moment Eva continued to replay, over and over.

Sitting in the boat, she seemed almost bored, complacent as she waited. But boredom was furthest from her mind. She wanted events to progress... but not too quick. Eva needed everything to play out as long as possible so she could revel in the ordeal bit by bit. Although confident in her situation, she remained guarded for her own protection. There was a small trace of uneasiness that she continued to mollify so she wouldn't give her position away. Certain energy sat nearby that she didn't trust; energy that could expose her and show her true identity. She had to maintain her composure. *Not a problem. Maintenance is my specialty.*

Her thoughts drifted across the water as she watched the divers gear up, readying to head out on the lake. She welcomed their orderliness as they considered equipment, rules and protocols of their skill; it piqued her interest. She liked that there were rules in existence to be applied, carried out and followed stringently. Including repercussions if broken. She also enjoyed it when people challenged the rules, broke them. She liked to rejoice in their consequences.

Eva liked to play games. She liked to play games for which she made the rules.

CHAPTER 11

Sarah

The ranger dropped a styrofoam buoy at the location where Gunner had given his strongest indication of the presence of human scent rising from the water's surface. After the buoy had been placed, the engine set in neutral and the GPS coordinates called in, the ranger pulled out an extendable grappling hook. He poked around the darkened waters bringing up long spires of aquatic growth and grasses. "With the clear spring-fed water and all the sun we had this summer, the vegetation is dense in several areas throughout the lake," he offered. "We've never seen it propagate like this before."

Sarah scrutinized her surroundings. She viewed the dam from where she sat in the boat. The structure towered over the water's surface like a formidable fortress. It gave her the impression of a medieval castle with its block-type construction and faded gray coloring. Over 750 feet thick at its widest point and close to 1700 feet in length from shore to shore, the dam appeared impressive and intimidating.

The lake was a product of the local paper mill and population that needed the efforts of a dependable water source—one to run the mill's facility and the other as drinking water for the inhabitants. The dam had been built in the mid 1960s to block Codorus Creek and catch the many natural springs within the valley. The resulting Lake Marburg was formed, named for the flooded town which slumbered under a hundred feet of lake water. The surrounding park opened in 1970 as part of the Project 70 Land Acquisition and Borrowing Act. Cultivated between the state and local townships, it had become a popular hiking, camping and outdoor destination, especially of late.

Chatter between base and the dive team came across their radios. It sounded like they should be headed in their direction in the next few minutes. This gave them a window to discuss what search efforts had transpired and the water area they had just finished covering. Kellee yielded a park map and the three looked over it as they waited for the divers. Sarah took the map from Kellee and stood up in the boat. She oriented it to their surroundings. Sarah and Kellee also produced notepads and started scribbling a few quick comments.

"Here is where Sam first hit scent along the south shoreline," Sarah spoke, referring to her other dog and the morning's task. "And here is where he barked and wanted to enter the water." Sarah commented as she pointed to the area along the rocky edge with the tip of her pen.

"This is where we started our sweeps in the boats and here is where we are now," Kellee marked the map with her pen and wrote a note on the border along the edge of the map. "How deep is it in this area?" she asked the ranger.

"Oh, we're probably looking at anywhere from 90-100 feet right around here, give or take 20 feet. This area closer to the dam is the deepest part of the lake. More'n likely, the coldest too."

"So how far down do you think the vegetation would be? How far can the ultra-violet rays penetrate to promote all of this plant growth?" Sarah asked.

"Not positive," the ranger replied, "but I'm guessing around 30 feet in the deeper portions of the lake. "It's been a real problem this year, but the younger fish and smaller aquatic life seem to thrive within it. The fishermen are having a lot of trouble though. It catches the props on the boats and tangles up their lines. We're in a heated debate between the recreational users of the lake and the conservationists. Trying to decide whether to clean it up or let it be."

All around there were small dark areas that dotted the water's landscape where you could see patches of weedy growth. They had avoided crossing through them when they were running their search patterns. It would have proved to be a mess if the plant life got tangled up in the boat's small motor.

Sarah turned toward the cove at the sound of another boat motor. Her teeth clenched automatically. *Stop it!* she told herself. *Relax. Our part is almost done here.* Gunner also looked up to the oncoming boat. He wagged his tail when he saw more humans headed in his direction. *Always the outgoing one, he's never met a stranger. Wish I could have a little bit of his confidence and demeanor.*

The dive team's boat pulled up along the ranger's Boston Whaler. Thankfully it was two of the senior dive team members *unaccompanied* by their commander. Sarah watched as the shorter, older diver maneuvered their boat into position alongside the whaler. Although both divers were suited up, the younger diver sitting on the stern was ready to go into the water with his tanks already assembled on his back and his face mask in hand.

I wonder why "he" didn't come out? Sarah thought regarding the dive team commander. *But I'm completely OK with that,* she smiled to herself.

The ranger and Kellee exchanged pleasantries with the divers. Sarah felt a tug as Gunner strained against his leash to get a closer sniff with his ever curious nose.

"Hey there, boy," the younger diver greeted the dog, "how ya doing?" He also gave Gunner a rough pat on his side as he continued to speak to him. The dog responded by licking the diver on the chin. *Guess they can't be all bad,* Sarah thought as she watched the exchange.

The older diver requested permission to board their boat. The ranger nodded an approval. The group gathered around an open map to discuss what had occurred with the dogs so far. It appeared the diver hadn't been given the full disclosure of the canine location of the clues from his commander.

"Okay, Sarah," the older diver started. "Where did your dog react? Can you give me some insight to how this works with the canine as we get ready to go in?"

So it seems everyone knows who I am. Not sure if that's a good thing.

"No problem," Sarah began, always happy to discuss the working and findings of their canines—*especially to someone who is interested.* Sarah watched the younger diver who had stayed in the other boat, continue to ready himself and the materials to submerge. She quickly gave an overview of how Sam had shown scent interest along the shoreline and then Gunner had followed it all the way to their current location and signified the find by barking. Barking is the dog's final trained response after locating the source of human scent.

The older diver listened with respect and intent as he tried to take in all the details.

"The biggest challenges I see right now," the ranger stated when Sarah had finished, "is the fading light and all of this vegetation. We don't know how far the weedy growth spreads out under the water's surface."

"We hope to make a hasty dive now just to look around. If we don't find anything in a matter of minutes, we plan on coming back by first light tomorrow. Everyone is suited up and ready to go, so let's see if we can find something." He pointed to the younger diver, "Matt's going to dive for us. He'll be carrying a Pelican system if there's any problem and he's got a knife on his belt." The Pelican system he referred to was an open line of communication between both men in case the submerged diver needed anything.

Sarah felt more at ease knowing the divers had a way to communicate with each other. She was glad they erred toward safety and were only planning a short, swift dive. *So tired*, she was fading. *Thankfully it's my four-day weekend and I can sleep tonight!*

The ranger grabbed the towline from the diver's boat and tied it off tight to his. Sarah got Gunner to settle down and the dog curled up in the boat's corner near the bow. Kellee stood along the console with the ranger, looking on as the diver dropped over the side of the boat, feet first, quickly submerging himself and immediately resurfacing. He grabbed the side of his boat and pulled his mask off. It had fogged up. He dipped it in the lake, swished water around the inside to clear it and re-fit it over his head. Once again, they all looked on as he disappeared below the water's dim surface.

Time seemed to pass slowly. Sarah found herself holding her breath as she imagined what the diver might find underneath their boat in the darkened waters. It had only been five minutes when he reappeared on the opposite side of the boats. He gave the other diver a thumb's up, then pointed straight down from where he had just come. Right away, everyone on the boats knew what that meant. The diver hadn't spoken it over the Pelican system in case the line was not secured and could be picked up by locals listening in other than base camp.

The diver in the water asked for the grappling pole from the ranger's boat. Once it was handed over, the diver re-submerged.

The older diver radioed to base. "Base, dive team here."

"Go ahead, dive team."

"Need to secure the net, secure the net." The diver let base know he had potential fragile information and they needed to move their conversation to a secure and private channel. Between recreational users and the media, it was wise to make sure confidential information was handled as professionally and securely as possible.

"Copy, dive team. Move to channel three-ohh-ohh."

"Dive team copies."

After the channel change, the diver reported the find. A body had been located about 30 feet below the surface. It was completely surrounded in dense vegetation. The body was suspended in the lake due to plant growth. The diver had tried to use the grappling hook to snare the body, but with the added weight of water and plants, it was too difficult to maneuver and free the body. They requested the smaller drag bar be used. The body itself wouldn't weigh much underwater so the hooks on the drag could snag the clothing, allowing the body to be pulled through the vegetation to the surface.

With both divers back in their boat, waiting for the drag to be ferried out, the ranger decided to head back to shore with Kellee, Sarah and Gunner. It was getting late. News of the find had still managed to quietly make its rounds through base camp, and the ground-pound teams were debriefing from their last tasks before heading home.

Sarah no longer cared if her team stuck around to watch them drag the lake tonight. She was satisfied they had located the body and that a retrieval plan was in place. It was validation. She and her canine team had been vindicated.

As the whaler headed in, they passed the boat with the drag bar going out to the dive team. The lieutenant was aboard. *Maybe she needs to be there when the body is brought up since it's a crime scene.* Sarah could see the mesh body bag as well that was used in drowning cases. Sometimes a body would be hooked and dragged all the way back to shore but that wasn't always a good thing. Dragging a victim so far might compromise forensic evidence. It was always better to bag the body at the site of recovery.

"Hey Sarah," Kellee called as they headed to the dock, "let's see if Joe and Garrett want to grab some dinner after we debrief." She turned to the ranger and added, "You're welcome to join us as well."

"Starving," Sarah replied. "Just want to get the dogs taken care of and get a burger and a beer somewhere." Sarah laughed. Her spirit had improved since the body was discovered. She felt like she could finally relax. She sent a text to her team members to see if they wanted to join them afterward for dinner.

The sun had just about settled over the western sky. A last few orange rays escaped through the hills and valleys intersecting the shoreline, illuminating sections of the lake. Sarah pulled her phone from its Ziploc baggy and took a few quick shots. *Perfect setting for the end of a long, stressful day.*

The boat rounded the last bend in the small cove on the way to the dock, and the radio crackled with static and chatter. The lieutenant's voice came across their still secure channel to base. She reported that the body had been recovered. She gave a quick description of a white male, approximately 5'9', 250 lbs., gray hair with a tattoo on his left arm. Base confirmed, then requested specific information regarding evidence retrieved that morning from the unmanned boat.

For a moment there was no response, only dead air. Sarah wondered what was going on as she paid attention to the radio prattle; they all were waiting on the lieutenant's response.

As the ranger expertly maneuvered the boat alongside the floating dock, the lieutenant's voice resounded over the radio, finally. They all realized the dive team must've been taking time to check.

"This may be the owner of the unmanned boat and the subject of our search, but he's not missing his frank and beans. I repeat, this body appears to be *completely intact*."

Surprised at the revelation, Sarah and Kellee looked at each other.

"What the hell?" Sarah let drop out. "So where's the guy who's missing his?"

CHAPTER 12

Sarah

Dave was waiting at the dock when the ranger navigated the skiff along the edge and secured it. Sarah smiled at Dave as he helped her and Kellee exit the boat. "You still hanging around? I thought your shift ended an hour ago?" Sarah teased. She felt comfortable enough with him to banter.

"Just thought I'd stick around to see how things went and if you guys needed any help. I see the divers can take instruction from the dog team after all," he sparred back.

Sarah tried to keep a poker face. Dave's comment was spiteful but funny, and she didn't want to give him satisfaction just yet. She wanted to make him wonder a little bit longer. He looked at her with a perplexed face.

She stared back for a moment and then broke into a grin.

"So that's how it's going be," Dave replied. "Next time, I might have to help out the *other* team," he said with a sarcastic smile.

Dave walked with Sarah and Gunner as they headed to her truck. "I checked Sam's water and gave him a dog biscuit while you guys were out on the boat."

"Thanks. Appreciate you looking in on him." She was grateful but suddenly felt smothered by allowing him this close to her personal world. She trusted him with her dogs, but she didn't want to feel like she owed him anything. *Maybe this was close enough for now.* Was she starting to have self-doubts when it came to the walls she had erected around herself?

Base camp came across the radio, "Debrief in 10 minutes. 1900 hours in the command unit for those teams just coming in from the field."

"Sounds like that has your name written all over it. I'll head over with you if you don't mind me tagging along," Dave offered.

Sarah considered. He'd been getting a little too close for comfort, but on the other hand, maybe Dave just wanted an excuse to be kept in the search loop. She didn't want to push away a fellow canine handler for the wrong reason. "I just need to finish up with these guys and then we can head over." Not sure about allowing Dave into her space any more than she had already done that day, she nonetheless heard herself invite him to dinner. Maybe she felt obliged.

"Not sure I want to be seen with the dog team," Dave retorted.

"It'll be your loss!" Sarah spat back, pointing at him with one hand and the other on her hip. She broke into a teasing smile and turned her focus on her two boys.

Dave stood back as Sarah took care of the dogs. She needed a few moments to check Gunner and take a quick peek at Sam. She made sure they both had fresh water and were secure in their crates. She put the tail gate up but left the cap door open for air flow. The dogs curled up in their crates. They were content from their day of work. It satisfied them physically and mentally. *So lucky,* she thought, smiling and taking one last glance at the dogs.

She turned to Dave and said, "Ready?" He nodded his head and they started to make their way to the command unit.

"I wonder how this will affect future dive team searches in this lake," Dave made a blank statement, "since the body was caught in the vegetation and never made it to the bottom. Will it make them re-think the use of side scan sonar with its limitations."

"Coming from another resource's point of view, I'm hoping it opens the dive team commander's eyes a little. The canine team is only here to work with them, not compete. Our team is happy that it was a successful recovery and we were able to be utilized. It will help to bring closure to the family. That's what we train for."

"I'm a believer. You're really good with your dogs, Sarah. It was remarkable watching you guys work together."

Sarah could see he was sincere. She was flattered, but didn't want to be emotional. She didn't want to appear weak. She needed to stay strong and professional on the outside. "Thanks. But it's all the dogs. It's because of them. They're the ones who get the job done."

"They wouldn't be here without you bringing them and leading the way."

"They would drive themselves if they could!" Sarah retorted with a chuckle. She kept trying to steer the conversation back to the lighter side. She was fearful of being too serious emotionally or letting the conversation take a deeper tone.

Dave followed as Sarah led the way. She had taken the bandana off her head and used it to tie her wavy, copper shoulder-length hair in a ponytail.

"Nice tatts," Dave complimented.

Sarah touched the back of her neck subconsciously. "Thanks," she sputtered, not knowing if he was sincere or judging her.

"Never seen paw print tattoos before. Is that Sam and Gunner's names inside them?"

"Hunh?" Sarah was caught off guard. She wasn't quite sure of his tone.

"Just saying there's no doubt what's most important in your life."

Sarah appreciated that Dave could understand how her world revolved around her dogs. They *were* the most important things in her life.

Clambering up the steps into the command unit, it was standing room only. There were five members of the dive team including their commander, the lieutenant, Kellee, Joe, Garrett, a few leaders from the ground-pound teams plus the rest of the communication and search management team. Sarah instantly felt like she would suffocate.

"Well, there's our little star of the search. Glad you could make it," the dive commander stated in a condescending tone as Sarah entered. She and Dave had been the last ones to make it to the debriefing.

"That will do," the lieutenant blasted back, her face sharp and pinched with infuriation. It didn't go unnoticed that she had grown tired of the man's immature antics.

Sarah shot the dive team commander a hardened look. *Enough already! He's nothing but a bully! He must feel threatened. I think we proved ourselves today. I shouldn't have to put up with his constant grind.*

"Okay, now that we're all here, let's quickly go over today's search event. I know everyone is tired and hungry and wants to get out of here," she began. "I want to thank all of the resources and volunteers for their hard work and time. We couldn't have done this without any of your teams," she said as she looked around the crowded unit.

Sarah's mind started to wander as the lieutenant droned on about the search assignments, the areas covered and outcome. She looked over to where Kellee stood with the rest of their team. She was proud to be a part of an organization that was both professional and good at their jobs. It had given her the confidence she needed to get through today's search tasks.

Having Dave as an alliance and support was an added bonus.

She was still lost in thought, only half listening to the lieutenant when she heard the recovered subject's name. It was familiar. It was a name from her not so distant past.

"The drowned subject has been identified as 65-year-old Thomas Brickner from the Penn Township area. We pulled ID from the deceased that matches the truck's registration."

Sarah's jaw dropped at the sound of the victim's name. Her breath became shallow.

The lieutenant continued, "The boat registration did not match up to the boat that was found which made it difficult to identify the owner and occupant." The lieutenant paused for a moment to look through her notes before she continued.

"We're at a complete loss as to why there was a dismembered male body part located in what appeared to be Brickner's boat. Brickner's body was complete—intact—as far as we could see. Though, he does appear to have received some sort of trauma to the head and upper torso. Trauma that could've happened from a fall of his own accord, or perhaps received from another human. We won't know cause of trauma until a full autopsy has been performed."

Sarah's muscles tensed and she felt her body go rigid. *Breathe,* she told herself.

Dave looked at her. He watched her clench her jaw for the third time today. "You okay?" he whispered.

The lieutenant flashed a look at Dave and continued. "We are handling both the drowning and the evidence found on the boat as suspicious and crime scenes. Since this will be an on-going investigation, we would appreciate everyone keeping this information quiet."

At first, Sarah didn't respond to Dave. She just concentrated straight ahead at the lieutenant. *Really? I went through all of this trouble today for* him? *How ironic is that?* Hateful thoughts crossed her mind when she realized it was her state-appointed foster father. Her abusive and degrading foster father. Her piece of shit foster father. It made her breath catch in her throat.

With a concerned look, Dave asked her once again if she was okay. Swallowing hard, she waved a hand at him and said she was fine. She crossed her arms and re-focused on what the lieutenant had to say.

She steadied her breathing. Sarah had become a pro at learning to conceal her emotions.

"Thanks again to all the first responder volunteer teams who gave their time to help with the search today. This agency as well as the county appreciates your services and dedication. If anyone has anything to add to today's search notes, please stay behind after debriefing. Other than that, you're all free to go. Make sure you sign out."

Since Dave and Sarah had been the last ones in the unit, and closest to the door, they were the first ones to exit. Sarah jumped down the last few steps and stormed away toward her vehicle. She could hear Dave follow in pursuit. She knew he would want an explanation. Heavy footfalls, he jogged to catch up with her.

"Sarah."

She didn't turn around.

"Sarah," called Dave more firmly.

She felt his hand on her shoulder as they neared the back of her truck. Sarah spun around on her heel. The look on her face stopped Dave in his tracks. She had a hardened expression she'd never shown him before.

"Sorry," he spat out. "What's going on?"

Sarah stood there for a moment. Blood pounded in her temples. *Calm down! He's dead! Why am I letting him have this effect on me now?* She closed her eyes and drew in a few deep breaths. Dave stood facing her, waiting and patient. "I'm tired, I'm hungry. That's all. It's been a long day. I guess I overacted to being stuffed into the command center."

Dave looked at Sarah. From the appearance of concern on his face, the sincere tone of his voice, she could tell that he was honestly worried about her. She didn't like keeping the truth from him.

"Are you sure? You just seemed to react when the lieutenant said the subject's name."

She studied Dave's face for a minute. *Should I tell him?* Did she want to risk the chance of being judged by him so soon? Lose the chance of him getting to know who she really is, not who she was due to the way she was raised. She didn't want to chance seeing the judgment reflect in his face like she'd seen so many times in the past. No, she couldn't bear that right now. *Too much explaining*.

"Yes, I'm sure."

"Okay, no problem. I just wanted to make sure you're going to be all right. Do you still want to grab some dinner?"

"I'll be fine. Let me check with Kellee and the rest of the team. I'm sure they're famished as well and ready to head out." Sarah looked around but didn't see Kellee by her van. She pulled out her phone and sent a text to Kellee, Joe and Garrett asking if they were ready to go. Kellee quickly replied with a message that they were almost finished in the command unit and would be ready to head out to eat shortly.

"Looks like they'll be ready to go soon. There's a great burger place just a few miles from here. We can meet them over there." Sarah sent a text to Kellee with the info on the diner so she and Dave could head out.

"Perfect, I'll follow you over." Dave headed to his police-issued SUV.

Sarah walked around to the back of her truck. Gunner and Sam looked up from where they were sleeping in their crates. "Hey guys, you were amazing today. I'm so proud of both of you. Good job!" The dogs' tails wagged lightly in gratitude as she spoke to them. She shut the cap of her truck and locked it. Once in her truck, she put it in gear and looked around for Dave. She saw a state police vehicle waiting at the entrance to the parking lot.

She headed out of the park with Dave following close behind. She was beyond tired. *This has been an interesting day. A fucking emotional rollercoaster.* Her thoughts were scattered as she headed to the diner. *What am I getting myself into? I need to tread lightly here. Not sure I'm ready for this. Just keep it simple,* she told herself. *At least I can sleep in tomorrow and maybe sort all of this chaos out over the next few days,* she thought as she looked forward to the rest of her four-day weekend.

CHAPTER 13

Sarah

Sarah headed home after dinner with Dave and her teammates. She had struggled to stay awake and coherent through discussions rehashing the search. Polite, but aloof, she remained quiet as she listened to her teammates' conversations. She paid attention when Dave added his thoughts to the day's events. She could tell he had respect for her team and regarded them as peers when it came to teamwork, canines and search strategy.

So tired! She had been awake for over 24 hours. The stressful day was finally coming to a close. The group finally parted, everyone headed in their own direction.

Arriving home, she let the dogs out in the yard to stretch and take care of business. She turned on the spotlight above the deck in the backyard. Looking out the kitchen window she could keep an eye on them as she prepared their evening meal. She watched them follow invisible tracks around the yard to the back gate where a path dropped into the woods. *They never stop. Their sniffer is always turned on,* she laughed to herself. *I wonder what type of animal they're tracking now.*

She called the dogs back in the house and locked them in their crates with their dinner. Heading down the hallway from the dining area to the bathroom, she grabbed a towel from the linen closet. Sarah could feel the dogs' eyes follow her. "You're not missing a thing, guys."

Once in the bathroom, she pulled off her team-issued ball cap and slipped off the red bandana that helped keep her hair in place. She carefully pulled up and removed a thick hairpiece and sat it on a pedestal on the counter. She pulled the strips of tape that held the piece in place, from her scalp.

Looking at herself in the mirror she realized it wasn't her past that kept her from getting close to men, but the conditions from her past that she still dealt with. *What would he think? What would anybody think? Damaged goods, no doubt.* What would Dave think if he ever were to find out she had *alopecia areata universalis*? She studied the small scars that wound their way along her upper arms and torso. *Damaged goods. That's what she was and always would be.*

Turning on the hot water, she let the shower run for a few minutes before stepping in. Steam filled the little bathroom. Once under the faucet, she leaned against the tiled wall, closed her eyes and drifted. She let the grime and stress of the day wash way, allowing herself to drift off and relax.

Feeling somewhat renewed, she dried off and pulled on an old, worn t-shirt. For a moment, she felt whole again. In the privacy and confines of her home, with her two dogs. She felt in control, comfortable. By herself, in her own space, where she would never be judged by anyone, especially her dogs, she felt the most at peace.

Letting Gunner and Sam out of their crates, they competed with each other to see who could get Sarah's attentions. "Settle down, guys," she chided. After checking locks on the door and switching on a nightlight in the bathroom, Sarah finally headed to bed with two dogs in tow. She fell asleep as soon as her body hit the bed. The dogs curled up on the hardwood floor close to their owner.

* * *

The early morning sun streamed in through the bedroom windows. Sarah pulled a pillow over her head to block the disruptive light from interrupting her sleep. The dogs heard her stir and were up circling, stretching and whining immediately. "Go lay down!" she mumbled with some exaggerated distinction. She tried to sound firm, even mean, but they knew better. Gunner and

Sam just looked at her, tails going non-stop, prodding her to wake up with their pitiful whines and willful stares.

"Okay, okay!" She gave into the dogs' demands and pried herself from her snug bed. She followed Sam and Gunner as they raced each other down the hall. They slid into the wall as they turned the corner on the hardwood floors, stopping at the back door. Sarah let them out, yelling, "Take it easy, guys," as they bounced down the brick steps. *They are so numb sometimes!* She watched as they playfully bit and bowed at each other, running across the deck and out into the yard. "Chaos as usual!" she laughed shaking her head.

Picking up the dog bowls from inside their wire crates, she could hear her phone buzzing. She'd been so tired last night she'd left it in her BDU pants pocket, dropped unceremoniously on the hardwood floor outside the bathroom.

Most of the time, Sarah kept the phone beside her wherever she went. Setting the bowls down on the counter, she found her BDUs and fished the phone out. She had missed that call plus a few more. Dave had called twice already, both recently. Kellee had called last night.

I wonder why he's calling? We just saw each other. Sliding the bar to unlock her phone, Sarah tapped on Dave's number. He answered the phone within a few rings. Sarah could tell he was on his Bluetooth, in his squad car, she assumed.

"Hey there, Sarah," echoed in her ear. "Hate to bother you so early on your day off."

"Oh, hey Dave. Sorry I missed your call." She stretched her whole body still trying to wring the sleep from her tired bones.

"Has anyone called you yet?"

"Uh, no. I'm just getting up. Called me for what?"

"Looks like we have another search," Dave continued, "and you will never guess where it is."

Sarah cast a silent smile. She knew Dave was trying to humor her. She was getting the idea that he was also a goofball at heart. She was happy he felt at ease with her enough to kid around. "How many guesses do I get?" she fired back. "The same park, maybe?" She retrieved her notepad from her BDU pants as well as her pen and waited for Dave to respond

"Well, aren't you the smart one. Is your team available again? Will they be ready to go out on another search this quick? Can Sam and Gunner work again?"

"Are you kidding? The dogs are always ready to go," Sarah laughed. "We have several certified members and I'm sure we'll have a couple dog teams available. You know I'm available and can help. Good thing I'm close to the park. Is this another water search?"

"Will be an inland search to start out with. Seems we have a despondent person whose vehicle has been left at the park for a few days. Apparently the gentleman has been known to drive to the area and hike so he knows the trails pretty well. Evidently his car has been in the lot since sometime on Tuesday. He hasn't been seen since."

"Okay. Will the state police be running the search again?"

"Yeah, it's our jurisdiction and with what was found yesterday, our agency is all over this one. I'll be there with Bella as well," he said referring to his new bloodhound. "I'm going to try and see if we can pick up a track from his vehicle. Hopefully Bella can figure out a direction of travel. We're heading there now."

"Okay, that sounds perfect. Would be great if she can pick up a track." Sarah jotted down a few notes. "Where is base camp set up for this search?"

"At the horse parking lot area. Do you know where that is?"

"Yep. Got it. I'll send out the info to my team and get back to you ASAP, Dave. Thanks for calling us again." Sarah hung up. She sent Kellee a personal text with all of the information on the search prior to sending out the team-wide text. Sarah wanted to make sure Kellee was up to escorting her and the dogs.

Wow, another call out right away! Finally fully awake, her adrenaline started to flow. Both dogs were on her heels. *They always know when something's up!* "You guys ready to go again?"

The dogs responded by running back and forth between the front door and Sarah. Gunner's body was shaking with excitement. There was nothing in this world these dogs loved to do more than go to work with their handler. They knew the game and that using their nose meant a huge play reward and interaction with Sarah.

She decided to give each dog a small portion of their morning meal since they would be heading out soon. She didn't think it would be a good idea to work them on a full stomach. But she also didn't want them going all day without something in their system. They each licked their bowls clean in a matter of seconds and looked up at Sarah and back to their empty bowls. The dogs had expected a heartier meal. "Sorry guys, I'll give you extra kibble tonight when we return."

She poured a cup of strong coffee and picked her uniform up off the floor. A quick "sniff test" told her it might be better to pull a fresh uniform from the closet.

Texts started to ping her phone as teammates responded to the call-out. Kellee replied stating she could escort Sarah and her dogs, but would not be bringing Meika today. A few other canine handlers responded available with an ETA of later in the day. Sarah responded with the address and directions and finished up with a call to Dave.

"Déjà vu," Sarah said out loud as she loaded her dogs up in the truck. *This reminds me of Groundhog Day,* she thought, referring to an old favorite movie. Once crated, Sam and Gunner broke out barking in full force. "You guys are so full of energy! Save it, you might need it today," she laughed.

I wonder what today's search will entail? She headed back in the house to finish dressing. *Hopefully everyone can work together without any conflict. Gaitors! Don't want to forget them,* remembering they were in the garage after the last muddy training. *I'm sure I'll need them today.*

CHAPTER 14

Dave

Dave pulled into the parking area where the abandoned car had been found. The missing subject's car still sat vacant and unattended. The small irregular-shaped lot was covered in gravel and met up with a large grassy knoll that bordered the lake. You didn't have to enter the park to come into this lot as it was directly accessible from the main road.

It was a favorite area for parents with small children just learning how to fish, and people who wanted to feed the local geese. The main trails were also easy to get to from there. During warmer months, although a small area, it could be very busy with lots of car and foot traffic.

There were a few state police units on site as well as the head ranger from yesterday's water search. They had secured the area and already scoured for possible obvious clues. Hunched together, coffees in hand, they were deep in discussion, waiting for Dave and his new bloodhound, Bella. Dave sat in the SUV that was outfitted for canines as he finished up paperwork for a previous call. They all pointed and laughed at him. *Up to no good as usual,* Dave thought, smiling back. He was used to their good natured harassment.

Dave had positioned his vehicle along the edge of the lot under a shady pin oak that still held onto its autumn-colored leaves. Since Bella had accompanied him today, Dave drove a late model SUV outfitted with insulated dog boxes in the back. The dog boxes had their own separate air conditioning as well as a security system. Bella rode in style. The boxes were padded and made of steel. They were top safety rated and could withstand a crash or rollover.

Dave and Bella had spent twelve long, arduous weeks in canine boot camp. Bella was just over a year old, already professionally trained for tracking when Dave had been paired with her. Dave had to understand how to work a tracking dog and then learn to work with Bella. They had to discover how to partner together as a successful team and pass stringent certifications before graduating from their class. Once completed, Dave had been transferred from traffic to canine. He took it on as a challenge and new adventure. He had never owned a dog in his life but delighted in just about everything so far.

Sarah called to let him know she and Kellee would join the search this morning with Gunner and Sam. Two more canine handlers would be able to join after 1400 hours. She gave him an ETA of 0900 hours for herself and hung up. Dave relayed the information to base camp and turned over the dispatch and contact duties to another officer. With the mystery surrounding yesterday's search, the state police wanted to keep a tighter hold on this undertaking. They only called out select teams that management considered capable to handle a high profile case: Sarah's team, a mounted unit, and a highly trained ground-pound unit consisting of volunteers from the local fire department.

From training and the few searches she had already worked, Bella knew the drill and began to bay. She was excited and loved her job. She did what came natural to her, sniffing a track. And when she was done, her handler rewarded her with food. She wasn't obsessed with toys like Gunner and Sam. She worked on a higher pay scale. Bella demanded rewards that consisted of hot dogs and roast beef.

"Hey girl, sounds like you're ready to go. Hang on a minute." He really didn't care if she continued to be vocal, he loved to hear her eagerness when they were getting ready to run a track.

Opening the rear passenger side door, Dave reached in and grabbed his police-issued vest. He pulled it over his uniform. The vest had several lined pockets where he could stash food rewards. A few pockets were reserved for scent articles and other search supplies. The vest was a hideous neon green color with Police Canine Unit printed in bold letters across the back. The color helped illuminate and make him more visible if he had to work along the edge of a road.

The other troopers and park ranger gravitated to Dave and began to lightheartedly harass him. "I see you brought your girlfriend today," one of his co-workers remarked.

"At least he brought a partner that can get the job done," another one teased.

"Stand back," Dave grinned at the other troopers, "or I'll have to unleash the fury of Bella on you."

"Fury?" one laughed. "What fury? Will she slobber us to death?"

In his mid-twenties, Dave was considered a youngster among his law enforcement brothers. Though they chastised him from time to time, they were his protectors and confidantes. He was still innocent in many ways, not as hardened as they had become. He had not seen or dealt with what his older brothers had yet. It was all part of the job.

Dave popped the hatch to expose the dog box and Bella in the back of his truck. She was standing in her enclosure, still baying. Her long, thick tail whipped the inside walls of her steel restrictions. Dave opened the front of her enclosure just enough to allow her head to stick out. He quickly attached a leash to her wide leather collar. She looked up at him with saggy, deep soulful eyes. He rubbed her ears and scratched her exposed neck as she stretched. Bella had grown quite fond of her handler in a short time.

Once the leash was attached, he allowed her to come out the rest of the way from her crate. She jumped down from the back of the SUV to the gravel. "Easy girl, be careful," Dave cautioned Bella. He spoke to her as he would another human. They had developed a great relationship in their short time together. He knew he spoiled her sometimes, but he felt she deserved it. Numerous arrests had already been made thanks to her skill. The arrests were directly due to Bella tracking and locating the subject.

Dave pulled a Kevlar vest over Bella's head, adjusting it so she could move freely. He attached her badge to the front of the vest. Bella wasn't just another canine, she was a state trooper—given the same rights and protection any human trooper was given. Dave was responsible for her care and protection. He took that responsibility seriously.

She didn't have or need the obedience Sarah's dogs had. Bella was a bloodhound, a different breed and worked in a slightly different capacity. Although they needed a strong, stern handler to take charge, they worked best with a calm firm partner. Someone who was forceful or overbearing could cause a bloodhound to become disobedient and disrespectful.

Close to 90 pounds, Bella was large for a female. Mainly black and tan, she had a black mask and saddle that lay over her dark tan body. She also had dark points along her ear tips and tail. She was fit and well-muscled, a handsome animal. Naturally, she would go to the ground to track a scent due to her history and breeding. The long ears and folds of skin helped hold the subject's odor and skin follicles in place to assist her scenting abilities.

"Were you able to secure a scent article from the subject's vehicle?" Dave asked the other troopers. He continued to ready himself and Bella, stashing a couple all-beef hot dogs into his vest. *Only the best for you, Bella.*

"Yeah, we pulled a hoody from the back seat that appears to belong to the subject. We used silicone gloves to pick it up and sealed it in a plastic bag."

"That should work," Dave replied. He outfitted her with a thick leather harness which he slipped over her protective vest. The harness had dense wool padding on the chest area and rounded brass buckles. He checked the pockets of his vest to make sure he had zippered the reward pockets shut. He checked his pants pockets to verify he had his phone and radio.

“Okay, Bella girl, ready to do this?” Dave spoke to her as he patted her head and sides. Appearing calm, Dave was really reeling inside with excitement. He couldn’t wait to show Bella off and get to work.

“Okay, we’re ready,” Dave addressed the other troopers and the ranger. “Once we do a thorough check around the subject’s vehicle, I’m going to open the car doors and let Bella check out the inside. After she’s finished with the car, I want you to bring out the scent article and let her take a good whiff.”

“Sure, will do. Just let us know when you’re ready for it and if you need anything else.” The troopers and the ranger stood back in a group, giving Bella and Dave plenty of room around the parked car to work. Standing with authority, they crossed their arms to watch their comrade work his dog. No doubt they looked like an imposing force, or believed they did. *More like the three stooges,* Dave thought.

Dave hooked Bella’s long leather tracking line to her harness. Unhooking her leash from her collar, he wrapped it around his waist and re-connected the leash back to itself so it fit snug around him so he wouldn’t lose it. Bella was in a sloppy sitting position at Dave’s side waiting for his command to begin her task. She didn’t jump around like Gunner or Sam. She didn’t seem to be that excited actually. She had energy and was ready to go, but didn’t waste it on unnecessary rambunctiousness. Her intensity was all in her gaze, her stare at her handler.

Looking down at Bella and her droopy, soggy eyes, Dave told her, “Okay,” and headed to the subject’s vehicle. He had her walk around the car a few times. Opening the driver’s door, he allowed the dog up into the front seat to sniff around. Slow and methodical, Bella took her time, taking in all the smells and scents within the vehicle’s confines.

When Dave saw that she had enough and was ready to exit the car, he had one of the other troopers bring the bag over with the hoody. Opening the top of the sealed baggy with gloved hands and making sure he didn't touch any part of it, Dave lowered the item to Bella and let her take in a good, long sniff.

Like a vacuum cleaner, Bella sucked in the smell, letting the scent of its owner pass over her receptors. She was a "scent specific" canine. They were trained to look for a specific human. Bella would now only track whoever had the strongest scent left on this article.

"Find him," he asked her. Bella put her nose back down to the ground. She turned in small circles around the gravel directly below the driver's car door. After a few moments, she started to move out from the vehicle, trying to follow a particular scent. It had rained since the vehicle had been parked which made tracking difficult. Also many people had hiked through, which was another added variable for the bloodhound.

Bella continued to work hard. She found a "hot track" and followed it several feet, lost it, cast around and found it again. She repeated this process several times and slowly moved forward toward a wooded area and a trail head. It was frustrating for the dog, but she was dedicated. She was still young in her work experience but proved to be an outstanding dog with her scenting capabilities and perseverance to her work. Dave stood by unobtrusive, offering verbal support where he thought she needed it, but mostly, he was patient and let her do her job.

After an hour of losing and re-picking up the subject's scent, Bella finally lost the track completely. She started to head down the main trail from the parking lot. With several attempts to re-start her, trying to pick the track up further down the trail, Dave finally called it and brought Bella back to the parking lot.

He pulled out a hot dog from a zippered pocket in his vest. He offered the reward to Bella. The food brought out another beast in Bella which she showed by almost taking Dave's flesh with the hot dog. "Easy, Bella, that's my hand too!" Dave warned her. It didn't faze the dog. She had swallowed the hot dog whole and gave Dave a look that said, "Is that all?"

"She's got your number," the fellow officers chided Dave. "I can see the headline now—Trooper gets mauled by his own canine."

Dave took it all in stride. It was good-natured mocking from his fellow compadres. It didn't bother him in the least. He kept his focus on his dog, checking her over before lifting her up into her dog box.

"Well, at least we have a lead in the missing subject's direction of travel. I need to call this into base."

Dave made the call. He checked to see if Sarah had shown up yet with her dogs. "Okay, perfect, I'm heading that way now. Can you hold off deploying Sarah until I get over there? I think she should work this area with her dogs."

The communications officer replied, stating he would let the lieutenant know the track that was discovered and relay Dave's request.

He finished packing up Bella and headed over to base camp. Dave had an ulterior motive regarding his request for Sarah and her dogs. He wanted to learn more about how air-scenting dogs worked. But mainly he wanted to spend more time getting to know her.

He would volunteer to work with her again as her escort. Hopefully Sarah wouldn't mind him tagging along again today. Aside from the dogs, he found her very interesting. There was something about her that really piqued his curiosity.

Chapter 15

Sarah

Sarah sat parked on the shoulder of the road intersecting the main highway and the park entrance. Kellee had asked Sarah to wait and lead her to the new base camp since she was not as familiar with that area. If they arrived at the same time, Sarah and Kellee could also park beside each other.

Even though Sarah had handled the stress of yesterday's water search well, she was grateful Kellee could accompany her and lead the team today. Kellee would be the liaison between search management and her team which meant less mental work for Sarah and made the whole search event easier on her. She would be able to concentrate just on the search work itself and her dogs. Feeling thankful, she smiled inwardly. A weight had been lifted from her shoulders.

Sarah rubbed her eyes and yawned while she waited. Removing her baseball cap, she tightened the bandana and pushed a few stray curls up under the material. She chugged down the rest of her cold coffee, wishing she'd packed a second thermos again. *Never enough coffee!*

Lately, it seemed she was always dragging, tired. She needed the extra caffeine boost to get her moving. *Maybe third shift is finally catching up with me. Maybe I need to eat better and get more sleep too,* she laughed, thinking of the burger and beer from the night before. *Easier said than done,* she thought.

Looking in her rear-view mirror, she spotted Kellee's maroon mini-van heading her way. *About time.* Although a little tired and irritated for having to wait, the sight of Kellee lifted her spirits.

Even though she was still fatigued, getting the chance to work her dogs gave her the motivation and a burst of energy to carry on.

It's what she lived to do. It had become her main passion in life. The bright blue skies and drier air gave her soul a much needed lift as well. *Another gorgeous day to work Gunner and Sam! This weather's perfect to be outside in the woods with the dogs doing search work.* Humidity levels were down; there was just enough breeze and dampness for the dogs to air-scent. Ideal conditions for this type of work. The trees were in all their autumn splendor. Harvest time, her favorite time of the year. Sarah could think of no other place she would rather be.

Sarah pulled off the gravel shoulder onto the asphalt road in front of Kellee. She knew the park well and hadn't needed to set her truck's navigation system. Turning onto the thoroughfare that would lead the way to base camp, Sarah spotted a county sheriff's officer standing along the roadside. *Wonder what this is all about?*

The deputy's car was positioned at the main intersection to the horse lot and its blue and red lights were flashing. Sarah slowed down. As they approached the intersection to make the left turn, the deputy stepped out and flagged them down along the shoulder. The dogs had settled and quieted in the back, but when Sarah pulled to a stop, both started barking wildly again. *Looks like they stepped security up today.*

Although both of the women's vehicles had search logos visible on each side and rear, the deputy demanded they each produce appropriate identification. Sarah pulled her driver's license from her wallet and her search team's identification that she wore on a lanyard around her neck. She also wore a name badge with "Sarah Gavin, K9 Handler" pinned to her team's bright orange authorized uniform shirt. It was obvious and evident as well.

"Are you here for the search?" the deputy questioned.

"Yes," Sarah replied. "The woman in the van behind my truck is with me also. She is my canine's flanker, her name is Kellee Durham."

The deputy searched a sheet of paper attached to a clipboard. Finding Sarah's name, he checked it off and wrote the date and time beside it.

Not seeing Kellee's name on the sheet of paper, he asked both women to wait while he radioed to base. The deputy asked Kellee for her ID and called in to clear her. Becoming a little apprehensive, Sarah felt her pulse quicken as she scanned the area. *Deep breath.* Her angst was due more to her need to move and ready for the search. There were steps she needed to take to get her and the dogs ready and she replayed them over and over in her head. It took her anxiety up a step. *Stop it!* she tried to tell herself. *OCD? You think*? Always worried she would forget something, she had to laugh at her own shortcomings.

After what seemed like forever, but was really only a few minutes, the deputy returned Kellee's ID. He stood to the side and waved both women through the stone gates to the base camp area. Sarah didn't realize she had been holding her breath. She exhaled sharply with a happy sigh of relief.

Sarah slowly drove along the access road. This area was one of her favorite spaces within the park. The horse trailer parking lot was a well-used area for avid trail riders. Many other park goers stopped there because the site lent well to dog walkers and hikers. The lot was large and open. There were several picnic tables available as well as wide well-groomed bridle trails that park goers liked to hike. The trails near this lot traveled close along the lake's contour.

The space was level with an entrance and an exit. The horse trailer lot featured crushed stone and sported a portable bathroom. It was the perfect location to be set-up for a wilderness search within the park parameters. The site would accommodate several searchers, their vehicles, media and the county's large command center if that was also being utilized.

Across from this site was a sizeable hay field that could hold overflow vehicles. There was also capacity for a helipad if the need arose. Helicopters were useful for searching areas with difficult to access terrain, and the use of infrared at times was beneficial as well. You never knew what a search would entail—or the outcome—even though you hoped it would be a good ending. But, that is why training involved as many scenarios as possible.

Searchers always kept their hopes up that it would end with a live find—subject found alive and well—and everyone goes home afterwards. But a helicopter would came in handy if a search victim was found with debilitating injuries, requiring emergency transport. Even that was better than a deceased subject find—which turned into a recovery rather than rescue.

Sarah followed the narrow road's twists and turns with Kellee trailing close behind. Amazed at the recent storm's devastation, Sarah spotted downed and uprooted trees. She made a mental note not to forget to wear gaitors over her hiking boots and pants to help protect her feet and legs from rough patches they might encounter while out in the field. Made of tough, waterproof Gore-Tex, the gaitors zipped up the side of her calf like a half chap covering from the top of her boots to the bottom of her knee.

Sarah passed the glistening lake. She marveled at how the morning sun bounced off the overflowing body of water. Her thoughts turned toward the water search for a moment. She was thankful there had been a portion of beach to run the shoreline searches yesterday. All the recent rains had swollen the lake and in turn, the water level was at its highest. Some of the lake's normal rocky shoreline that met the grassy edge had completely flooded the beach on this side of the lake.

Close to 0900 hours, Sarah and Kellee arrived at the lot, already at capacity and full of activity. The area was full of deep, wide puddles. The ground looked soft and muddy where it met the crushed stone. Sarah quickly scanned to find an open and less soggy spot where both vehicles could park side by side. She also wanted a spot away from most of the activity. If she could back the truck in, the dogs would not be as distracted by the comings and goings of other personnel attending the search. The less motion the dogs took in while in their crates, the more they could relax, or so she thought.

Heading to the back of the lot, Sarah spied the perfect spot. Dropping into four-wheel drive with the flip of a switch, she executed a three-point turn and parked on the soggy grass between the porta-potty and a small clump of trees. Kellee opted to park her front-wheel drive van on the gravel in front of Sarah's truck. *Good thinking,* Sarah thought, *no use getting stuck and causing a second rescue today.*

Sarah saw the local media and a news commentator heading her way as soon as she put the truck in park. "Great!" she voiced out loud with a bit of irritation. This was the last thing she wanted to deal with at the moment. *Calm down,* she told herself, *don't let the red-headed attitude show through. You can handle this.* Taking a deep breath, she thought back to her training and how they were taught to deal with the media. She slowly opened her truck door to step out.

Luckily for Sarah, Kellee sprang from her van to intersect the reporter and entourage. Although at times, the media can be positive for a search, they can also be a hindrance, trying to glean information from search responders, especially at the most inappropriate and inopportune times.

I wonder why and how they got in. I thought this was a "closed" search? Maybe it's to show the public how their taxpayer dollars are being utilized.

Kellee blocked the reporter and the cameramen. Sarah could see the spokesperson continue to point toward Sarah's truck. Sarah made busy with the dogs and her gear until Kellee could satisfy them. Finally, the news team turned and headed toward another group of searchers who had just pulled into base camp. Kellee threw her hands up in the air and smiled as she walked to Sarah. Sarah responded by rolling her eyes and shrugging her shoulders and a slow, sly smile crept across her face.

Sarah let out a sigh of relief. "Thank you, thank you, thank you!" Sarah gave Kellee a quick hug. "I owe you big time!"

“Oh, don’t thank me,” Kellee retorted with a smirk and a wink. “I said you’d give them a full interview after the search was concluded. Including all about how your dogs work, what’s involved with training air-scenting canines—and even a demo.”

“Great, Kellee. I know I can always count on you,” Sarah said sarcastically. “We better go sign in.”

The command unit and sign-in table were not far from their vehicles. Sarah felt confident leaving the dogs unattended for the short time she would be away. She opened up the back of the truck to allow air to vent for Gunner and Sam. The dogs stood up in their crates. They had stopped barking but were still whining. “Okay, guys, I’ll be back in few. Just chill out for now.” The dogs tilted their heads at Sarah as they listened. They stopped their whining for a moment as she spoke, but it picked right back up when she turned to leave.

Sarah looked around base camp. There were units already on scene from other volunteer search organizations she and her team trained with on occasion. It looked like the ground-pounder team and mounted unit had already checked in and were headed out on search tasks. She saw a couple gentlemen who were highly skilled man-trackers. Even though her anxiety was high and her adrenaline was pumping, she felt right at home among all the other searchers and frenzy of activity.

With such a large turn-out from the search community, Sarah hoped for a task far from base. Or at least an area up-wind of other searchers for Gunner and Sam’s sake. If there were less people for the dogs to check out, it would make it easier for her to control their whereabouts since they would work off-leash.

Sarah knew her boys would waste valuable time checking out any human they caught scent of who might be working close by. Sam and Gunner weren’t trained to scent discriminate like Dave’s bloodhound Bella. She would only search for a certain person’s scent. But the German Shepherds were taught to search and locate any unfamiliar human that happened to be in their assigned search area. And dogs didn’t understand search task boundaries.

If there were searchers in an adjacent area they wouldn't check the GPS before following whatever human scent blew their way.

Sarah noticed the state had brought its larger mobile command post today. It was centrally positioned in the parking lot. *Geez, an impressive bit of a beast.* The mobile unit was a large Class-A motorhome that had been morphed into a highly utilized resource center, complete with the county's 911 logo and other contact phone numbers emblazoned on the outside.

Several large antennas sprouted from the sides and top of the vehicle. Its windows were darkened glass so no one could see in, but people working inside could easily peer out. Spotlights were attached to the sides of the unit, as well as a huge awning. Generators were running, but were semi-quiet and barely audible. They made a low humming noise and a low rumble Sarah could feel through the ground.

Normally on a search, there was a certain "hurriedness" to getting there and being ready, but usually, there was a lot of down time as well. It was pretty much a "hurry up and wait" game. Most searchers would use the down time to check packs or take a nap and get as much information on the area and the missing subject as they could. Today's search resembled the norm more than yesterday's water search. To Sarah, it epitomized the atmosphere of a regular call-out and search. *Thank God,* she thought, *doubt I could handle the stress that surrounded yesterday's deployment two days in a row.*

Both women headed over to the crowded sign-in table and stood in line behind other first responders waiting to check in. Sarah was fidgety and the line seemed to move slow. *Finally,* she thought as she made it to the table. "Sarah Gavin, local county canine team," Sarah began when it was her turn. The officer manning the table looked up when she stated her name.

"So you're Sarah," he said. He smiled at her and she returned the smile.

Sarah wasn't expecting her name to bring recognition from someone she didn't know. It surprised her. Taking a deep breath to control rising anxiety she returned the exchange. "Am I on the wanted list?" she laughed.

"Oh no," the officer replied with a grin. "Seems a few people are pretty impressed with you and your dogs."

"Is that a fact?"

"Yes, it is. The lieutenant was very happy with the job and support your team provided yesterday."

"That's nice to hear. Good feedback's always welcome," Kellee piped in. "Our team trains and works diligently to make sure we can provide a reliable resource." Sarah could tell Kellee was trying to take some of the pressure off of her. Her friend knew she didn't always like being in the spotlight.

"Well, we really appreciate you joining the efforts again today."

"Not a problem. Glad we can help out." Sarah handed over her ID so the officer could check her in as they continued their conversation.

"I believe the lieutenant is waiting on you guys. When we're done here, go ahead in the command center and check in with her."

"Okay, appreciate your help." Sarah tucked her ID back in the case that hung around her neck on the lanyard. She waited for Kellee to finish up and they headed to the door at the end of the command unit.

Although Sarah knew she and her dogs were ready for today's search, she still had apprehensions left over from the previous day and the water search. She was worried her nervousness would show through or she would say something stupid in front of the lieutenant. *Chill out*, she told herself. *We'll get through this fine. We're all human.* She didn't understand where all the angst was coming from. Kellee opened the door and both women entered the unit.

Chapter 16

Sarah

The moment Sarah and Kellee entered the state police command unit, they were impressed. The hulking RV had been a recent purchase—over $500,000 of federal money spent upgrading to a newer, higher tech model. Not as expensive as many other states, but it was still a large chunk of money.

This unit was much more glamorous than the smaller, older county unit they'd used for yesterday's water search. It sported the most up-to-date computers, communication and internet systems available, as well a full kitchen and bathroom. They were tied into the state's computer-aided dispatch (CAD) system which allowed search management easy access to all databases.

Kellee looked at Sarah and mouthed, "Wow."

Sarah nodded her head. *Overkill,* she thought. *This place is nicer than my two-bedroom shack.*

The unit was pulsating with commotion. It felt like it was its own entity possessing private energy. A ground-pound team stood near the front receiving a briefing on their search assignment. Communications buzzed with the sound of radio transmissions from teams just heading out or starting their task.

On one side of the command center, a huge area map covered most of the wall. A trooper was writing "LKP," Last Known Point, in red letters on the spot where the car had been found. There was a red circle encompassing the immediate search area with the acronym "RoW" written just outside of it. The acronym stood for Rest of the World, the portion outside of the immediate search area. Their efforts would be concentrated within the red circle. Eventually, if the subject was not found within that immediate search area, sectors within the RoW would be the next step. *We will be searching somewhere in that area,* Sarah thought as she made a quick study of the map.

Everyone had a job to do and was acting on it. No one was standing around idle. All the fervor sent Sarah's energy level up another degree.

"Well good morning, ladies. Didn't think we would be meeting again like this so soon," Lieutenant Langenberg greeted them.

"Good morning," Sarah and Kellee returned in unison.

"Glad we could help out again," Kellee added.

"Are your dogs up for a search again so soon?" the lieutenant asked. "Isn't this tough on them mentally and physically?"

"They're ready and waiting. They would be here without me if they didn't need a chauffeur," Sarah laughed. "It's really not that tough on them. Since we split the search tasks up yesterday, Sam and Gunner had plenty of downtime. It will be more physical for them today, running through the woods, but it will help use up some of their excessive energy. Maybe they'll sleep well tonight," Sarah added.

"The dogs are pretty physically fit. We wouldn't deploy with them again if it jeopardized or compromised their health and well-being," Kellee stated.

"Okay, I just wanted to make sure. You guys did a fantastic job yesterday. My team and I were pleased with the work your organization provided—and the level of professionalism."

Sarah looked up and met Kellee's gaze. Both women smiled. The weight of what the lieutenant was saying was not lost on them. Kellee nodded in response.

"Thank you, we appreciate the opportunity to help out and utilize all of our training," Kellee stated.

"It's refreshing to work with 'drama free' teams as well. Since we're treating this area as a potential crime scene, we expect that same work ethic today. We don't know if today's subject is in any way tied to what we found yesterday, but we don't know that he's not either."

The lieutenant pointed to the table as she spoke. Sarah and Kellee obliged, heading to the desk full of paperwork and maps. They sat down across from each other, but Lieutenant Langenberg remained standing at the head of the table. Search management personnel continued to interrupt the lieutenant, peppering her with questions regarding placement of resources and other decisions that needed to be made. *No one realizes how much work and energy goes into a search effort,* Sarah thought.

Turning her attention back to the two women, Lieutenant Langenberg closed her eyes and gathered her thoughts. "Okay, we have a lot of information to go over. Some new knowledge has just come in from our K9 Unit as well. We'll wait for him to make his way over here from the LKP. After we're done going over the map and the subject's details, I want you to meet with him so you can go over what he and his tracking dog found."

"Are you talking about Trooper Graves?" Sarah questioned.

"Yes, that would be the one."

"Was he able to work Bella this morning successfully?"

"He worked her over at the LKP and I believe the pair found some information that will be useful in determining where we'll task you and your dogs. But let's go over the map and the subject first. Then we find out what he's learned. You three can discuss all the canine jargon."

"Sounds like a plan," Kellee added.

The first map the lieutenant opened up and straightened out across the table was a topo map. "Here we are," she pointed to a cleared area with an unimproved road running alongside it, a small stretch of trees and the lake on the tree line side.

"Here is the LKP where the subject's car was found." In red letters, LKP was marked in a small clearing along Sinsheim Road and a small finger of Lake Marburg. A black circle had been made around that portion, indicating the initial search area that Sarah had noticed on the wall map on her way in. From there, arrows and notes had been drawn regarding the main trails, the most popular points along those trails and other frequently visited sections of the park.

"This is the area our K9 worked this morning." The lieutenant continued to point at the black-encircled area with the tip of her pen. "The dog was able to pick up a track on this trail head, and follow it several hundred meters, but then apparently lost it. Dave can give you greater details. He should be here any minute."

The door to the command unit opened. Dave's booming voice could be heard as he spoke to the search management team on the way in.

"Hey there, guys! How's it going this morning? Any luck yet?" Dave asked management, making his way toward the group of women. The management team just shook their heads as he passed.

Sarah was quiet as Dave approached. He seemed to be in a great mood. *Beaming's more like it,* she thought. His smiling face did nothing to hide how he felt.

"Bella worked great this morning," Dave said as he looked at the lieutenant, hands on his hips. "The conditions were difficult though. With all the major storms that have passed through there's been a lot of rain since the car was left in the lot. And tons of foot traffic through the area as well. But Bella never gave up," Dave said proudly. "Although we lost the track, she did give us a clue as to which direction the subject went after he exited his vehicle."

"That'll be very helpful," Kellee responded.

"Good thing Bella's on our payroll," the lieutenant teased Dave.

Sarah couldn't help but smile at him. Dave was excited and full of enthusiasm as he described how Bella had worked and found the track, giving every detail of their search effort from earlier. His energy was infectious as he used his hands to describe how Bella worked and the track she picked up. He was very animated. She could tell he was completely absorbed with his canine partner and doing scenting work. *It was hard not to be.*

The lieutenant however, didn't seem to share their fascination in the minutiae of canine search. "Has anyone briefed your team on the subject yet?" she asked Kellee and Sarah, obviously trying to wrestle control back from Dave.

"No, that would be helpful, along with the tracking dog's clues. Those will help us choose a sector to work the dogs. The subject's physical shape, health and mental well-being can help us determine how far he might hike," Kellee suggested.

"Knowing how he was dressed could help, too," Sarah pointed out. "And what about friends, or someone who might've come by and picked him up? Does he have a cell phone?"

"Hang on, hang on, ladies. We have some interesting information on our subject. First off, he's wanted by the authorities."

"Wanted? What do you mean?" Kellee asked with deep concern in her voice. "We're an all-civilian volunteer team. We don't normally deploy for wanted criminals. "

"Hang on, slow down," the lieutenant repeated. "Seems he has a long rap sheet for petty stuff from juvie, but now he's wanted due to a domestic altercation with his wife. Just wanted for questioning—there's no warrant, and he's not listed as dangerous. The wife won't press charges. Yet again."

"Does he have a license to carry? Do we know if he could be armed?" Kellee pushed for more information.

"No license to carry, but that never rules out any kind of weapon on him," the lieutenant stated.

Sarah lowered her gaze to look at the map. She didn't want her expression to give away what she was thinking. *I thought today would be stress free but it seems this area's a shit magnet.*

The heated conversation between Kellee and the lieutenant continued. Kellee was seriously looking out for the team. She needed to make sure the canine handlers and their dogs would be working in a safe environment.

Or at least as safe as one could be with high-powered German Shepherds working off-lead in the middle of a forest,

Sarah thought sarcastically. A wicked grin crossed her face and she looked away again.

"So why is he wanted for questioning?" Kellee asked the loaded question.

"Seems this domestic altercation took place Tuesday evening between the subject and his wife. It wasn't witnessed by anyone, and she won't press charges, but the neighbors could overhear the argument and fighting. One neighbor called 911. When the police arrived on scene, the wife needed a ride to the hospital and the subject could not be found. The same neighbor also heard the missing subject threatening to kill himself. He's a known drug addict as well, so overdose is a possibility."

Sarah jotted down a few notes as she listened. There were standard questions to be asked and she knew Kellee would ask them. It was her responsibility to record the information.

"Has the subject attempted suicide in the past?" Kellee inquired.

"Not that we are aware of, but we are checking his background for that information."

"As far as drug information, do you know what kind of drugs he regularly uses or has used in the past?" Kellee continued with her litany of questions.

"From what we have been able to gather, he is a regular marijuana user, but has used other harder drugs in the past."

"Sorry, one last question. Does he have any medical conditions or is he on any medications that we be should be aware of?"

"Currently, we are not aware that he is on any medications. He does have a history of depression. Any more questions right now?" the lieutenant asked looking squarely at Kellee. It was clear that she wanted to move forward. Kellee just shook her head.

"Okay, as I was saying, the subject left home in his vehicle and hasn't been seen since. His whereabouts are unknown, no clue until his vehicle was identified. Being it's now Friday, he's been missing for three and a half days. He's listed as endangered and despondent."

"Okay, now that we've got that out of the way," Kellee sighed, "do we have a description, up-to-date information or a picture of our subject?"

"Of course," the lieutenant smiled sarcastically. She gestured to the entire mobile unit. "We have the latest and greatest databases available. Wouldn't do us much good if we couldn't access the information we needed."

Turning toward the printer that sat a few feet from the table, the lieutenant leaned down and pulled off a handful of documents. She handed one flyer to Dave.

"Dave, I need your search task report and a map of where your canine tracked. Do you have your paperwork with you?" the lieutenant asked.

Shaking his head Dave answered, "Hang on a second while I go retrieve it." He headed to the door and out to the parking lot.

Another officer stepped up to the lieutenant, whispered something and pointed to an area across the unit. Lieutenant Langenberg answered him patiently, "Alright, just a minute," then turned back to Kellee and Sarah. "Take a look at the subject's info. I'll be right back." She placed another copy of the flyer between the two women and headed to the rear of the command unit.

Sarah looked down at the paper. She froze. Her eyes rapidly took in the subject's picture, and her mind processed the specific details listed below. Sarah felt all the blood drain from her head. She stared at the flyer longer and her head started to spin. *Stop it!* she told herself. *What the hell? No fucking way!* Sarah involuntarily sucked her breath in sharply.

Kellee, whose eyes had followed the lieutenant across the unit, had just looked down at the flyer, but turned immediately to Sarah at the sound. "What's wrong?"

Sarah pointed to the name above the picture. She couldn't believe it. *This must be some kind of sick joke.* Her mind raced out of control. She tried to regulate her breathing.

Kellee grabbed Sarah's wrist. "Sarah, what is it?"

"It's him," Sarah mouthed under her breath so only her teammate could hear.

"Him?" A look of confusion crossed Kellee's face.

"From foster care."

It took Kellee only a few seconds. Sarah had told her about some of the demons from her foster care life. Understanding dawned on Kellee's face. There was one guy in particular Sarah had told Kellee about—but she'd never mentioned a name.

It hadn't been important. Then.

Now was not the time for Sarah to unravel. She needed to stop this physical reaction to her emotional response. Hyperventilating, she bit her tongue, and tried to hold her breath. She had to keep it together. Falling apart at a search event was a surefire way not to get invited back. *We've trained too hard for this! I can't blow it now. If I walk out and leave the search, they'll never call us back.* Word would get around; no other agency would use the team either. *Think*, she thought, *calm down and get all the information first.*

Kellee could tell that Sarah was about to lose it. Kellee looked at her teammate. Alarm registered in her eyes. "Look at me," she put her hand on Sarah's shoulder. "You'll be with me, Gunner and Sammy," Kellee told her. "You will be safe. We can handle this."

Sarah closed her eyes for a moment. *Deep slow breath, control yourself.* She tried to think of a calm, safe place. Gathering her composure just for a moment, she opened her eyes and refocused. *Knick of time*, she thought. Lt. Langenberg and Dave were heading back to the table.

With the flier still in front of her, Sarah forced herself to read all of the information printed below the missing subject's picture.

In bold lettering underneath the image of an unshaven, gruff looking man it announced:

AT RISK

DESPONDENT MISSING PERSON

Dwight Harrison, 27 years of age, 5' 11", White male, wavy mid-length brown hair, mustache & goatee. Full-sleeve colored tattoo on left arm depicting the devil. Several scars across torso and upper arms.

Sarah and Kellee read through all of the information the paper offered. Sarah drifted back to her days in the hands of foster care. She had shared some information from her previous life with Kellee, but not everything.

Sarah tried to calm herself down and push away her immediate fears.

Dave handed his canine report to the search management team while the lieutenant read through it as well.

When finished, they both re-joined Sarah and Kellee at the table where the maps were spread out. No one commented on Sarah's expression, so apparently she'd done a good job of outwardly hiding her fears.

Lt. Langenberg interrupted Sarah's thoughts. "Our missing gentleman was last seen at approximately 1800 hours this past Tuesday when he left his residence. As you know his vehicle was located at the lot adjacent to the lake and Sinsheim Road."

Sarah and Kellee reviewed their map as the lieutenant spoke. Sarah used a pen to pinpoint the area where the car had been located. She made a note in the sidebar. It helped her to relax as she continued to scribble remarks. Her shoulders began to relax. She felt the tension ease up for a moment.

"So far," the lieutenant continued, "we have two mounted teams and a handful of ground teams running hasty searches of the immediate area around the LKP. Those teams will run the trails and report back. Dave, I want you to show us on the map where exactly your dog found tracks."

Sarah was glad that she wasn't given the task of running a hasty task. Her dogs moved too fast and worked too far from her to be of much help on the quick initial information-gathering chore. The mounted team, in her opinion, was always the best option for this duty and she was happy they had already been deployed.

"Sure, sure thing," Dave pointed to the map. "I ran Bella on the vehicle first, let her scent and sniff around it for several minutes. Then we offered her a scent article, and she picked up a solid track from the driver's door. She cast about a few times but finally was able to follow the track from the car, through the parking lot onto the main trail heading northeast."

Dave pointed to the area on the map where the LKP was marked. He showed the group where Bella had crossed over a small stream and picked up the main trail that headed past the horse trail parking area and wound its way east. "We were able to make it about 300 meters down the trail. There are numerous smaller trails that drop off the main one, but we think he passed several of those pathways and remained on this trail at least this far. So I'm thinking maybe that was his ultimate goal. He could've traveled all the way to the furthest point of the park and maybe even back toward the lot where he had parked his car."

Sarah and Kellee studied the map, paying close attention to the main trail and how it wound its way through the whole park at some point. There were loops and shortcuts that split off, but they were not as wide or well-groomed as the main trail. If the subject continued as he had, he could have made it all the way over to the furthest northeast edge of the park.

With the predominant wind blowing from the north again today, this area might just be the best place to start working Gunner and Sam.

Kellee looked up at Sarah. "You thinking what I'm thinking?"

"I believe so," she answered, her throat constricted and dry. After studying search theory and training canines for years, they both thought on the same plane, though Sarah deferred to Kellee. She was still unraveled at the thought of who they were being deployed to find. Kellee took the lead and gave an overview of their search strategy.

"If I start the dogs from here," Kellee said pointing at the area on the southern boundary of Lake Marburg, toward the northeast corner of this side of the park, "we can grid from east to west working our way back north. Then we would be able to cover a large area efficiently depending on the terrain and how thick the ground cover is."

Dave and the lieutenant listened as the two dog handlers discussed how they would work their dogs. "Are there any searchers working in this area?" Kellee asked pointing to the edge of the park.

"No. The mounted teams plan to ride the main trail first and report back to base. Then their plan is to ride all of the smaller trails and loops that drop off the main trail. We also have a few of the mounted teams running a perimeter of the park to catch the subject if he's still mobile. Most of the ground teams are closer to the LKP and working the foot paths in that area. Will it disturb the dogs if you happen to run into any of the horse teams? They plan on riding the trail eventually through the area you're talking about. The teams might run into each other."

Sarah finally piped into the conversation. "No, the dogs will be fine with the horses. We've trained with a mounted team and know how to work our dogs around them. Gunner and Sam know most of the horses and team members here today." She found it calming to focus on something other than that worthless piece of shit that was the subject of the search.

Finally, their search sector was solidified, and they received boundaries of the area to grid. Their task would also cover part of the trail where Bella determined the subject appeared to be walking.

The lieutenant left to have management write up their search assignment and to retrieve a 7.5-minute topographical map of the area for Sarah and Kellee.

"Do you mind if I walk with you and the dogs on your task?" Dave asked. "I could be your escort." Sarah knew Dave was interested in seeing Gunner and Sam work together. Most handlers only worked one canine at a time.

"Oh no, that would be fine. I'm the strike team leader for the task," Kellee responded. Dave would know what the term strike team leader meant from NIMS training. Kellee would be in charge of the field team.

Maybe a man, especially a cop, would make it safer to be in the woods (with HIM possibly out there somewhere), was Sarah's initial thought. *On the other hand, the less info Dave knows about my past relationships the better.*

CHAPTER 17

Sarah

Sarah and Kellee were handed maps of their search sector. The management team went over their task assignment, discussing terrain, borders and search strategy.

"Your search assignment is at least two miles from base camp as the crow flies—even longer by winding roads and trails," Dave mentioned.

"Geez, you're right," Sarah agreed. *Far from the safety of base camp,* she thought. She knew what the subject—the creep—was about and what he was capable of. They would be the furthest team from base camp. Not unusual in itself, but it added additional concern for Sarah today.

The women stood up to exit with Dave in the lead. *Need to get outside!* Sarah felt like the walls were starting to cave in around her. She craved the fresh air and a chance to stretch her legs.

Kellee gave her a concerned look. Not wanting to worry her friend, Sarah smiled and whispered, "Ocean King." That was their team's code words used to indicate everything was okay.

"Do you think we can get a ride out to the sector?" Dave asked the management team before leaving the command unit.

"Shouldn't be a problem," one of the officers replied. "Let me find out where the mule is and if we have a driver." He turned to Sarah and Kellee. "Can the dogs handle riding in that?"

"Of course," Sarah attempted to smile as she answered. *We'll see,* she thought. "As long as it's the kind of mule you ride *in* and not *on*," Sarah laughed thinking of a vehicle commonly used on local farms. Though slightly larger than a golf cart, there still wasn't a lot of room in them and they usually were a bumpy ride. *Should be interesting*. Although both dogs had ridden in the back of an open pickup truck bed, they had never traveled in an all-terrain vehicle like a mule.

The officer pushed his chair away from the radio equipment. He shifted his police-issued leather belt, adjusting it around his considerable gut. He looked up to the dog handlers before he spoke as if he had something tremendous to say. "I can have a driver on his way over here with the mule. How soon will you and the dogs be ready to head out?"

The officer delivered his message in a monotone, but smug voice. Sarah felt like this was the last place on earth he cared to be and for some reason it added to Sarah's feeling of uneasiness. It unsettled her and she felt guilty for asking the man to do his job. *Asshole.*

"Give us 15 to 20 minutes" Sarah said, still trying to keep her composure.

Standing still, she was trying to hold herself together professionally. *Torn.* That's how it felt. Between giving into her anxieties and keeping her cool, she felt like she was being ripped in two. She knew once she could get outside, walking and focusing on the search task would help. She needed to be in motion.

"Okay, that will work," the officer from search management continued. "They'll be here when you're ready."

Finally. Sarah, Kellee and Dave were once again outside and moving. Dave headed toward his vehicle. "I need to grab a few things from the car and check on Bella. Don't leave without me."

"We won't," Kellee retorted, "but make sure you bring plenty of water."

Sarah held it together until they were far enough away from prying ears and suspicious eyes. Her face pale, sweat covered her forehead. Perspiration started to show through in patches through her shirt. All of the horror and memories had re-emerged when she saw Dwight's face—the missing subject—on the flier.

Sarah's signs of uneasiness were obvious. "Keep moving. Concentrate on getting the dogs ready," Kellee advised. "Don't think about the past. Focus on working your dogs and the task at hand."

Sarah felt numb inside. All of the painful memories flooded back in a rush. It made her head spin. *How could this be happening? Out of all the people in the world?* Sarah needed to pull herself together. Her reputation as a first responder and canine handler depended on how she performed—something she dwelled on over and over. Sarah never wanted to be the reason her team wasn't called back by an agency. She needed to calm down for herself and Gunner and Sam's sake.

If the dogs detected there was a problem with their handler, they wouldn't range as far while out on task. It would hinder their work. The dogs were apt to pick up on her emotional stress. Sarah tried to steady her nerves. She took a deep breath, stood taller, straighter and mouthed under her breath to no one but herself, "I got this, I can handle this."

Sarah could hear Gunner and Sam barking as she headed back to her truck. "Hey, guys," Sarah addressed them, her voice stressed and cracking. The dogs responded with high-pitched whines and the pounding of tails against their crates. Kellee headed to her van.

Sarah saw Kellee pull out her backpack and rummage through the contents. In slow motion, Sarah took in her friend's detailed preparation. Kellee refilled her containers with fresh water and made sure she had a working pen and notepad. Satisfied all of her supplies were in order, she secured the enclosures and placed the pack on the hood of her van.

"Do you need critter spray?" Kellee offered, holding the can of bug spray out to Sarah.

Sarah answered with a nod. The ticks were especially bad in this region of the country and in light of all the tick-borne diseases, it was best to be overly cautious. Thankfully the dogs were already well-protected with a monthly treatment that controlled ticks and fleas.

Sarah finished with the bug spray and handed it off to Dave once he rejoined the group.

Sarah pulled out one dog at a time to give them a quick bathroom break. It took Gunner and Sam a moment to settle down and get to business because they were so excited. She struggled to put their search vests on. Hugging Gunner around his neck, she held him tight to snap his neon collar.

Although today was another real search and they were "technically working," the dogs still thought of it as a game. They couldn't wait to play Find-the-Human-in-the-Woods. Sam and Gunner enjoyed any type of search work, but the terrain and environment of the woods was their favorite.

All of their search training had been carefully tailored to each dog's personality and drives, instituted through a completely positive program. To them, it was a fun outing in the woods with their owner, handler and partner. They couldn't wait to get the game underway.

The dogs' energy was contagious and their antics comical. Sarah's mind raced with the tasks that lay ahead. *Settle,* she told herself. *Take a few deep breaths and just chill.* She tried not to second guess her prep work regarding supplies, dog training or navigational skills. *Trust Gunner and Sam,* resonated in her thoughts. Seeing her dogs helped ease her mind. Slowing her breathing, Sarah smiled at her two clowns now back in their crates.

"Anything I can help you ladies with?" Dave asked.

"Think we're good for now," Sarah answered, "but thanks anyway."

Sarah stood unmoving surveying the contents inside the truck bed. The dog crates were attached to a platform. Under it were metal drawers filled with training and search equipment and supplies. There were racks along the inside of the truck cap that held several different types of leashes, collars and various other canine paraphernalia. To the untrained eye, it appeared to be in disarray, but actually the gear was well organized and easy to access.

Her wilderness backpack, the dogs' water bottles and several other pieces of search gear were spread across the open tailgate. Sarah had made sure all of the gear was clean and in good working order prior to storing it. She mentally primed herself for the search ahead. *You could never be over prepared,* she thought.

Dave peered into the back of her truck to admire some of her canine gear. He was in awe of how much stuff she'd fit in the bed. "From the looks of things, you have everything but the kitchen sink," he teased.

Nervous, Sarah joked back. "If you look hard enough, I'm sure you'll find that's in there too."

Exasperated with herself for being anxious and slightly on edge, she continued to keep busy, organizing and re-organizing her previously readied supplies. Finally, she straightened her back and shoulders once again to stand taller and give off an air of confidence, more for herself than for Dave. Her awareness shifted to trying to figure out the trooper's true intentions. She felt mixed signals coming from him.

Looking at her watch, Sarah realized they needed to get moving. "Okay, is everyone ready?" Sarah looked to Dave and Kellee. They nodded.

She could see the mule pulling up in front of the command unit. She grabbed Gunner and Sam's beta leashes from where they hung in the back of the truck. One excited Shepherd was enough to handle, but two doubled the joy. Sarah needed to pull the dogs out, straighten their vests which had shifted while they lay in their crates and attach their leashes.

She pulled Gunner out first and tried to get him to stand still long enough to reposition and tighten the straps on the dog vest. He was so excited, it was beyond difficult.

"Settle!" Sarah firmly command, continuing to try to get the vest to fit properly. Gunner pretended not to hear her and continued his capers.

Kellee laughed at the dog's antics. After Sarah was finally able to attach his leash, she saw Kellee pull a cookie from her vest. She held it in a fist in front of Gunner's nose. Instantly he settled down and started to push his nose into Kellee's tightly gripped fist to get at what she was hiding. Both dogs possessed a huge food drive as well as their play drive. Times such as this were perfect to use this food drive to advantage.

Sarah quickly adjusted the dog's vest. "Thank you," she mouthed silently to Kellee. She handed Gunner off to Kellee and moved to pull Sam out of his crate. Sarah quickly attached his leash and straightened out his vest. Sam was more of a gentleman and allowed Sarah to do what was necessary. She handed Sam's leash off to Kellee as well. Sam could smell the cookies in Kellee's hand and started pushing for them too.

Due to the tough terrain the dogs would be working in today, the vests they wore were different than the previous day's. Each was made of a rugged canvas material that discouraged briers or sticker bushes from catching. "Search Dog" was embroidered on both sides of the vest and the team's logo patch was sewn alongside. The orange vests contrasted with the dogs' neon yellow collars which read "Search and Rescue." Emergency contact information, in case one of the dogs went missing during a search effort, was also embroidered. Each dog also had a specific tattoo inked on its underbelly which was registered with a working canine agency.

Both collars were outfitted with a GPS tracking device so Sarah could download the exact area each dog had covered. Management liked to have this information to verify map locations of the dogs' exact search coordinates. Each dog also wore a "trail bell" that Sarah had already attached to the collars.

"Hurry, Sarah! Get your pack and whatever else you need while I still have these guys' attention," Kellee admonished.

Sarah picked up her wilderness field pack with all of her search supplies; she put her left arm through one of the straps and swung it up on her shoulder with a little effort. Heavy, the field pack was bright orange and made of a durable, waterproof material. Neon yellow reflectors adorned the sides of the pack. It was loaded with necessary first responder gear such as first aid materials for herself, the dogs and the missing subject if they should locate him in their search area.

There were many miscellaneous survival tools in her pack including a knife, various bits of wires, foil and batteries and even a tarp should she need to make camp for the night. While there were some supplies she used over and over, she found others to be useless as she never used them and forgot they were even in her pack.

Sarah attached the radio holster across her chest and secured it tightly. She dropped the freshly charged team-issued radio into its pocket. Her knee-high, black Gore-Tex gaitors were zipped up over her hiking boots and BDUs. She carried a Garmin GPS in a front pants pocket with fresh batteries, but she also carried a Ranger Silica orienteering compass as a back-up in case the GPS malfunctioned.

Satisfied she had everything she and her dogs would need, Sarah grabbed Gunner and Sam's black beta leashes with quick-release brass snaps. While the dogs were pre-occupied with Kellee and the treats, Sarah checked to make sure the leashes were snapped onto each of the dog's fitted prong collars as well as their leather flat collars.

Bells were hung from the dogs' flat collars since they would wear them throughout the search assignment. Sarah only used the primitive looking prong collar while in base camp to keep better control of her energetic beasts. When they were in exciting surroundings it helped keep them from burning up their energy too quickly. Sarah would remove the prong collars once they arrived at their search sector. They weren't appropriate while the dogs were working in case they snagged on a branch or got caught on something else.

Even so, the collars looked worse than they actually were. Because they applied even pressure on the neck and throat, they were actually less severe than a choke collar. Like most "tools," it was all in how it was used.

Kellee met Sarah's eyes. "Do you have them?" she asked, still teasing the dogs with the hidden treats.

"Yep," Sarah replied, "at least for the moment."

Kellee rewarded the dogs with a piece of a small treat she'd kept hidden in her hand.

When the dogs were finished with Kellee, they turned toward their handler. "Platz," Sarah commanded. Both dogs responded quickly, settling into a sphinx-like position on the ground beside the truck. They kept their eyes glued to Sarah. They were having a difficult time trying to contain themselves.

Panting and antsy, Gunner could just barely stay in a down position. He continued to flip his hip from the right side to the left never taking his eyes from his handler. Sam stayed in his original position, but an occasional tremor surfaced across his body as he tried to remain in place.

"Settle, Gunner," Sarah quietly commanded the dog. "Good boy, Sam."

"Ready to head over?" Sarah asked Kellee.

"I'm ready. Looks like we have everything." Kellee scanned the area immediately surrounding herself, Sarah and the dogs. She wanted to make sure no one had dropped any equipment or left anything out.

"Watch." The dogs looked at Sarah. They locked eyes with her. Sarah waited a moment. She looped their leashes around her hand. "Free," she told them. The dogs jumped up to run, but hit the end of the leash and their prong collar. They immediately caught themselves and settled down, keeping an eye on their handler.

The merry band walked over to the mule beside the command unit. Sarah recognized its driver from a search-and-rescue class but couldn't recall his name. *If he had been one of the search dogs,* she thought, *I wouldn't have a problem remembering his name!*

"You sure you don't mind me tagging along?" Dave politely asked again. "I think it would be a good idea just in case the dogs find something."

"Just in case?" Sarah said with a smile. "I hope you have more confidence in us than that!"

"Oh I do," Dave quickly replied. "But to be honest, I really want to see you in action. Working two dogs. I mean see the dogs in action," he backpedaled with a grin.

"I'm sure the dogs won't mind," Sarah replied back, testing him. *I wonder...*

CHAPTER 18

Sarah

The small band of humans and dogs made their way over to the mule that was parked outside the command unit. Sarah sucked in a deep breath of fresh air. She scanned her surroundings. Fluffy white clouds dotted the azure skies above Lake Marburg. The temperature hovered in the mid-seventies, a mild breeze drifted through base. Bits of sun bounced off the lake's water and reflected through the trees. Sarah couldn't imagine a better time of year or a better place to be. She loved the outdoors. Autumn was upon them, harvest season. Her favorite.

Reality set in when they reached the all-terrain vehicle that was to be their ride to their search task. *I can't believe we are searching for him!* Dark thoughts of the victim crossed her mind again. It angered her to think he was the subject of the search and all the effort and commotion. *The creep really wasn't worth this endeavor,* she thought. *Stop it! Focus on being positive. Positive energy!* With that notion, she refocused on the task at hand and why she was in this business.

Contemplating her assignment, Sarah considered the area they had been assigned to search. Sarah knew as a first responder, it took good search strategy combined with pure luck to actually find the lost subject in your sector. History of the missing person as well as interviews of family and witnesses was always a big help in deciding on an area to search—all items they had taken into account.

Search management was still trying to glean as much information on the subject as possible. New details were always emerging during a search. They were still trying to determine how the subject was dressed, what type of foot gear and shoe size he had. His wife hadn't proved to be much help. Aside from some possible mental issues, alcohol and drug abuse, the subject didn't appear to have any other major health concerns. *Like that wasn't enough.*

Dave sidled up beside Sarah and Kellee. "What can I help you with?" he asked as he looked down at the dogs lying by his feet wagging their long bushy tails.

Sarah had them lay down when they reached the mule. Gunner and Sam stretched as far as they could to sniff Dave and his pants. It was evident that Bella had left her smell all over Dave. With her oily skin and coat, it was hard not to be covered in her scent after working or caring for her.

"Hey guys," Dave offered to the dogs as he bent down to ruff them along the side of their heads and scratch their ears. The dogs continued to wag their tails in response.

"You can throw my field pack into the back of the mule," Sarah said as she let the heavy, densely crammed backpack slide from her shoulder and arm onto the ground beside the vehicle. The pack hit the ground with a heavy thud.

"Whoa," Dave remarked. "Glad I don't have to carry a pack like that while working out in the field. What in the hell do you have in there?"

Feeling confident at the moment she replied, "Everything," with a smug tone.

"Well, I sure as hell don't doubt it," Dave replied. "Especially after what all I saw packed into the back of your truck."

"You can also run the radio today if that's okay with you." Without waiting for a reply from Dave, she started to remove the radio apparatus from her body. She ripped the Velcro strap open, removed her cap and carefully pulled the radio harness over her bandana that fit snug around her head and hair.

"Oh hey, not a problem. Would be glad to," Dave replied as he accepted the equipment and responsibility.

As they loaded up the gear and dogs into the mule, Kellee grabbed a few more bottles of water and granola bars from the table in front of the command unit. Both women checked to make sure their GPS units were set on the same Datum as search management. There were different longitude and latitude measurements available and they needed to be sure that their units were set on the same one the management team was using. If not, their GPS coordinates would not match what was used in base camp.

Sarah pulled her compass from where it hung from her belt loop. She used a little key that was attached to the lanyard and placed it in a keyhole in the back. She turned the key until she had added eleven degrees to her compass bearing. Search management was using magnetic north instead of true north. Confident she had set the declination correctly, she dropped the compass back into her BDU pants pocket.

Dave and the driver went over the best route to their search sector. The two men were deep in discussion debating who knew the best track.

Sarah looked at Kellee. For some reason Kellee was wearing a huge grin. She appeared to be in a great spirits.

"So what's got *you* in such a good mood?" Sarah asked kiddingly.

Kellee made sure Dave and the driver were still distracted, and answered, "Well, actually, if you must know, *you*."

"Me?" Sarah asked quizzically. "Am I really that interesting?" She flashed her eyelids and lifted her chin mockingly

"Just thinking about how far you've come since our first meeting. How far *we've* come. I'm so proud of you," Kellee continued.

Sarah felt like Kellee was trying to give her a boost of confidence and also make her take responsibility for today's mission. She knew Kellee wanted to make her stand up and be ready for whatever they might find out in the woods today.

"Proud?" Sarah asked.

"Yes. You've done so well becoming a first responder and training Sam and Gunner. I'm also impressed you're taking this on and standing up to the challenge. I know it's not gonna be an easy task for you. I'm glad I'm here with you. Just the thought of going out on your first wilderness search as the lead dog handler is enough to make anyone nervous," Kellee retorted lighthearted. "This search is more involved physically and mentally than yesterday. Between the amount of ground and the terrain we need to cover and follow a map, this will not be an easy undertaking."

"Oh, I know. But I love working the woods and forest the best. It's Gunner and Sam's favorite type of problem and terrain."

There had been a time in Sarah's past where she could have gone either way on her path and direction in life. She had the choice to overcome her dark past and move on to a better life. Or she could have succumbed to it and repeated that misery all over again.

It was a chance meeting six years earlier when Sarah had first encountered Kellee. Sarah, a young redhead, had held herself with defiance and at a distance. She knew she was witty and intelligent but she kept her emotional and personal distance from everyone, never allowing anyone into her personal space. She carried an internal sadness, a kind of deep darkness in her soul that followed her everywhere. Sarah called it her "baggage." Weight she hoped to rid herself of one day.

Sarah had opened up to Kellee little by little when Kellee gained her trust. She had shared some of what she'd had to endure in her years in the foster home system. No one else knew or cared to know. And that was fine with Sarah, the less people knew about her past life, the better she felt about herself. But Kellee had been there when Sarah needed someone. She had helped Sarah bloom into a responsible person. A strong person.

Helping Sarah into the back of the mule, Kellee turned her attention to Gunner and Sam who were still in their down command beside the vehicle. She picked up both leashes and braced herself to trudge after the joyful animals. "Free," Kellee told both dogs when they met her eyes.

Sam and Gunner jumped up and bolted toward Sarah and the mule, which was only a yard from where they had been. Dave dropped the mule's tailgate as the dogs closed in.

"Hup!" Sarah commanded. Both dogs jumped into the back of the mule as Kellee let their leashes go. "Good job!" Sarah lavished praise on them. She in turn picked up their leashes, and gave them time to find a comfortable spot to settle down.

Dave and Kellee clambered up the steps on the side of the vehicle and found a spot to sit and hang on.

"All aboard? Ready?" the driver asked and Sarah nodded her head. The driver took off in the direction of the search sector.

Boy, I hope I'm ready for this.

CHAPTER 19

Eva

Perfect. Eva smiled. She was content with how the event was playing out. She was also content with Sarah, at least for the time being. Eva was happy with how well Sarah had received the news as to who the subject of the search was. Yes, Sarah did squirm at first, but she regained her composure and that was what counted. It wasn't the initial reaction that mattered, but how well she recovered.

About time! About time you toughened up and took on the challenge. Eva wished Sarah was more emotionally savvy and stable. She was better than she had been in the past, but still not as tough as Eva. This was the main reason Eva still stuck around to keep an eye on her. If only Sarah would take matters into her own hands. But Eva knew she wouldn't. So she stayed. Eva was close enough to watch, but far enough to be physically out of Sarah's life.

She watched as the searchers loaded the mule with equipment, people and the dreaded dogs. She hated the dogs. That was one thing she really didn't understand about Sarah. They were stupid animals. She would be so much better off without them.

The closer the search party got to deploying to their chosen search sector, the more excited Eva grew. It was hard to control her pleasure and satisfaction. *I can't wait for this to unfold!*

CHAPTER 20

Sarah

Lurching forward, the mule pulled out of the horse trailer parking lot. It groaned and struggled at first from being so weighted down. Sarah sat facing the rear and watched as the incident command unit and base camp disappeared from view. She stared off, deep in thought.

"You okay?" Dave asked.

He touched her shoulder. Sarah jumped. "Did you say something?" Sarah tried to regain her composure. She scrambled for words and tried to make up for flinching at his touch. "Sorry, contemplating today's search strategy."

"Just seeing if you were still with us," he laughed. "You seemed lost in another world. You doing okay? You and the dogs had a long day yesterday and right back at it today."

"Oh, I'm fine. Wondering what we may encounter, what the dogs may find. That's all. Isn't it about time to do a radio check?" Sarah changed the subject to shift his attention.

"Yep, on it." Dave picked up the microphone. "Base, Team Echo calling in for a radio check."

Releasing the call button, he waited a few seconds and was rewarded with, "Base copies Team Echo, coming through loud and clear."

"Team Echo leaving base, heading out to starting point of search sector," Dave continued with the transmission.

"Base copies. Check in again when you are ready to begin task." Base repeated back the information Dave had given and asked them to check in every half hour.

"The area we're headed to has a few hills and ravines. Nothing major as far as steep or too difficult terrain. Radio signal should stay strong throughout the search area," Dave explained.

Sarah barely listened as Dave went on about the radio. He seemed happy to have something to talk about. It was another responsibility she had delegated and put all thought of it out of her own head.

As the driver headed east, he crossed an open field, followed a horse trail as far as he could and then had to get back on the asphalt road because the mule couldn't fit along the trail. They crossed a bridge that spanned a small branch of Lake Marburg.

The driver wound through another parking lot by the southeast edge of the lake and headed down to pick up a section of the main trail where it had been theorized the subject might have hiked. This part of the trail consisted of a well-groomed bridle path that would take them to an area of substantially tall, un-timbered soft pines.

The ample stand of pines had originally been planted to be harvested for the local paper mill. But that was years ago, back before the park existed. Once they dammed the creek and turned the area into a park, all the lands surrounding the lake became state property. Any trees within the new boundaries of the park were no longer allowed to be timbered.

The once fertile farmland within park boundaries was now at nature's whim. What resulted was mainly scrub with a few scattered hardwood trees dotting the landscape here and there. Thirty years later, a forest had grown and there were now several mature trees, but the scrub was still plentiful. It had grown up along many tree lines and caused several trees to slowly die as vines and scrub eventually choked them out.

This stand of pines would be the southwest boundary—the initial starting point of their team's search sector depending on a few determinates. First, the search party would need to check if the predominate wind continued to flow from the north within the tree line. Sometimes the air flow differed within diverse areas of terrain.

Next, they would need to consider other hazards or difficult areas the team might encounter in their direction of travel. If all looked good, they would start out from this point to begin to grid their sector—walking in straight lines from one end to the other as the dogs were turned loose to search for any humans.

Sarah and Kellee pulled their maps out as they bumped along in the red and black mule. Kellee was studying the Codorus State Park map which showed all the man-made trails and other park information pertinent to visitors. The park map was on a different scale than the topographical map Sarah was using. Although the park map was pretty and offered good information, it wasn't drawn to any specific measure. Its purpose was simply to help visitors and hikers stay on marked trails.

By contrast, Sarah's topographical map was referred to as a "7.5-minute map." It was the size and type of map her canine team trained with and utilized while deployed. Most search teams used that scale because of its availability and accuracy as far as terrain. Every inch of the United States was mapped and set up in this style. They were called 7.5-minute quadrangles because they showed an area 7.5-minutes of longitude wide by 7.5-minutes of latitude high. Each inch on the map was equal to 24,000 inches on the ground—or 2,000 feet.

To the average civilian, these maps looked like a foreign language. But seasoned search responders understood their mysteries and were grateful to be issued them—especially if the maps were printed in color.

Opening her topo map fully, Sarah looked over their search sector again. Her map not only showed the layout of the land, but also the elevations in grid lines. All of the details of the lake boundaries, forestation, swamp areas, creeks, roads and nearby buildings were noted. The map was further broken down into 1,000-meter boxes with 100-meter grid ticks. This would help the search team identify their exact location within their sector down to the meter.

They had been assigned an area which started at the large stand of pines and extended well over 900 meters from west to east. It ended at the park's northeastern border where another set of pines backed up to private property. The western border was the lake itself and would not be even because the shoreline zigged and zagged. The width of the sector would change depending on how far the shoreline turned in or out from north to south.

Their northern boundary was the peak of one of the park's most elevated hilltops. Running north to south, the sector was about 800 meters wide. *A pretty large wooded area to cover,* Sarah thought, *but between three trained search personnel and two trained air-scenting canines working as a team, we should be able to take our time and clear the area well.*

Taking a closer look at the map, there didn't seem to be any difficult natural obstacles that stood out. As far as Sarah knew, downed trees, low-lying scrub and sticker bushes would be their biggest adversaries today. At least as far as the terrain. But Gunner and Sam would be tempted by the lake. She wasn't sure how she would manage that one yet. Nor had Sarah completely come to terms with how she'd feel if they actually located her scumbag foster brother.

Gunner and Sam loved the water and would swim at any opportunity that presented itself. She hadn't let them swim during yesterday's water search though because she was still on guard. She was afraid search management might have frowned upon it. Sarah had been lucky to keep Gunner restrained in the boat during his entire water search. He had been known to abandon ship during training for a fun romp in the water.

I can see the headline in the local news now, "Search Dogs Abandon Lost Man to Play in Lake." Sarah laughed out loud. Kellee turned to look at her. "Just thinking my biggest problem today will be keeping two furry searchers out of the water!" Sarah grinned.

Dave gave both women a puzzled glance.

"They're both avid swimmers," she shouted over the whining of the mule's engine. "Sam and Gunner love getting in the water. I bring them over to the lake to swim during the summer months."

They continued to roll along to their destination. Dave smiled at Sarah, looking at the dogs and shaking his head as if he understood.

"The lake will be a good resource to cool the dogs off if they get overheated," Sarah commented. "They'll be working physically harder today than yesterday. This is a pretty large sector. The dogs have a lot of ground to cover." *And so do we*, Sarah thought.

After a twenty-minute ride to their sector's starting point, the driver pulled up to a wide open area along the trail, not far from the pines and the lake's edge. The mule came to an abrupt stop. The dogs shifted and scattered for a moment, then stood up to regain their balance.

"Easy," Sarah whispered to them as she held their leashes tight. She didn't want the dogs to exit the mule suddenly. She took a quick 360-degree glance of the area before disembarking. She noticed several large puddles from recent thunderstorms. "Slight miscalculation," she voiced to Kellee as she pointed to the standing water. "I thought most of the water in this area of the park would have been swallowed up by the loamy soil."

"I guess so much water came down so fast that the ground couldn't soak it all up," Kellee retorted. "We just need to make sure to keep Sam and Gunner from drinking out of those puddles if we can. Looks like mosquitoes have already been here," she said, pointing to the puddles full of larva.

The driver of the mule jumped out and opened the tailgate. He helped Sarah, and then the dogs unload from the rear of the vehicle. Sarah took both Sam and Gunner to a shady area and had them lay down. "Stay," she commanded. She returned to get her supplies and backpack and set the equipment on the ground beside her dogs. Dave and Kellee grabbed their field packs and did a quick check of the vehicle.

"Got everything? You guys all set?" the mule driver asked.

Dave turned to Sarah. "You good?" he asked.

Sarah rolled her eyes over the back of the mule, her dogs and her pack.

"Looks like we're good to go," Dave stated.

The driver put the tailgate up with a loud smack. He hopped back up into the front seat with a little effort. "Okay, if you all are sure you have everything you need, I'm gonna head back." He deftly maneuvered the vehicle around and shouted, "Stay safe!" as he started back west to base camp.

Yeah right. With that asshole out here? Sarah looked over to Gunner and Sam. *I guess I'm the only one here who knows what this guy is really capable of.* She would never forgive herself if something were to happen to her boys.

CHAPTER 21

Sarah

Sarah pulled the container of baby powder from a front pocket of her BDUs. She kept it in a close spot for quick access. She liked to check the air flow and wind direction frequently while running a search in the woods. Even though the predominate wind direction normally didn't shift, when trees, ravines and changing elevations came into play, they added further variables to how the wind blew and how the dogs worked.

As a canine handler, you needed to be able to "read the air movement" to support your dog in solving a scent problem. It could mean the difference between your dog making a successful find or possibly overlooking the subject.

Twisting the top open, Sarah held the powder at arms-length downwind of the other searchers and dogs. She squeezed off a few puffs forming a small white cloud. She watched how the powder moved. It danced and flowed and slowly spread through the pines until it gradually dispersed and altogether disappeared. Sarah mentally noted how the air pulled the cloud up and dropped it several meters away. *Hmmph,* she thought as she studied the movements. "Well that's interesting."

"Are you going to share your findings with us or will they remain top secret?" Dave mused.

"Oh, I don't know. What's it worth to you?" Sarah teased back.

"Does the powder really tell you that much?" Dave inquired. "How much effect will it actually have on how you're going to work the dogs? I thought you just used it to tell the direction of the breeze?"

"Mainly, but it can tell you so much more. Air movement does all kinds of neat little things."

"Okay," Dave acknowledged sounding unsure.

"Since the prevailing airflow is from the north as it was in base camp, we can keep the search strategy pretty much the same as we had planned. But we have to keep in mind that there are more variables in the woods that could have many different effects on how human scent can pool in areas or be dispersed."

"Oh." Dave replied still not totally getting it, but he seemed to understand they didn't have time at the moment for a deeper lesson. "Maybe we could discuss this more in-depth at a later date?" he asked more as a suggestion than a question.

"Sure," Sarah responded automatically as she concentrated on what she was doing. *Date? Did I just say, "Sure," to a date?*

She needed to work the dogs across or into the wind to maximize their efficiency and effectiveness for locating a lost person. Since the follicles, or rafts, from people's skin traveled with the breeze, having the dogs work into the wind, or across the wind, would give them the greatest opportunity to intersect a missing subject's scent cone. It would put the dog in the best position to be successful. The further out a dog caught the scent, the wider its scent cone generally became. Air-scenting dogs are trained to work within these scent cones and follow them to the source, the subject.

Canine handlers know the subtle signs and changes in their dog's body language and behavior. They can read when their partner has discovered human scent, as Sarah had proven the day before during the water search. There was no doubt in her mind when Gunner or Sam came into contact with human scent that didn't belong to their search party. Handlers can also tell when their dogs are not working or are goofing off. Sometimes a canine needs to be re-focused, re-started on their task—but that was never the case with Gunner and Sam. They were devoted to getting paid by finding the subject and getting rewarded.

The dogs began to let out barks of frustration. Gunner and Sam were having a difficult time staying in a down. They were both shaking with anticipation. Gunner had started to whine obnoxiously. Tired of waiting for the game to begin, they broke position and stood in place.

"Settle," Sarah spoke softly, but firm. Both dogs stopped moving for a moment and focused all of their concentration on her. They knew the command was meant for them to chill out and calm down, but it only lasted a few seconds.

"Hey guys," Sarah directed to Kellee and Dave, "We need to go over the search strategy quick so we can get started. I really need to get the dogs going. They are on edge and tired of waiting."

Sarah pulled the folded topo map out once again from her BDU pants pocket. She opened it just enough to show the 1,000-meter by 1,000-meter square they were in. Using the tip of a small twig, she pointed to a spot on the map. "We are here right now. We're going to grid from this point west to east starting from this stand of pines to the park boundary here," she continued to use the twig as a pointer to show the direction and area of travel. "We head out using a 90-degree bearing, turn north which will be a left turn, head about 30-50 meters on smaller sweeps, then head back on the opposite bearing to work back west on the long sweep."

She pointed to the boundaries. "Kellee, can you keep track of our direction of travel, marking our boundary corners with flagging tape as we hit each one?" Kellee nodded and pulled her compass out of her pocket and set the bearing using the topo map to acclimate herself and the settings. Sarah shoved the map into a plastic casing that hung from a lanyard and put it around her neck. Now it would be protected from the elements and she could access it in seconds.

Sarah had stepped up. She had taken full control of her search task, the dogs and her team's responders. The group was known as a strike team and Sarah had deferred to Kellee as the strike team's leader. Kellee still let Sarah run the show and was in total support of whatever Sarah would need. Sarah was feeling more confident as she concentrated on the task at hand. It kept her mind from creeping back to the past. *This feels good, feels right,* she thought. *I just need to stay in control. Everything will be okay. Stay positive.*

Dave's job was to continue to man the radio and communicate with base. Handling a radio was second nature to him since he did that during his job. He asked Sarah where he should tread in conjunction with Sarah and Kellee and the dogs as they walked their grid pattern.

"Just stay to my left and Kellee will stay to my right, about 10 or 20 feet off my side and a few feet behind. Don't get in front of the dogs, though. They may come around behind us and check our scent or come in for a water break, but let them lead the way. Try not to interact with them in any way. I like to stay quiet while the dogs are on task, other than calling out the lost subject's name, but let's keep the chatter to a minimum."

Sarah looked over to where Kellee was standing, compass in one hand, GPS in the other. Kellee had been busy checking her bearings and plugging map coordinates into her GPS. "Are we r-e-a-d-y?" Sarah spelled to her two team members in a low, slow voice. The dogs were looking for any recognizable word to tell them to take off and start running through the woods. Kellee and Dave nodded their assent.

Dave picked up the microphone once again and pressed the call button.

"Base, Team Echo here." Dave released the call button and waited a few seconds.

"Team Echo, this is base, go ahead."

Dave called in the beginning coordinates and a loose basis of what their search strategy was. He let base know that Team Echo was starting their task.

Base read the coordinates back, stated Team Echo's start time of 1000 hours and gave protocol for the team to check in every half hour from this point with their status, condition and coordinates.

Dave copied base, ended the transmission and clipped the radio microphone to the strap of the holster that wrapped around his neck and shoulder. Packing the rest of the radio back in the pocket of the holster, he turned to watch Sarah release the dogs.

Sarah faced east, the direction of travel she wanted to head off in. She picked the dogs' leashes up slowly. Gunner and Sam turned to face Sarah, their eyes locked on her. The energy was thick as the dogs anticipated their release command.

They knew the start of the game had arrived and they shook with anticipation. Sarah had already removed their prong collars, refastening the leash to their flat collars. She didn't allow them to work with much hardware. Sarah stood behind the dogs, their bodies facing east.

With her thumbs on each of the dogs' quick-release snaps, she was ready to let them go. When they turned to look east in the direction of travel, finally, Sarah commanded, "Go Find!" She pressed down on the snaps to unhook them and not get in the way. Even so the dogs still managed to almost pull her forward into the wet soil. Sarah caught herself before falling face first into the dirt. Kellee stifled a laugh as the dogs kicked pine needles up in their race to begin. Teammates reveled in seeing their partners do face plants thanks to their working canines.

"Too bad I forgot my camera," Kellee commented as she watched the dogs race away.

Kicking up loamy soil and a bit of mud, both dogs sprinted off in a frenzy. Sarah helped guide them in the direction she was heading by pointing and swinging her arms toward the southeastern line of the stand of pines. "This way," she yelled. She over-exaggerated her body language at first to get their attention. It helped the dogs make the connection of the direction she wanted them to head.

Sarah, Kellee and Dave stepped into formation. Sarah situated herself in the middle in front with Dave on the left and Kellee on her right checking her bearing as they headed out in a quick pace.

Kellee set her sights on the furthest point she could see, a large pine that was cracked in the middle of its trunk several meters down their immediate line of travel. "See that split tree?" she pointed. "That's where we're we heading to. I'll keep pace count as well," Kellee offered.

Even though they had an idea of what to look for in terrain changes as they approached their eastern boundary, it helped to keep a pace count. It kept their travel distance more accurate. Kellee's pace count was approximately 65 steps to every 100 meters traveled, more or less. She had beads that hung on a cord on the front of her pack strap. For every 100 meters they traveled, Kellee would pull a bead down to the bottom of the cord. This way, she wouldn't have to remember in her head exactly how many hundreds of meters they had traveled.

"Off on a new adventure!" Dave stated enthusiastically as they started their task.

Sarah smiled at Dave. She thought his energy and outlook were thoughtful, almost innocent. *Sometimes hokey,* she thought, *but always in a good way.* She knew he loved the outdoors and was fascinated by the working dog discipline. It was hard not to get caught up in Dave's eager vigor.

But thoughts of who was missing, thoughts of past memories almost made her shiver. Sometimes she could feel the physical pain that worthless POS had inflicted on her just with a memory. Without thinking, she touched a round scar just inside the small of her right collarbone.

Pushing those thoughts aside, she concentrated on what she was doing. She needed to stay alert and ready. *On the defense!*

She looked up toward the split tree where they were heading just in time to see both dogs disappear deeper into the woods and out of sight. For a moment her anxiety shot up and she breathed in deep. *They will be okay, let them do their job!* Sarah tried to calm herself with her own words of wisdom. She lengthened her stride and quickened her pace following Sam and Gunner's lead.

CHAPTER 22

Sarah

Sarah's nerves settled down each time she caught a glimpse of the dogs as they hunted for the lost person. Sarah wore a huge smile. The missing subject had put a black cloud over the day, but she couldn't help feeling proud of Gunner and Sam. Watching the dogs take off with purpose and loving what they were doing was pure joy. They meant the world to Sarah. More than just pets, they were her whole life. She didn't know how she would react if anything ever happened to them.

There was always a bit of apprehension when you turned your working canine free to work a search. Especially in a wooded area where the visibility was limited. You had to trust them. It was no different for Sarah. There were always unforeseen dangers. One never knew what they would ultimately encounter while working in the field on a search.

She wanted to get through this with no injuries to her team or her dogs. They had worked so hard to get to this point in their search career. It had taken almost two years to train Gunner and Sam to be able to pass all of the tests that led up to the final evaluation and become a certified team. It had been challenging and demanding, yet rewarding work.

She was finally to a point in her life where everything was looking positive. She had a good job she felt made a difference in people's lives. People counted on her to make quick, correct life-saving decisions in her emergency operations position. She had gotten her degree and was looking forward to a possible career with "the agency," as she referred to the FBI. As a part of the canine team, she witnessed not only the benefits her organization had to offer, but also the camaraderie between first responders.

She thought of her county position co-workers and her search teammates as the closet thing she had to a family.

Sarah looked around to Kellee at her right and Dave a little behind her on her left. Dave smiled. She couldn't help but know by now that he was interested in her. *Interested in me? Or my dogs?* She liked Dave. She liked him as a co-worker and friend. *Nothing more, nothing less. At least for the moment.* Sarah still wasn't ready to open any in-depth emotional doors.

It had been hard enough to let Kellee through and open up to her emotionally. To allow her into Sarah's personal space. It had been a relationship which developed over years. She found Kellee to be a very trusting friend and confidante. A good person.

But most important, Sarah saw the care that Kellee gave to her dogs. Sarah had learned early in life that the way people cared for their animals told a vast amount about them as a person. She had seen the animal brutality in her past from the same people who raised her. Their treatment of animals reflected the same as their treatment of children in their care. Sarah was forever grateful that Kellee was in her life. She felt extremely lucky to have found her.

Sarah concentrated on the terrain in front of her. She stepped over several downed trees and broken branches. They had been ripped from the few hardwoods that stood intermittently among the native species during the recent thunderstorms. *The winds must have been pretty violent through here,* Sarah thought as she navigated through the obstacle course.

Most of the downed tree limbs were covered in heavy, hairy looking vines. There were thick sticker bushes wound within the trees and broken branches. To add to the situation, the mosquitoes and no-see-ums were out in full force. They seemed to be thickest among the jumbled piles of disarray, hovering right at the height of the searchers' faces. *Thank god for gaitors and bug spray,* Sarah thought. *Glad I remembered to treat Gunner and Sam as well.*

"Heading to that large oak," Kellee stated, pointing toward a big, mature tree with leaves that were just starting to announce autumn. The trio was close to the end of their first sweep. This one would finish at the eastern boundary of the park. Sarah knew what trails intersected near the boundary. She knew the forest would dead-end, opening up to private property.

Between being familiar with the area and understanding the topographical map, she was aware of what landmarks to look for. She also knew they wouldn't have to walk all the way to the end of their boundary. The dogs would have already covered and cleared the area. Gunner and Sam helped save time and energy. This allowed the search team to start their sweep back toward the western boundary quicker.

When the team came to where they would turn in a 90-degree angle to their bearing for their shorter grids, Kellee pulled out her fluorescent orange roll of flagging tape. She unraveled a long strip and tore it off. Locating a branch to attach it, she hung it just above head height.

"Need help with that?" Dave offered.

"Nope, got it," Kellee replied as she pulled the branch down lower to make it easier for her to tie. She pulled out two more strips and hung them along the same branch.

The flagging tape marked the team's turn near the boundary in their sector. They would be using quite a bit of flagging tape during this mission since their sector encompassed a large area. They would not come back to pick up these strips of flagging tape so their team made sure all of the tape they used for training or during searches was biodegradable. It would take time, but eventually the tape would break down and deteriorate altogether. Once Kellee had tied the tape off, she took out a black permanent marker and wrote along one of the strips of flagging tape. She marked the team's ID, date and area.

The team trudged on. Sam and Gunner had settled into their air-scenting work and were staying on task well. Sarah and her team couldn't see the dogs all the time, but could hear their bells in the distance.

If the dogs happened to be several hundred meters away though, they might no longer be within earshot. If it had been a while since she'd heard the bells or the saw the dogs, Sarah would stop and listen closely until she could see or hear them before she moved on again. Each dog wore a bell with a different tone so she could tell which dog was where. Gunner's tone was low and had a longer ring to it while Sam's was higher pitched and shorter.

Most canine handlers worked only one dog at a time. Sarah hadn't planned on allowing both of her dogs to work together on the same problem or search as they did now. But somewhere in their training, it was realized that Sam and Gunner had such different searching styles that once on task, they worked independently.

The dogs didn't interfere with each other's working ability. They actually ended up complementing one another and this helped to clear an area quicker and more effectively. Although it was unorthodox in normal air-scent canine training circles, it worked and the team had allowed Sarah to continue to use both dogs in this manner.

"Hey Kellee, we're going to go about 50 meters to the north on the short grid before heading back west for the second long sweep. I don't think we need to run the long sweeps too close together since the dogs are covering the ground well in the open pines."

"Sounds like a plan. If we run into a thicker area or more downed trees, we can always tighten the space up and run the sweeps closer together," Kellee responded.

It was close to noon. The sun was high in the early autumn sky. Sarah looked up toward the tops of the towering pines. They were taller than they should be and stood planted in rows like soldiers standing at attention. This was one of Sarah's favorite places within the park. It reminded her of a setting for a horror movie. It was quiet and serene, but felt as if something lurked deep in the forest, waiting, just beyond their grasp, watching.

She heard the dog's bell before she saw him. Sam returned to Sarah and banged his head hard against her leg where the water bottle hung off her belt loop.

"Easy, Sam!" Sarah reprimanded the dog as she rubbed her thigh. "I'm sure that will be black and blue tomorrow."

She called and whistled for Gunner. He eventually came bounding back with his tongue dragging the ground. Covered in mud with a vine stuck in his bushy tail and dragging behind him, he looked bedraggled. "Well, you're a sight!" Sarah laughed. Gunner was like a bull in a china shop. He would plow through anything to check a scent or cover his sector.

"Hey guys, I'm going to make the dogs take a short break, give them a quick check over and some water. Dave, can you call into base for any updates and give them a safety check on us?"

"Will do."

Sarah asked both dogs to lie down. She pulled out two soft collapsible water bowls and poured a small amount of water into each one. She sat the bowls in front of the dogs. Sam tentatively lapped his water up and took his time. Gunner on the other hand, drove his whole snout into the bowl spilling most of it. Sarah started to reprimand Gunner, but ended up laughing at him instead.

Both dogs had such opposite personalities and Sarah thought that's why they got along so well. Sam, always the more cautious, methodical dog, complemented Gunner who just threw everything to the wind. But as far as air-scenting and working dogs, they each had a tremendous work ethic.

While both were trained to air-scent, if they came across a "hot track"—a recent track from a human—Gunner would check it out, but Sam would put his nose to ground and follow the track as far as he could. Gunner would continue to keep his nose high and work what scent he could find floating on the air currents.

Occasionally, Sarah noticed the dogs come across a strong scent clue during training and she could see their different behavior unfold. Other than cleaning out a few burrs from the dogs' coats and pulling the vine from Gunner's tail, they were fine. Once they had consumed enough water and cooled down a bit, Sarah was ready to release them to get back to their job. Everyone seemed rejuvenated by the break; the searchers each drank water and ate a granola bar as well.

Sarah grabbed both dogs by the collars allowing them to stand up from their downed position. She pointed them in the direction she wanted them to head. The dogs pulled to be let loose, but didn't tug as hard. They were easier to handle since they had burned off a lot of energy, but eager to get back to the game. When both dogs were looking west, Sarah commanded, "Go Find!" and released them. The dogs raced off together at first, but quickly fell into their own rhythm and search pattern.

"Okay, let's do this!" Sarah exclaimed with enthusiasm. She looked at her two sweaty partners with a hint of sarcasm. When she saw Dave she couldn't help but laugh.

"What?" Dave had dirt smeared across his forehead and cheek. He must have wiped his pants after sitting on the ground, and then wiped his brow, leaving a few dark streaks across his face.

"Oh, nothing," Sarah responded and looked at Kellee who was also trying to stifle a smile. "Maybe you need to look in a mirror."

"We can't take you anywhere!" Kellee added teasingly.

"What?" Dave touched his face with the tips of his fingers and could feel the dirt stuck to his skin. "Oh, this is just my last-minute camouflage paint," he said laughing at himself. "The dogs won't be able to see me now."

"Good thing they rely on their nose and not their eyes," Sarah joked back.

The three picked up their packs, hiked them up on their backs and headed off in the direction of the dogs. Dave did a quick 360 survey to make sure they hadn't left anything behind. He then looked around the area they were headed. Keeping safe was a number one concern. Taking care of your own safety first while on a search task was top priority, then your teammates and the missing subject. You were useless to help others if something happened to you.

Moving forward on a long sweep, Sarah continued to dodge spider webs and low hanging tree branches. She was shorter than Dave and Kellee which made it easier. When the other two ended up walking face first into a web, Sarah couldn't help but laugh. After walking through one, it was hard to get over the feeling that there was a spider on you. It would give you the creeps. Sarah knew by experience and it gave her the heebie-jeebies just thinking about it.

Sarah was lost in thought as the trio moved along, quietly following the compass bearing. She was getting ready to call out to the dogs to check their location when she heard a sharp cry from one of them. The trio stopped in their tracks.

Sarah's anxiety shot up and she called out with alarm in her voice.

"Gunner! Sam! Come on guys," she yelled and whistled as panic rose in her throat. *Oh my god,* she thought. *I hope they're okay.* Anxiety caused her to break into a sweat as the search team stood waiting and listening. Everyone held their breath not making a sound as they listened intently for the dogs. Sarah could hear her own heartbeat pulsating in her head.

CHAPTER 23

Sarah

Silence. *Not a good sign,* Sarah thought. Dave stood still, looking at Sarah for guidance. He was genuinely worried but not sure what to do. Kellee helped call for the dogs. It seemed like forever, but finally they could hear two bell tones ringing as Gunner and Sam came busting through the woods and into view. Sarah let out a breath of relief. She called the dogs over to her and had them lie down beside her. The women bent down to inspect them.

"Sam looks fine," Kellee stated after she gave him a cursory inspection.

"Gunner has blood on his front right paw. He won't let me look at it. Can you hold him still for me, Dave?" Sarah asked.

"Sure, anything!" It was easy to tell that Dave was concerned, but wasn't sure what to do.

"Grab him by the collar and wrap your other arm around his chest like this," Sarah gave a quick demonstration.

Stooping over Gunner, Dave held the dog by the collar with one hand and held onto his right leg with the other.

"That'll work." Sarah bent down to inspect the pad on his paw closely. Gunner wriggled in Dave's grip.

"Settle," Sarah said with clenched teeth giving her meanest sounding command she could conjure up. She needed the dog to stay still so she could work on him. Gunner stopped moving for a moment but wasn't fazed by her tone and then tried to pull backwards out of Dave's hold.

"Yo, Gunner," Dave started a one-sided conversation with the dog. That seemed to calm Gunner and he remained stationary.

"There's blood coming from this right pad." She took out a small bag from her pack. From that she pulled out saline, an antibiotic ointment and vet wrap. "It looks like a small puncture, maybe from a sticker or a twig."

Sarah cleaned the wound by flushing it, adding ointment and wrapping a thin piece of vet wrap around the paw to prevent dirt from entering the area.

"I know that won't last long, but I still want to see if it will stay on for a while," she said referring to the bandage. Gunner would tear it off eventually with the way he dove through the brush and pushed off the ground.

"It's better than nothing. I'll help you clean it out and rewrap it when we return to base," Kellee offered.

With great relief, Sarah re-started the dogs on their task. Terrible thoughts had run through her head when she'd heard her dog cry out. It brought back thoughts from long ago and memories of what she had witnessed *him* inflict upon animals. *Not just animals, but humans as well.* Some of the memories were vivid and clear while others she'd barely hung onto. Sarah questioned her sanity, wondering why she was participating in a mission to rescue that asshole.

The search team was now on their sixth long sweep. As they headed back west, the terrain had begun to transform. The neatly planted stands of soft pine gave way to mixed forested trees that provided a canopy. Common hardwood trees shaded most of the area, keeping the light from reaching the dark rich soil.

In areas along the edges of the trail where the sun could reach, abundant dense scrub brush, consisting of sticker bushes and vines had grown thick and tall like a wall between the woods and the trail. The women had to pull out their small bypass pruners from their packs. They used them to cut holes through brush patches, making it easier to get through without getting hung up or caught on sticker bushes. Once out on the trail, it was open and clear, part of the bridle path system along the main trail that the park kept maintained for equestrians. But the search team was running sweeps perpendicular to the trail so at this point it wasn't an advantage.

"A machete would have come in handy today!" Dave quipped as he stood by and watched the women cut through the sticker bushes once again. "I would help out, but forgot my pruners today," he teased.

"Oh, no problem, we women are used to doing all of the work," Sarah kidded back.

The middle of their search sector was more open and had better visibility. It would have been easier to traverse but they were now heading up an incline on the side of a large hill and ravine. The three searchers were wearing down, fatigued. It had been a long couple of days. Normally a hill wouldn't be a problem, but it was soggy and slippery from the recent storms.

"Great," Sarah commented with a bit of edge in her voice.

Sarah could hear the dogs' bells; sound traveled further in the open woods. Occasionally she caught sight of their bright orange vests as the dogs went flying by in the distance. When they were thirsty, they would come in to Sarah and bang into the water bottle she kept hanging from her waist. The team continued to take breaks as needed to make sure the dogs were well-hydrated and relaxed. Sarah added electrolytes to the dogs' water as well to help keep their system balanced and to replenish their energy reserves.

The search party had just begun their sweep across the bottom slope of the large rise. They were nearing their northern boundary, which was 100 meters past the crest of the hill. Kellee readjusted her compass bearing so the searchers could walk the side of the gradient at an angle to make it less physically demanding.

Kellee looked up to set a point to traverse to and caught a glimpse of Gunner.

"Sarah," Kellee whispered as she walked closer to Sarah.

"Hunh?" she responded looking in Kellee's direction. Kellee pointed to where Gunner was.

Sarah witnessed the dog suddenly snap his head back as he was running across the side of the hill. It was a telltale sign that he had caught human scent which differed from the scent of the three searchers who trekked after him.

The dog had stopped and now stood along the hillside. Dave watched the women from where he stood. He followed their gaze. Sarah and Kellee remained silent so they wouldn't cause Gunner to look back at them. They didn't want to disrupt his concentration. Sarah motioned to Dave and put her finger to her mouth to make sure he stayed quiet. Then she put her hand in the air to signal to him to stay planted where he was. Dave nodded that he understood.

While the search party stayed silent, they watched the dog work. Gunner closed his mouth and stuck his snout up into the air. The dog had located another human's scent. His body seemed larger, his tail flagged straight up from his back. There wasn't any doubt he was trying to figure out where this new human smell was coming from. Gunner continued to suck in deep breaths as he concentrated on the scent picture.

Sarah could tell without fail he was working hard. She knew the dog's body language well. He was speaking volumes that he had picked up a new and different human scent that hadn't already been on his radar system.

Sarah was elated. It made her forget, at least for a bit, who the subject was and just allow herself to be in the moment. Watching all of her hard work and training unfurl was beyond words, especially when working in her favorite environment.

Gunner stood up on his hind legs trying to catch more of the "scent picture." He sniffed the ground and checked out a few trees near where he had originally caught the scent. The dog moved back and forth across the hillside, stopping in the same area and lifting his snout to the sky again to sniff.

Sarah looked up the hill, thinking the scent must be rolling down the incline instead of rising up as it should be doing during the heat of the sun. *But there's a lot of canopy from the trees making this area shady. Maybe that's throwing a variable into the scent picture.*

During daylight hours, scent should rise with the heat and sun. But during early morning hours and late evening hours and nighttime, scent had a tendency to hug the ground and not rise up any higher.

Kellee whispered, "Chimney effect." Sarah nodded in agreement.

Sarah pulled her powder out of her pocket, squeezed off a few puffs and watched as it was sucked up a few feet vertically, moved several feet laterally and then dropped several more feet away. A light bulb went off in Sarah's head. *The scent must be further up the hill. It's being carried from its origin and then being dropped over the side where Gunner is picking it up.*

Dogs "see" scent through their nose. As the air pours over their olfactory, the dog can differentiate what that scent is and break down all of the scents into the specific items. Their noses are 100,000 times more sensitive than a human's nose. They can discriminate each detail of every item.

Sarah kept her eye on Gunner as he persisted in trying to work out the scent problem. When a dog hits on or encounters scent from air flow that's experiencing a chimney effect, it presents a difficult picture for the canine to figure out. When faced with such difficulties, there were a couple ways the canine handler could manage the situation. Either they could get involved and try to send the dog out further, or they could stay out of the problem and just encourage the dog to continue to try and work it out.

Sarah usually chose the latter, especially when it involved Gunner. She didn't like to intervene if she didn't have to. She didn't want to influence her dog in any way. Sometimes if a handler got too involved, they created other unwanted behaviors in their attempt to shortcut the process.

Both of her dogs had the stamina and work ethic to continue to try anything to find the source of the scent. But ultimately, it was the dog's deep desire for the reward he would receive for locating and pinpointing the scent source that drove him. That was the main reason the dog was so committed. It was a means to

Gunner's favorite toy and play session with Sarah—and he wouldn't quit until he'd solved the puzzle.

The searchers were closing in on the western border as they finished their sixth sweep. This had put them close to the main trail and bridle path. While all three continued to watch Gunner closely, Sarah caught Sam in her peripheral vision. The dog was running toward the main trail with his nose close to the ground. She watched him circle around in a small open area and go back to the trail. Sam appeared to be very interested in a track. He was intently checking it out. The hair along the back of Sam's spine had risen. It stood up from the nape of his neck to the base of his tail line. A tell-tale sign that Sam had also found human scent.

Each dog had their own natural body alerts that Sarah intimately knew and understood. Sam was a more serious dog than Gunner and could sometimes be more cautious when closing in on a missing subject. He tended to be more aloof.

Sarah looked over at Kellee, pointed at Sam and smiled. Kellee returned the smile, acknowledging that the dog was no doubt on human scent and following a hot track. There was no uncertainty in Sarah's mind. *Trust your dog,* she thought as she tried to keep an eye on Sam who was following the trail. She had complete and total confidence in both of her dogs' working ability and devotion to their job.

"Can you tie flagging tape off to that tree?" Sarah whispered to Kellee pointing at a nearby hardwood. Kellee nodded and pulled the roll of tape from her pocket. By tying a strip of flagging tape off at this point, they would know where to return if they had to resume the search from where they left off. There could be a number of reasons the team might have to return to this point in their sweep: if the dogs followed up on human scent but couldn't locate the subject, or if the missing subject was on the move and possibly no longer in their sector.

Turning to Dave, Sarah asked, "Can you check the GPS coordinates and call them into base? Let them know that the dogs have both picked up human scent and are showing natural body alerts. Advise base that we are following up on the dogs' alerts."

"Got it."

Dave pulled his GPS out and started his transmission. He let base camp know all the pertinent information. He told management he would update them once they had followed up with the dogs.

Search management also cleared the radio line which meant they were on standby waiting for Team Echo to get back to them with whatever information they were able to find. Other search teams would only call in if they had clues, an emergency or had located the search subject. There would be no radio checks, safety checks or unnecessary transmissions during this time.

Once Kellee had the flagging tape tied in place, she pulled out her black permanent marker and recorded the date, their team name and coordinates on it. She was excited as well—hard not to be when a dog hit human scent and went into major alert mode.

"Can you follow Sam?" Sarah asked Kellee, "while Dave and I follow up with Gunner?" Sarah was almost breathless, her excitement obvious.

"Yep. Call me on the FRS radio if we get separated. Let me know where you are," Kellee asked.

"Okay, will do."

Kellee took off in the direction of Sam and the trail. Dave followed after Sarah as she headed up the hill where Gunner was working.

Gunner continued to work back and forth on the hillside near the top of the incline. He tried to stand up on his hind legs and use a low tree branch to support himself, sniffing the air higher off the ground. After a few more attempts of intense nose work, the dog appeared to figure out what direction the scent was coming from. He took off toward the crest of the hill in a direct line.

Sarah's anxiety level went into overdrive. "Hurry, we're gonna lose him," Sarah yelled to Dave. She turned around just in time to see Gunner head over the top of the hill and disappear from sight.

CHAPTER 24

Sarah

Sarah was in a panic. The dog had solved the direction in which the scent was coming from and now was on a mission to get to the source of the scent.

Breathing heavy, Sarah and Dave sprinted after where they had last seen Gunner. It was tough terrain, straight up a steep, wet incline. The loamy soil was deep and slippery. Finally busting through the trees, Sarah let branches whip back. They caught Dave in the face as he followed close behind.

Winded after barely making it to the top, Sarah shouted, "Wait." Dave stopped in his tracks. They had completely lost sight of Gunner. The dog must have taken off swiftly in the direction of the scent source. He could really move quickly when he wanted to. It had been much easier for Gunner to make the ascent and continue moving toward his target.

Sarah couldn't hear the dog's bell; she wasn't sure which direction he had gone. They stood still for a long moment and listened. *There it is!* She heard Gunner's ring tone. Instant relief. She pointed off to the northeast, but before they could move, the bell stopped again.

Another wave of panic set in. She remembered who they were searching for and immediately feared for her dog. Sarah saw Dave unclip the top of his leather gun holster. *Does he know more than he's letting on?* Sarah wondered. Their eyes met, still holding their stance, listening and waiting. Suddenly a dog could be heard barking in the distance.

"Gunner! It's Gunner!" Sarah choked out. "He's found someone! That direction," Sarah pointed as she took off running.

Dave followed close behind. They could barely make out the sound of a dog barking furiously in the distance. Sarah was confident he had made a find—a human find. But she couldn't know who, at least not yet.

She was frantic. She wanted to get to Gunner as quickly as possible. Sarah silently feared for her dog. Images from years past crept into her mind again as she thought of the missing asshole and his capabilities.

Holding her breath as she ran, her head became dizzy. *Stop it! This is craziness.* Mentally, she tried to regroup. She didn't want Dave to see her unwind. *Breathe deep. The dogs need you in a solid mental and stable condition.* The dogs would be able to tell if she was not at her best. They would question her leadership role in their relationship. Gunner and Sam would feed off her nervous vibes and might not work as well. The dogs depended on her to take control of the situation. They needed her to be confident and be there to reward them if they made a find.

Once they had topped the hill, the woods had given way to a more open forest, dotted with a few large, mature hardwoods. There was very little scrub or underbrush. Several young saplings had taken advantage of the area. The forest floor was covered with rotting leaves from the previous autumn.

Sarah stopped again to listen. She looked around and observed the area for a moment. Remembering the first rule was to keep yourself safe, *Don't rush in,* crossed her mind. *Make sure the area is safe.* She looked around in a full 360 degrees and listened. She didn't see anything suspicious or signs of would-be danger. She could only hear Gunner as he continued to bark. His voice was becoming rougher and raspy. It sounded like he was putting everything he had into his indication.

Dave and Sarah took off in the direction of Gunner's barks. As they closed the distance between themselves and the dog, Sarah could just see Gunner's bright orange vest through the shorter and sparser trees. She could partially make out a barking and bouncing German Shepherd as he pounced off his front feet with every bark.

The dog was on the other side of a very large, downed tree. The old hardwood partly blocked their view of Gunner.

Sarah could make out the dog's head and top of his back, but she couldn't see who or what was the subject of Gunner's indication. Whoever or whatever it was, was lying on the other side of the tree as well.

As Sarah and Dave closed in, Sam headed across the top of the hill from the main trail. He ran parallel to the crest following a hot track. His nose was down to the ground tracking whoever lay on the other side of the downed tree where Gunner was parked.

Kellee, out of breath, had slowed down to a jog trying to keep up with Sam. Sam was moving too fast. He made it to the downed tree, circled it and came running toward Sarah. He took a flying leap at her torso and bounced off her chest. Making eye contact with Sarah, Sam took off back to the tree. Gunner's attention and indication never faltered as Sam came back and circled once more.

Jumping up on Sarah was Sam's indication that he had found someone. Instead of barking and staying with the subject as Gunner did, Sam did a recall, re-find as his indication to make sure Sarah was paying attention to him. He was telling his handler, "Follow me."

Both indications were natural behaviors that the dogs presented while in training. Sarah just brought the behaviors out more in-depth, and rewarded Sam and Gunner when they offered them naturally. She had allowed the dogs to use their own "strong points" and cemented them until they were proven and reliable. Gunner unsurprisingly was a barker and Sam loved to jump, so inherently, the actions worked well.

Within seconds, all three of the searchers were closing in on the dogs and the downed tree. As Sarah approached, she verbally rewarded them. "Good boys! What a great job!" She was caught up in the moment. *The dogs had made a find! They worked so well!*

Then reality hit. A real subject was involved. *Check yourself, Sarah,* she told herself. *Calm down.*

She saw construction-type boots sticking out from the end of the tree. It appeared one leg was pulled back slightly while the other leg was flat against the ground.

"Hello, hey? Search and Rescue. Can we help?" Sarah yelled.

"Dwight, Dwight Harrison? Hello? Dwight?" Dave called out the subject's name in his booming voice a few times.

Sarah shouted again, "Hello. Search and Rescue."

They called out a few more times without a reply.

"Police," Dave called out half a dozen times without a response.

Kellee pulled her GPS out to allow time for it to adjust to the surroundings.

Each searcher tentatively moved forward to make sure the area was completely safe.

Gunner glanced at Sarah as she approached. He turned back to the subject and continued his indication. His barks were becoming whiny, stressed. The dog was still excited, but also starting to fatigue. He kept his indication up knowing that his reward was coming soon. That motivated the dog even more.

Sam and Gunner whipped their tails with vigorous excitement. Covered in mud with burrs stuck in his coat, Gunner had drool and spittle around his snout and down the front of his chest. Sam appeared to still be well-groomed aside from his chest where he had laid down in a mud puddle to cool off. Sarah watched as they continued to bark and jump at her with eagerness.

"Good job, guys!" Sarah continued with verbal praises. Regrouping, she spoke calmly and with confidence to the dogs. The subject hadn't responded and didn't appear to be conscious. She needed to make sure the dogs didn't disturb him. Or his body.

As the searchers got closer to the subject, they could tell the man was face up, lying on his back. There was a faint yet unmistakable smell. A mass of flies swarmed the body. The soil was darkened around him, leaves wet with a dark sticky substance. It didn't appear to be from the recent rains.

Sarah's eyes widened. The wind shifted and sharply wafted her way. A clearly identifiable smell hit her. Her nose scrunched, assaulted by the stench. She instinctively covered her mouth and nose with her forearm and shirt sleeve.

The subject didn't look right. In fact, he looked really messed up. She turned her head sideways as if to change the setting. His skin had grayed, almost waxy and thick. A look of terror stood frozen upon his face. The mouth hung agape with eyes fixed, staring straight up at the sky.

Sarah was glued in place, fascinated. She had subconsciously grabbed both dogs by the collars. She stood staring fixedly at the subject. The dark, sticky substance seemed to be everywhere. Her eyes took in the scene, but her brain had a difficult time understanding and processing exactly what she was looking at.

"Sarah? Sarah?" Dave called a few times. "You okay?"

Finally, Sarah took a few steps back. After a couple deep breaths, she tried to clear her head. *Bad idea.* Coughing, gagging, she glanced over at Dave and Kellee.

"Oh my god," Kellee whispered faintly, "unbelievable." Kellee closed her eyes, shaking her head as she looked away.

Sarah needed to reward the dogs. They had done their job and done it well. But Sarah found it hard to move, to take her eyes from the body. She was mesmerized.

"Not at all what I was expecting to find when we started out a few hours ago," Dave stated as he surveyed the body.

"I don't think any of us were expecting to make a find like this," Kellee seconded.

"Should we check for a pulse?" Sarah asked. Dave and Kellee both just gave her a blank stare then smiled.

"Uh, doubt seriously this man has a pulse, Sarah," Dave shot back with a laugh. "He looks like he's seen better days."

Kellee finished noting the GPS coordinates. Tree cover had made it difficult for satellite reception and it had taken several minutes for the location to update. She pulled out her notebook and jotted down several bits of information like the time, their location and the find. She noted everything she could think of.

"Make sure you hold onto the dogs okay, Sarah? We need to keep this area as undisturbed as possible," Dave said.

"Sure thing," she responded automatically, continuing to stand in place holding onto the dogs. Dave's words weren't registering. She wasn't connecting the dots.

"Maybe you should take them out to the trail to play with them so they don't disrupt the ground around the body any more than they already have."

"Okay," Sarah said. "In a minute." Her feet felt cemented in the ground. She was in awe.

It had taken time for Sarah to realize what had transpired. She had been completely caught up in the moment of her dogs' find. All of the relevant details hadn't registered at first. Her brain wasn't processing. It had been several years since she had seen her foster brother. But she recognized him. He appeared to have aged quite a bit.

She looked the area over again and observed the body closer. *Oh my!* It finally clicked.

CHAPTER 25

Sarah

Holy crap! Thoughts ran wild through Sarah's head. It had taken her a moment to process everything. The scene was in disarray in her mind. *Could the subject have committed suicide?* Something didn't look right. The sight wasn't adding up. *But search management had reported him as being despondent.* Then it finally hit her. *This dude's been taken out!*

She began to sort out each detail, slowly scanning the body and her surroundings again. From his facial expression, or what was left of it, it was clear he wasn't expecting to meet this unfortunate end. His neck appeared slit. It was laid open, slashed from ear to ear.

The open laceration around his neck was surrounded by fly activity. His arms extended outward from both sides. It seemed he had tried to grasp at the ground, leaves and dirt still partially clenched in his hands. Pants and briefs were below his waist and past his knees. His heavy leather belt with a large brass buckle lay to the side. A long silver chain full of keys poked out from underneath him.

The body was dark, bruised around his loin area, but what really caught her attention, was that it looked like his penis and testicles had been severed. At least what she could see of the area due to the swarm of flies there. *Oh my god, what the hell happened here?*

She couldn't take her eyes off of the body. Flies buzzed about, landing on the searchers, irritating the dogs. They were everywhere. The shiny, metallic pests with wings hovered above the man's body in small erratic frenzied clouds. There were several of the insects around his head and face. Some were throughout his eyes, nose and mouth. Sarah was fascinated by their activity.

The searchers moved closer to the body. The wind continued to change and whip in different directions on top of the hill. It sucked the smell in one direction away from them but a moment later the pungent scent was pushed into their faces again. It hit them hard. Bile rose up in the back of Sarah's throat. She took a physical step back still clinging to Gunner and Sam's collars.

"I need to move away from this," Kellee stated, "we've done our job here."

Sarah looked up at Dave who was already on his cell phone, not the radio. She could overhear him speaking with search management. He looked at Sarah as he spoke and put his hand up. Sarah stayed in place as Dave discussed the scene with someone in base camp.

"I'm sure, I'm sure. No, there is no possible way he did this to himself. No, I'm not mistaken." Sarah watched Dave as he continued to survey the surroundings. "Yes, yes, it's the subject of the search." Dave was beginning to sound annoyed. He slowly spun in a full circle. It was evident he had switched from search-and-rescue mode to officer-in-charge mode. His stance and the tone of his voice made it clear he was now the one in control. Sarah had no problems with that. She was happy to defer this mess to someone else.

Kellee came up behind Sarah and offered to help leash the dogs. Sarah handed her Sam and his leash while she snapped Gunner's to his flat collar. Both dogs were quiet, but staring at Sarah, wondering when they were going to get their toys and play session. Sarah knew what they wanted—what they were waiting for with their intense looks. But she needed to wait for Dave to give further instructions. This was a crime scene. They may have already disturbed evidence and she wanted to keep that to a minimum.

"So?" Sarah asked as she watched Dave pocket his cell phone.

Dave directed his attention to Kellee. “I need you and Sarah and the dogs to head out to the main trail and wait there. Do you think you can find the way you and Sam entered and try to follow that trail back out?”

Kellee looked over her shoulder in the direction they had come. “I won’t be able to follow our path out exactly, but will do my best.”

“Do you need help with anything?” Sarah directed the question at Dave.

“I’ll need more flagging tape. Think I’ll need all of your rolls if you don’t mind. I need to cordon off the area,” Dave explained, waving his arms and pointing his fingers, “and secure this whole area.”

Kellee fished her one roll out of her pants pocket and tossed it to Dave. Sarah pulled the roll out of her pocket as well. She located another roll in her backpack and chucked them both at Dave’s feet. “Do you think that will be enough?” she asked in a serious tone.

Dave gathered up the rolls. “Think so. Regardless, it will have to do.” He stuffed two rolls in his pocket and started to tie the end of the other one to a tree. “Try not to disturb much on your way out to the main trail. I’d appreciate it if you could draw your map and write up any notes or comments you have about our search sector and what you saw.”

“Will do,” Kellee replied.

“Okay, we’ll be careful. You okay with us rewarding the dogs once we make it out to the trail?” Sarah asked. Due to the nature of what was discovered, she didn’t want to appear brash. But she also needed confirmation that he didn’t think they would be disturbing anything by rewarding the dogs out on the trail. Sam and Gunner were energetic, boisterous during a good play session and would end up moving dirt around and dislodging patches of plants. Sometimes they brought a little bit of earth back with them when they would fetch a ball or Frisbee.

“Oh no, that’ll work. You make sure the dogs get a great reward. They did an awesome job. The mule driver should be able to drive all the way up the main trail to pick you guys up. It may be a while though; the lieutenant will have to wait on the crime scene technicians and the ME to show up. They will be coming by way of the mule as well. Can you check Bella when you get back to camp? Make sure she has water and is okay? I'm sure she'll be wondering where I am. I'd really appreciate it." Dave looked around again at what he was facing. "Who knows how long this will keep me," he said in an exasperated tone. Clearly, it wasn't what any of the searchers had planned on.

"Okay, not a problem. I'd be happy to check on her when we get back to base camp. In the meantime, while we're waiting up here for the mule driver, we'll take care of rewarding the dogs and do our maps," Sarah responded. She had gained her full composure finally. This was the first time she had come across a dead subject so far into the decomposition process. *Dave must think I'm some kind of an idiot,* she berated herself. *Check for a pulse?* Smiling, she laughed at herself.

"What's so funny?" Kellee asked.

The more Sarah thought about the situation, the more she couldn't contain her laughter. "Oh, I dunno. Maybe that statement I made about checking for a pulse when it was so obvious the man was dead?"

Kellee laughed as well. "What gave it away? The cloud of blow flies or the smell of rotting flesh?" she asked smiling at Sarah.

Sarah held Gunner's leash near his collar to keep him close to her body. She turned around to follow Kellee and Sam out to the main trail. Kellee moved slow and deliberate, carefully placing each step as she made her way. The women remained observant in case they saw anything that could turn out to be a clue. Neither spoke as they concentrated on getting themselves and the dogs out to where they could relax.

They had more than 100 meters to traverse between where the body lay and their endpoint. Sarah was thankful the dogs were cooperating. They walked quietly like two well-behaved gentlemen. Sam and Gunner seemed to be able to read the situation well.

As they neared where the edge of trail met the woods, Kellee found the hole in the wall of scrub and brush she had cut through earlier to follow Sam. She turned around to point at it, showing Sarah where they could crawl through the sticker bushes to get through to the trail.

"Boy, it's thick through here," Sarah stated, referring to the vines and plants that blocked the forested area from the main trail.

"I think just enough sunlight comes through where the trail was forged that the sticker bushes and undergrowth get a chance to grow up along the trees here. The overgrowth chokes out a lot of the mature trees and eventually causes them to die."

"Not to mention, it's a pain in the ass to get through." Sarah held onto both dogs as Kellee went through the cut out area first. Once Kellee was on the other side, she called to the dogs. Sarah let both dogs through one at a time.

Finally it was Sarah's turn. She started to step through the debris trying to be careful. She let out a few choice words when her backpack caught on some thorns, making it more difficult for her to get all the way through. More thorns and stickers poked through her long-sleeve shirt and tore at her skin. Pulling as hard as she could, the sticker bushes gave way and Sarah gracelessly came crashing down into the dirt, tripping over the rest of the vines. Kellee couldn't help herself. She laughed so hard that Gunner and Sam backed away thinking there was something wrong with her.

"It's okay, guys. We know she takes delight in seeing her teammates make a fool out of themselves." Sarah stood up and tried to brush as much of the mud and debris off her pants, shirt and pack. Teammates reveled in seeing a member do something stupid. "Thankfully she forgot to pull her camera out," Sarah continued to speak to the dogs. "Payback is hell, just remember that!" Sarah stated with a twisted smile.

CHAPTER 26

Sarah

Once Sarah and Kellee made it to the trail, they were able to give Gunner and Sam an intense play session—their reward for working so hard and for making a find. It's what the dogs lived to do. Sarah was glad they had a little time on their hands. It allowed them to have a moment to get silly and whoop it up with the dogs. They threw the Kong for Gunner until his tongue was dragging the ground. He kept insisting on just one more throw. Sarah had to command him to lie down. Sam finally tired of his own accord and lay down in a cool spot with his soft Frisbee between his front legs.

Kellee squirted a little water into each dog's mouth. She needed to wait until they cooled down before allowing them free choice water. Each woman chose a dog and checked them over from nose to tail. They removed their vests to allow for better air circulation to help cool the dogs down quicker. Gunner and Sam had used up most of their energy reserves. The dogs lay quietly, allowing the women to inspect them without a fuss.

Gunner was even quiet as they cleaned the small cut on his paw for the second time and re-wrapped it. It was barely visible which could mean the wound was a puncture—keeping it clean would be a priority. Once home, Sarah could soak the area and leave the bandage off while Gunner was in the house to let it air out in sanitary conditions. She was thankful that was his only battle wound from the day.

Both women drank, sipping from their water containers slowly. Finding a semi-dry spot near trees to lean against, they sat down and pulled out their maps, notepads and pens. They wore serious expressions as their maps were drawn and notes were made. Sarah hesitated for a moment as she studied her work. She wanted to include every detail she could think of. This wasn't like making notes for a "normal" search. This search had concluded with a dead body—and that dead body had turned out to be someone she had feared most in her life, for almost all of it. It was someone she had known. *Someone I wish I'd never known.*

"Do you think I should inform search management that I... know, I mean, *knew*... the subject?" Sarah posed the question to Kellee as they continued with their paperwork. "Could this complicate matters somehow?" *So far, these last few days have been full of nothing but stress and conflict. What else could possibly happen to make it even more interesting?*

Kellee pondered the question for a moment before she spoke. "Does Dave know that you knew the victim?"

"No, I never said anything. I was concentrating on holding my shit together."

"I'm not sure it really matters, Sarah. It's not like you had seen him in years or he was somehow part of your life now."

"I would rather not. They'll want to know everything and I just don't think I can go there again. Pretty much left that chunk of my history behind me—or as much as I could."

"Well, I wouldn't offer the information up then. If they ask you, then be honest. If they don't, then don't say anything, even to Dave. I would just leave it alone."

"Sounds fair." Sarah turned her attention back to her paperwork. "So how is your map coming along? What are you putting down as the time we located the subject?"

"I have 1420 hours."

"Great, thanks."

"Make sure you put down on your notes that Trooper Dave Graves took over the scene so we have information regarding chain of command. It will be important since this looks like a homicide. Eventually, it will make it to court and we will be summoned. You might even have to do a demonstration with the dogs and produce your training records. So make sure everything is up to date."

The women finished up with their notes and drawings of their recollection through maps and how they traveled. Every so often Sarah looked through the hole in the scrub they had cut, toward where the body and Dave were. She could detect his movement and see his neon green vest reflect through the trees. She hated to leave him alone with the dead man, but knew he had to stay until he could turn the scene over to another authority. *He's a big boy, a cop, he should be fine.*

A whining engine could be heard in the distance. *The mule must be loaded down. How many people were necessary to take care of the crime scene?* Sarah and Kellee leashed up both dogs. Sarah put the dogs' toys in the backpack and finished cleaning up their supplies from the ground. Kellee had one small piece of flagging tape stuck in her pants pocket. She pulled it out and tied it to the area where both women had come through the wall of brush.

"At least they'll know where we traveled. They may have something larger and sharper to open up the brush," Kellee stated. "Or they can head down the trail a bit further and find a better place to enter the woods. I had to follow Sam and this is where he squeezed through."

The mule was closing in. It continued to whine and groan, growing louder as it climbed toward them. Sarah and Kellee waited, standing on the trail at the crest of the hill holding onto the dogs. Gunner and Sam stood rigid like sentries, as if on alert. The dogs closed their mouths, stuck their snouts to the sky and started to sniff deep at the air as the ATV approached. Both Sam and Gunner looked back at Sarah behind them then turned their attention to the approaching mule.

"It's okay, guys. They're with us." She spoke in a low voice. "Always checking things out," Sarah observed smiling at the dogs. *They always had her back. At least someone did.*

The mule rose up over the crest and into view. It was completely loaded down with passengers. Arriving at the top of the hill where the canines and their handlers were standing, the driver abruptly stopped the vehicle. The dogs eagerly pulled Sarah and Kellee closer to the people haphazardly departing the mule. "They always want to get their 'sniff' on," Sarah offered to no one in particular.

Two crime scene investigators from the state capitol's lab jumped from the back of mule. They looked too young and immature for this type of job, like they had just graduated high school. Carrying two camera bags, leather messenger bags and large tool boxes, the CSIs had a lot of gear to tote. They wore field lab coats made of canvas material. Several pockets sewn in the lab coats offered up spacious areas to carry more equipment.

The ME who had shown up to yesterday's water search was the same one who came today. She would want to make sure the CSIs captured as much evidence as possible. Her job would be to oversee the whole operation from evidence gathering to removal of the body. The CSIs' feet had barely hit the ground when she was already on their ass about what they needed to accomplish.

"You guys doing okay? How're the dogs? We should put you two on roster!" Lieutenant Langenberg had ridden along as well. She should be here, at the scene of the body. She's the one in charge. Her body language exhibited tense excitement. She could barely contain her aroused energy. She seemed to live for this type of action. "What're we looking at here?" she asked, wanting details on what direction and how far it was to the area. She had a difficult time standing in one place.

"The dogs are doing fine and so are we," Kellee answered.

"See the flagged area over where the wall of scrub brush is growing up from the forest floor along the trees?" Kellee pointed to the small strip of tape. "That's where I followed one of the dogs originally. I had to cut the brush to get through. Trooper Graves and the body are directly east of the trail. About 100 meters."

"Is it all scrub brush? How difficult is it to reach the body?" the lieutenant asked.

"It's not bad at all once you get past this area. The brush is only about fifteen feet deep, then it opens up to less dense forest.

If you don't want to fight your way through the brush, head up the trail about 50 meters and I think the woods open up more. It might make it easier to traverse over to where Dave is."

The last person to exit the mule, a well-dressed gentleman sporting a tailored suit, silk tie, and wearing expensive leather dress shoes appeared miffed. He looked out of place. *Didn't he know where he was going? Not exactly dressed for a hike in the damp woods. Why does he look so familiar?* Sarah thought to herself. She knew she had seen him someplace before.

The smart-garbed man looked at the ground before stepping onto the soggy laden soil. His expression gave away his unhappiness at having to ruin a good pair of Italian leather shoes. His disdain was apparent.

"It was my understanding that I was to only view the scene and would be driven directly to it," the gentleman could barely contain his contempt for the situation.

Sarah looked at Kellee, whose eyes had locked with the gentleman. Kellee's face turned ashen. All of a sudden, Sarah remembered where she knew him from and memories started to fall into place. *Oh my god, that's him! I'm so stupid!*

CHAPTER 27

Sarah

It all came back to her like a freight train. Like a freight train bearing down a long straight hill. With the brakes out. Realizing her mouth was open and she was staring, Sarah swallowed hard and looked away. At first, she remembered him from an investigation into her foster home when she was a teenager. She had been somewhere around 15 years of age. He had been the final straw why Sarah had given up on the system... and trusting adults... and "authority."

But then she realized he also had a history with Kellee. Sarah had never pulled it all together until now. His title had been Detective Durham at the time he came out to Sarah's foster home but now he was the state's attorney, Prosecutor Durham.

He and Kellee shared a turbulent tragedy from the past. They had been married for several years. Most of those were spent focused on Bill's career while Kellee maintained their little family and household. His ego helped build his profession, but it frayed their marital bond. And when the couple faced a major heartbreak, it proved to be disastrous. Instead of strengthening their connection, they grew further apart.

Years prior, several young children had gone missing over a period of years from Sarah's foster care home. Enough kids to finally send up a red flag. *Like one wasn't enough!*

Authorities were notified to check out the foster home and parents. The disappearance of children should warrant an investigation. Detective Durham had been assigned the case. He was to look into the complaints and see what was involved. If he found evidence of wrong-doing or if it justified a deeper probe, he would decide.

He had interviewed all the children who were currently staying in the foster home under the care of Tom and Judy Brickner. All of the children were fearful; they only answered in yes or no replies. Except Sarah. She was defiant, always holding out hope that one day her life would be better. She carried a reason within her for wanting a better life. When it was her turn to be questioned, she dropped heavy hints of what was really going on in the foster home. She tried to tell Detective Durham those kids didn't run away, there were other things going on. Sarah had never heard the term "human trafficking," or how its use might have helped her cause. She also didn't know what the detective was going through in his own personal life, but he seemed uninterested, preoccupied.

The foster parents had told authorities that the older children had run away. The teenagers all had juvenile records and a history of running. Their answer regarding what happened to the younger children who disappeared over the years was that their parents had come for unsupervised visits and stolen them back.

It all made sense to the detective. And at the time, he really didn't care about those kids. They were throwaways, unwanted children to begin with. Many parents of foster children were in prison or addicted to drugs.

The detective himself was in the middle of his own living nightmare, his own tragedy. His teenaged daughter had gone missing and he was obsessed and consumed with finding her at the time. She had been a wanted child—a dear and precious daughter. Not a worthless juvenile that no one cared about.

Eventually, after several months of her disappearance, Kellee and Bill Durham's daughter's body was found. Lindsey had been sexually assaulted, murdered and left to rot in a lonesome patch of deserted woods. What was left of her decaying body had been uncovered by a farmer and his dog. The farmer had been staking out a place on the back of his property to set up a deer stand in early summer. His dog had run off to investigate a patch of ferns and wouldn't return to him. When he went to fetch his dog, the farmer discovered what the dog had been so interested in.

Lindsey's murder was never solved, her murderer never found. It tore apart an already stressed relationship. Kellee and Bill grew apart and ultimately their marriage dissolved. Bill Durham was consumed with work, studying law and trying to solve his daughter's case. Kellee was eaten up with the loss, the loneliness of not caring for her only child. Lindsey had been everything to Kellee; her whole life had revolved around her daughter. Lindsey's case was the reason why Kellee had founded the search and rescue canine organization. She never forgot the way her daughter had been located. It projected Kellee into a brand new world and gave purpose back to her life.

Sarah watched from a short distance as Bill and Kellee exchanged awkward courtesies. She had never witnessed Kellee looking so exposed, so out of her comfort zone. Kellee was always so well composed. Nervous, Kellee held Sam who had started to pull toward Sarah. Sarah had kept her distance out of respect for her team member. She wanted to give her space.

A troop consisting of the CSI, ME, Lieutenant Langenberg and Kellee's ex-husband made their way up the trail a short way. They decided it would be easier to forgo climbing through the wall of scrub and vines. They turned off the path and headed into the woods toward the area Dave had cordoned off with flagging tape. Sarah rejoined Kellee, and they watched them stomp away.

"The lieutenant wants us to wait in base camp until she gets back. She wants to question us about our search sector and the find before we leave," Kellee instructed. "Search management needs our paperwork, too. They want to go over our notes and hand-drawn maps. We won't be able to debrief until the lieutenant makes it back to base."

"Okay, guess that's fine. I hope she's not up here forever with the rest of activity."

"The ME and CSIs will be here long into the evening. They already plan on bringing in lighting if that's needed. They have another team of CSIs on standby. I think as soon as the mule driver takes us back to base, he'll be heading back to pick up Bill and the lieutenant. I have a feeling neither one of them will want to stay up here very long."

"I don't live very far from here," Sarah hinted with a smile of innocence. "Maybe I could run home for just a little while." She smiled sheepishly at Kellee. "I really need some good coffee! Not this instant crap that's being served here."

"Oh no, you're not leaving me alone here standing around with nothing to do."

"You guys ready to head back to base?" The mule driver was about to leave for camp. The driver was someone new, an employee from the county emergency services system. Sarah knew him from work. She had seen him on occasion during emergency response meetings. He had been standing by patiently, quiet as the women finished gathering up their packs, dogs and checking behind them.

"Hey there, how're things?" Sarah couldn't remember his name.

"Oh, not bad," he answered. "Base camp went crazy as soon as you made the find. They're not letting anyone leave. Search management is questioning everyone and making sure they have contact information. You never know, lots of times the person who committed the crime comes to help out at searches. It keeps them in the loop. Lets the one responsible look at their accomplishment through the eyes of others."

"Yeah, I guess," Sarah offered up. "Can't believe the monster that did this would be walking among us. But I guess you never..."

"Enough said, Sarah," Kellee interjected. "Remember, this is a crime scene. No discussing with anyone except search management and the authorities."

Sarah quickly shut her mouth. She looked at Kellee with a well-practiced poker face. She held her emotions in check. *Dumbass!* Mad at running her mouth, she silently berated herself. She hated when she did something she considered dumb—or times when she felt she looked stupid in front of someone. This was one of those times.

The driver got out and dropped the tailgate so Sarah could load the dogs and her pack. Gunner, still full of himself, had plenty of energy to jump up into the back of the vehicle. Sam had to have a little more convincing. "Hup, Sammy, Hup!" Sarah said with exaggerated enthusiasm as she tapped the downed tailgate. Sam finally found the energy and jumped up behind Gunner. They both found open spots and lay down, stretching out on their sides and taking up much of the ATV's bed.

"Shotgun" Kellee called out immediately as she claimed the front passenger seat.

Sarah knew she was messing with her. Kellee knew Sarah would ride in the back of the ATV with her dogs. She wouldn't have it any other way. "Thanks, guys." Sarah tried to find room between the dogs' bodies so she could place her pack and sit in the back with them. Once Sarah had everything loaded and got herself situated, the mule driver started the vehicle up, turned it around and headed back to base camp.

Sam was curled up in a corner of the mule's bed with his back leaning against Sarah. Gunner laid his head on his handler's lap. He looked up at her as they bumped down the trail. His tongue hung out of his mouth and his eyes showed the whites around them, giving him the look of a crazed animal. "Such the comedian," she softly laughed at him while she caressed his head and rubbed his underbelly. "Have to always be the center of attention."

Lost in deep thought while they rolled closer to base, she cherished the time with her dogs. They made her feel secure. Most of the time. The last few days though, part of her felt like she was unraveling. Like everything was falling apart or coming unglued. She couldn't figure it out, she didn't understand why. *Maybe I'm so used to having an agenda or schedule or having some control over my life since I left home. Maybe it's finishing school and waiting for news from Quantico. Or maybe I'm just plain tired!*

She wasn't completely mollified. She felt as if she were standing on the edge of an overhang. Like she was standing on the edge waiting to get pushed over. And she had no idea why.

Sarah held onto the side of the mule's bed to keep from sliding around as it climbed up and down a few hills. In her other hand, she held the dogs' leashes in a tight grip, but rested her arm on one of their bodies. Gunner and Sam stayed sprawled out and appeared to sleep on the twenty minute ride.

As soon as the mule got close enough to base, the dogs lifted their heads and stuck their noses up into the air to catch as much scent as they could. Reading the wind, they knew exactly where they were headed and who was already there. It never ceased to amaze Sarah how good their scenting abilities were and how she was able to access them to work for her.

The mule driver pulled up to the command unit and stopped. The dogs stood up in the bed of the vehicle. "Hang on, guys," Sarah commanded in a firm but gentle voice. Gunner and Sam held their stance. They looked up to her eyes and waited for more instructions.

"You guys are tired!" Sarah stated. "They're never this quiet nor listen so well."

"They got to work today and yesterday," Kellee declared. "Couple satisfied dogs, I would bet."

Jumping out of the driver's seat, the young man turned to Sarah. "Let me help you and the dogs out."

Sarah waited until he came around and dropped the tailgate. He reached in and grabbed her pack without asking if she needed help.

"Thank you," Sarah responded. "Appreciate you helping out and coming to pick us up."

Kellee took Sam's leash from Sarah. After getting the dogs' attention, Kellee asked Sam to jump down. Gunner waited for Sarah to disembark. He jumped off the tailgate once she gave the command to do so. Both dogs stood at the end of their leashes observing what was left of the activity from the search. Neither dog showed the same excitement as they had when they'd first arrived. They'd had a busy few days. They had expended a lot of energy on the wilderness search today.

"You guys did a great job today," Sarah praised the dogs. Gunner and Sam tilted their heads toward her and wagged their tails. "Steaks for both of you." *If I have the energy once this is over.* Sarah couldn't wait to get the dogs home, give them a good brushing after they ate and then just relax.

The day wasn't even close to being finished yet, though. Once the lieutenant returned from the scene, everyone would debrief. In the meantime, she would put the dogs up, clean up her gear and put her pack and other equipment away. *And check on Bella.* She was sure Bella would need a bathroom break by now.

Exhausted. She felt like she hadn't slept in days. *Thank god I have the next couple days off so I can recover.* She had two more nights and days off before she had to return to her late-night position with the county. *My paying position. At least tomorrow I can relax. I don't think I could deal with any more drama added to this weekend.*

CHAPTER 28

Sarah

Sarah drove home in the muted evening light. She had spent the entire day and into the evening at the wilderness search. She couldn't believe it was already this late in the day. Famished, she swung by the local pizza shop on Blooming Grove Road. She ordered a sub and fries for her and the dogs. She had promised them steak, but decided to cheat and give them a roast beef sandwich instead. She didn't have the energy to go by the grocery store. *They won't hold it against me.* The closest grocery store was several miles out of her way. *Part of living in the country.* She was completely drained. Too tired to go anywhere out of her way at this point. She knew the only reason she was still awake was due to the hunger pangs that threatened to engulf her from the inside.

Once she picked up the subs, she turned her truck toward home. Thoughts of the search and the debriefing clouded her mind. She mulled over the entire last few days. From the call-outs to the searches, to how they ended. For some reason, she felt anxious. But she couldn't figure out why. There was no reason to. She still found it strange that both search subjects had been from her foster family. *That makes no sense.*

She couldn't help feeling the murders were somehow connected to her and her past. *But how? And more importantly, why?* Her mind raced in an endless loop. *Tired, I'm just tired,* she told herself. "Good night's sleep after we eat will do us all good."

After she fed the dogs and ate her sub, Sarah managed to find the energy to throw her soiled uniform into the washer and pick up her mail from the last few days that was stuffed in her mailbox. She rummaged amongst the few bills and solicitations looking for any word from Quantico. Disappointed that she still hadn't received her appointment letter for her physical and psychological evaluations, she hastily threw the envelopes on the dining room table. *What the hell? I should have heard from them by now!* She felt like she could cry. Her stretched and tired nerves were showing through.

The dogs stepped warily around her, not sure what to make of her bad mood. They lay on the cool hardwood floor looking up at her with their deep soulful brown eyes. Confusion and concern showed through their penetrating stares. They weren't used to Sarah being so moody. The dogs yawned several times—their way of trying to defuse the situation.

"Sorry, guys, I'm just completely exhausted and I can't seem to shut down." Sarah let out a deep sigh and leaned down to the dogs. She slowly petted Sam's long lean sides. Gunner sat up and leaned against her leg and whined. "Okay, okay, boy. I'll pet you as well. Sorry I'm in such a shitty mood."

Sarah stood up and walked to the back door. The dogs followed. She opened the door, the dogs headed out. Leaning against the screen she spoke to them as they headed down the steps. "Go do your business, guys. Hurry up and make it quick." She stood by the backdoor watching and waiting. The dogs were worn out as well and didn't bother to seek out any scents or try to entice her to come out to play. Once their call of nature was taken care of, they headed right back up the steps to their waiting handler.

The dogs were rewarded with a cookie and praise as they entered the house. She felt bad about being in such an awful frame of mind. She knew it made Sam and Gunner tentative and anxious. She gave them a treat because she felt like she owed it to the dogs to show them her bad mood had nothing to do with them. It made her feel guilty.

She ran the slicker brush through their double coats to make sure there wasn't anything hidden in their plush double-coated hair. She made sure they had fresh water after she checked them over from head to toe once more. Now that they were taken care of, it was her turn to shower and get ready for bed.

Pulling a few well-placed pins from her hair, she carefully lifted her thick mop of copper curls off her head. She placed the hairpiece on its stand, making sure the hair hung just right. Her wig was made from human hair and had been costly. Besides her house and truck, it was her only other big expense. It looked authentic. No one from work or the dog team had ever questioned her hair. She felt it was a justified expenditure. She pulled the adhesive tape from her head

Looking in the mirror, she laughed. "What a mess," she mumbled to herself. Her scalp was covered in what looked like fuzzy orange baby sprouts trying their best to be real strands of hair. The skin on her practically bald head was dry and itchy from years of using rubbing alcohol prior to applying her wig cap and hair.

"Lucky you got a pretty face," she spoke to the mirror then turned to step into the shower. She had just about grown to accept her condition, but was still trying to learn how to make the best of it. A condition she had to live with didn't mean anyone else had to accept it. She continued to hold out hope that one day her hair would grow back. *What a pipedream. Get over it, girl!*

It was late by the time Sarah was able to crawl into bed. The dogs took up residence on the floor beside her. Lying on the hardwood was cool and comfortable to them with their thick double coats. They preferred its harder surface to their own dog beds. Sarah wished they would stay in the beds she had positioned near the windows, though. She worried about stepping on them when she exited her bed. She thought the padded beds would be better on their joints as well. They were always up first and out of her way and never seemed stiff.

Sarah closed her eyes. She tried to command her brain to slow down and shut off so she could drift off to sleep. Dreadful thoughts, horrible images from the day continued to replay in her mind. She couldn't get the smell out of her nostrils. Visions of her foster brother lying dead and mangled in the woods haunted her. Bile rose up in the back of her throat and she choked it down. She wondered what kind of monster could do that to another human being.

But then again, he had been a beast to live with. Maybe it was karma.

It appeared he had matured into a piece of shit as an adult as well. He'd always been the monster in the back of her mind, but she had never given him a second thought once she left the foster home. *What else had he been involved in later in life?* Sarah realized she hadn't been the only one abused by him growing up in that home. There were others. *Could someone from the past be seeking vengeance?* Sarah had never stayed in touch with anyone. She had wanted nothing to do with any ties to the system.

Reflections of Kellee and her personal tragedy, Kellee's ex-husband Bill, and Dave spun out of control. Lindsey Durham had been 15 years old when she had gone missing. Sarah had been the same age when it happened. Lindsey's face had been plastered all over the media. So much energy had been invested trying to find Lindsey. Sarah remembered thinking at the time, "Why is she so important? Kids go missing every day from my neighborhood and they don't get any attention."

No one gave a damn about the kids that were dumped in foster care. She didn't know Kellee back then and didn't remember her story until a few months after she had joined the canine search and rescue organization. One of her teammates mentioned it during routine dog training. Sarah still didn't understand the weight Lindsey's search carried until she put it all together today—when she finally realized who Kellee's husband had been. Just the fact that he had been part of a police department would warrant much interest in his daughter's case.

Sarah was having a hard time shutting off her brain and going to sleep. She wondered how Dave made out at the crime scene. How he had dealt with the whole situation. Sarah pondered the thought he might call to check on her, but he never did. Even a text would have been nice. Of course, she could call or text him as well. Not wanting to push the issue, she still wasn't sure where the two of them stood. She thought there could be something more. But she was still leery either way. She valued his friendship and hoped for more in one way, but feared getting close to anyone. She also didn't know how he would perceive her physical shortcomings.

Her heart and mind continued to race. She felt like the room was spinning. Late into the night, completely exhausted, she was finally able to slow her thoughts down enough to fall into a deep and fitful sleep. Her brain conveyed dreams that were dark, torturous memories of the past trying to link themselves to the present. Her nightmares morphed into dramatic scenes of being chased by vicious four-legged devil creatures with fire red eyes. Out of breath, she felt as if she couldn't stop running. Apparitions of scarred and dirty hands grasped for her from shadows cast just inches from her body as she continued to flee. It was as though she were trying to escape not just from something dark and twisted, but from someone evil and demented. They were reaching for her...

Chapter 29

Eva

Eva had viewed her handiwork with captive interest. She had taken time to make sure all the details were perfect. Just the way she had planned. She hadn't rushed any of her efforts. There had been no need. Everything was laid out perfectly. Eva fashioned herself as an artist and this was one of her masterpieces. She commended herself for having patience and staying the course, sticking to an agenda. She was satisfied—like she had filled a void in her life which had been empty.

He never recognized who she was, or if he did, he never let on. It had been dusk when they first met up, darkness falling fast before they entered the woods. Maybe the dimming light cast shadows, or her overall appearance had changed. With short dark hair, her body thin and more fit—she didn't look the same as she did as a teen.

He had been so easy to persuade. *Almost too easy.* She'd thought he would've disputed her in some way. She liked to be considered. A little deliberation. It added challenge, an obstacle that made her use her wits. Show a little leg and tit, they were all the same. She had hoped for at least some sort of discussion after they had smoked weed. All worries went out the window after that.

He had been so easy to lure off the marked trail and deep into the forest. It felt like it was meant to be. Predestined. That she was doing the right thing. He was getting what was due to him, even though his actions in his prior life had not been his choice. It didn't matter to Eva, this poor excuse for a human being had caused great pain to others. He needed to pay. It was the only way for him to be redeemed, Eva justified. It would set him free as well.

Her interactions with him as a teenager were always abusive and violent encounters. She stood in for others who couldn't take the agonizing and harrowing confrontations. Although he didn't orchestrate the abuse, he was actually a tool in the whole situation; it was still his body that carried out most of the mistreatment and cruelty. He never refused or backed down when he was told to conduct the abuse. Somewhere deep inside of him, he enjoyed it. At least to a point. A primal lust lured him to do as he was told. *Or just the fact that he would get his ass taken care of, literally,* she thought, *if he didn't do what he was told.* He really had no choice in the matter; he was a pawn that the foster parents used.

Eva had become a master manipulator, even with him. When they were all still in high school, Eva had told him there was a beautiful young girl in one of her classes who liked him. She told him the girl's name and that she was always asking about him. That she liked guys with a bad-boy attitude and reputation. At first, he didn't pay attention to what Eva told him until she pointed the girl out to him one day.

The young girl was gorgeous, smart, but a bit spoiled, an elitist. She had it all. Well-off parents, an only child. She was given everything. She was the type of person Eva couldn't stand and usually steered clear of. The girl flaunted her good looks and entitlement without a care. It was her normal behavior. Really, she wouldn't have anything to do with the trash from the foster home, but that didn't matter to Eva. It only mattered what Dwight believed.

Eva had managed to get him to listen to her after repeatedly dropping hints. The power of a perfectly dropped word in the right setting at the right time. She didn't push it. The bait had to be prepared just right and used to lure him at just the right moment. He started to ask questions about the girl. He started to think he could actually be normal after how he had been raised within the confines of his dysfunctional foster family home.

Eva laughed internally when he started to chase the bait. She had expertly crafted the situation so he would be made a fool.

What she didn't anticipate was his reaction. Eva never counted on what Dwight would do when the girl rebutted his attempts to interact with her... that he would take it as far as he did.

When the girl unsurprisingly refuted his attempts—called him white trash and asked where he ever got the idea she had the time for someone like him—he became infuriated. Eva was fascinated with his reaction. It fueled her confidence that she had power over others. That she could influence anyone to do what she wanted—whether for pure enjoyment or for her benefit.

The young girl ended up dead in the woods, left behind for the animals and bugs to discover. Her body broken and desecrated. Left in the cold to be discovered by the farmer and his dog several months later. He had crossed over to the red zone. He had to live with something he had done of his own accord. He was truly a monster now.

But the strangest part of all of it, Eva thought, was Sarah was indirectly *and* directly linked to what happened to Lindsey as well. Even though it was Eva's words, and Sarah had no conscious knowledge of what had transpired, she was still forever linked to the events which unfolded and caused Lindsey's brutal death. *Ironic for her to be best buddies with the girl's mother now.* Eva sniggered at how absurd the whole situation had become. *Weird how things work out. No one will ever know, though.* She had kept it a secret from Sarah to protect her. And planned to keep it that way.

Chapter 30

Dave

When Dave finally managed to leave the site, it was well after dark. He was happy to turn the responsibility of the murder scene over to Lieutenant Langenberg when she arrived. Chain of command had to be followed. Never leave the scene unsecured. Someone of authority had to take charge of the area at all times. Of course the medical examiner took complete control of the situation from the lieutenant immediately after that. When the ME shows up, the crime scene always becomes her—and her office personnel's—full responsibility.

Since Lieutenant Langenberg wasn't needed anymore, she and most of her troopers left the area before dusk and returned to base. When Dave finally left, the crime scene investigators and ME were still on scene and would be for several more hours. They had brought extra help from the lab: generators and field lights to illuminate the area. The lieutenant ended up staying at base camp for several hours to debrief searchers and coordinate the movement of personnel back and forth between base and the incident scene. She kept Dave on hand to help out where needed. He reluctantly agreed, but Bella was in the truck and Sarah was on his mind.

Bella had spent almost the entire day and late into the evening in her crate. Dave felt guilty that she had to endure the confines of her crate for such a long stretch of time. *The life of a working canine.* Giving her a quick bathroom break, he refilled her water bowl and threw a couple dog treats into her dog box before lifting her back up into it. He couldn't wait to get her home and let her out to run and stretch, but he had one more stop to make.

Headquarters was on the way home, a place where Bella enjoyed full rights as a trooper, and her freedom. They both needed dinner as well. He was famished. Couple bottles of water and granola bars didn't go very far after he had spent hours hiking through the woods searching just to turn around and spend hours at the scene helping out.

He pondered the known facts regarding the two Codorus murders as he headed out of the darkened park roads. He mulled over all the events surrounding them. There had never been homicides like this in the area. Surely they were looking at a serial killer. *A serial killer? Really?* The sound itself had an air of awe. The FBI would still have to link the cases together to confirm they were related.

It was difficult to believe this type of case in the small town area of Codorus. High profile. It meant more prestigious and weighted agencies such as the FBI would be involved. This case was going to occupy many people and many hours in the near future.

Dave and the rest of the agencies assumed the male organ that was found on the boat had to belong to the second victim. It hadn't been verified or confirmed yet, but it was anybody's bet. They still needed to run DNA to confirm. Even though they had access to a DNA lab, it still took several days to run and then to search the system looking for matches. At best, you could have a two-day turnaround. But since "the agency" —the FBI—was involved, it would push the lab to get results right away.

After leaving the search area on his way to the interstate, Dave swung by the drive-through of a fast food restaurant. Once he picked up food, he headed to headquarters so he could finish filling out his police report. He would pass right by the office on his way home.

Maybe the coroner's report would be in from the drowned victim and the flesh they had found on the boat. *I'd like to get my hands on both of those reports tonight if I can.* Even though the FBI would be taking the reins on these cases now, Dave would be stuck in the middle of the investigation. He would be the lead trooper from start to finish since he was already deep into it between attending both searches and finding the second victim.

Dave pulled into Troop H's large back lot and parked his SUV under a street lamp. Bella started to whine as soon as he pulled into the barracks. She knew where she was. A few squad cars dotted the lot. Aside from those, the area was quiet, deserted from the day shift and administration employees whose vehicles usually filled the entire space during normal business hours.

Dave had papers strewn all across the front seat of his vehicle. "Hang on, girl, just give me a minute to get all my paperwork together."

Bella's whimpers and whine turned into a full-fledged howl. She added volume that was deafening within the confines of the vehicle.

"Okay, okay! Just like every other woman out there, Bella! You have to have your way!" he teased her. *But you know you're worth it to me, whatever you want.*

Dave stuffed all of his paperwork into a backpack as quickly as he could. Making sure he had everything, he exited the SUV and walked around to the rear to open the hatch and drop the tailgate. Dave grabbed her long leather leash, opened the door partway on her dog box and slipped the leash in, snapping it to her flat collar. Opening the dog box all the way, he allowed Bella to jump out on her own. She wasn't used to taking orders or commands like Sam or Gunner, just suggestions. She pretty much ran the relationship.

"There. Is that better, girl?" Dave questioned the dog. She wagged her long slick tail in response and then her nose went to the tarmac. If she could talk, she would've been able to tell you everyone who had gone through the lot within the last few days... and what direction they had gone in.

Dave and Bella crossed to the sidewalk. They passed empty picnic tables and benches. He stopped for a minute to allow the bloodhound to check out a scent she found interesting. He looked up toward the few offices with their lights on. Graying concrete and faded dark glass reflected back. Dave thought the building was ugly. It stood out like a sore thumb now that other businesses had moved next door and built new, modern structures. Updates and renovations were soon forthcoming, but it would still be the same old tired building within.

"Come on, Bella. Let's head upstairs and get some work finished up." They entered the building after Dave swiped his badge and pressed his thumb to the reader.

The duo stepped off the elevator at the third floor. They headed to the far end where several troopers shared a small office space. There were a few other officers milling about on third shift. They loved seeing Bella, and a few bent down to pat her on the head.

"See you have a lovely date for this Friday evening," one of the other troopers harassed him.

"At least she listens well, doesn't cost me much and I can put her in her crate when I get tired of her," Dave spouted back with a smile. "And she thinks I'm the greatest man alive. Make that the greatest human alive."

Dave unhooked Bella, giving her freedom to roam the area unsupervised. She would go visit with the other officers to see if they had any treats first. Then she would take her time sniffing around the rest of the floor for a bit, eventually tire of it and come back and lay down under the desk. She liked to be close to her handler. Dave thought she just didn't want to be left behind or left out. Bella liked to be in the middle of whatever was going on. She was social and liked the limelight.

Dave turned the desk lights on and started up the computer. It took the screen a few minutes to warm up and display the sign-on prompt. He pulled his paperwork from the day out of his backpack and laid it on the desk. Grabbing a steno pad from the shelf above the desk, he flipped through it until he came to a patch of blank pages. He planned to jot down notes, some mental reservations he had and queries regarding the murdered subjects. There were many unanswered questions as per the usual in a murder investigation. It was more than that. Things just didn't add up. Maybe it was gut instinct. Dave felt like the answers were on the tip of his tongue, just out of reach. He needed time to do some investigating and mull over the events.

Entering his employee code and page after page of difficult to remember passwords, Dave gained access to several databases within the state's and the nation's systems. Having a high security clearance allowed him into the FBI's CODIS system where suspects' DNA was recorded. He would work on checking DNA records at another time. He was unsure if their DNA testing had even been completed or entered yet. He moved on to police incident reports he needed to finish. There were other research items he planned to do first. His intention was to start building a file on both subjects from the Codorus Park murders.

There were gnawing suspicions he couldn't push out of his head. The harder he focused on ridding himself of them, the stronger they came back to nag him. They were more than a gut feeling. He knew he shouldn't discount the thoughts. There was something in the back of his mind. Like a faint warning signal that told him to tread lightly and watch his back.

Dave brought up the correct form online and began to fill out his paperwork and official police reports. He wanted to have a clean, fully typed report as well as his handwritten ones to turn in to the other agencies. These typed reports would look more professional and much easier to read than his scribbles. He wanted to make sure everything was done as correctly as possible. Dave had a wariness, almost a foreboding that this case would be big—and possibly be followed nationally. Nothing like this had ever happened in his unpretentious jurisdiction. Serial killings were always a big news topic no matter where they happened. *If in fact these murders are related.* The mutilation of the second body would also add sensationalism to the coverage.

As he continued to work particulars of the most recent discovery from the day, he brought up the Department of Motor Vehicle site. He entered the second victim's name—Dwight

Harrison—and several details popped up on his screen. He was able to view a history of past motor vehicle violations as well as links to other branches of the court system.

There were several pages of information regarding the victim. Dave decided to print it out so he could read it when he wasn't so tired. He could scan through it tomorrow in his SUV while working the day shift in between calls. He accessed the district court systems and found several more pages of court cases, past and present, for the subject and printed them off as well. Dave rubbed his eyes. He checked the time on his phone. It was getting late and he was still scheduled on first shift for a few more days. It was time to finish up and head home. He shoved all the paperwork back in his pack once again.

Bella was snoring on the floor beside him. She twitched and jerked as she dreamed. "No worries hunh, Bella?" he said softly as he watched her. She never shifted, completely oblivious to the rest of the world. "I wish I could relax that easy." He smiled at her. Just watching the dog seemed to take away any anxiety or worries.

Signing off the computer he called to Bella. "Hey, girl. Time to go home." She just lifted her head and looked at him. Her tail lightly beat the old tiled floor. Standing up, Dave enticed her by picking up her leash and pulling a dog treat from his pocket. Bella took her time, shifting over to her other side. She rolled around on her back for a moment and then stood up and slowly walked over to Dave. She was in no hurry. It was all on Bella's clock now.

Dave gave her the treat and a quick scratch behind the ears. He leashed her up, grabbed his backpack and turned off the desk lights. He talked to her as they headed down the hall to the elevator. "So far this weekend has been an exciting one, hunh, Bella? I wonder what tomorrow will bring. Never a dull moment on our beat."

He thought about all the reports he had pulled on both victims. They brought up more questions than answers. The DMV report not only gave recent and current information on a subject, it also gave past history such as all recorded addresses based on driver's license and renewal information. The murdered subject from the woods shared the drowned subject's address—and showed he had been a foster child for most of his life. That piqued his interest. Dave knew Sarah had come from a foster care background. He didn't know the specifics—it was not something she discussed. *She never really discusses anything about her past, or her life in general,* he realized.

The database also showed each person's license picture, enabling the viewer to see a photographic progression. He had decided to enter Sarah's name. It was a gut feeling, more than a hunch.

Dave hadn't actually want to find anything, but got more than he bargained for.

As he and Bella walked to the car, Dave pondered the results from the computer inquiry. It had retrieved information dating back several years. At first he had scanned quickly, but details popped that demanded to be taken in slowly. Obsessively, compulsively, he had devoured the remainder of the data, struggling to make sense of it.

What he saw left him reeling. Dave hoped it could be explained away. He decided to give Sarah the opportunity first to explain everything before he would add anything to his report.

But there better be a damned good reason.

Chapter 31

Sarah

Sarah had slept in. It was much later than the hour she normally rose. Late morning sun streaked across her hardwood floors. Dust danced and shimmered in the tiny bands of light. She woke slowly. Curled up in a fetal position, she faced the wall beside her bed. Rolling over to confront the day, she was surprised to find the dogs across the room from her, sleeping in their dog beds. Not in their normal place on the cool hardwood beside her. *They're not even up bothering me for breakfast. Odd,* she thought.

Sarah groaned in a loud manner and stretched her tight, sore limbs. She felt every step of the previous day's wilderness search in the deep tissue of her muscle. From her shoulders to her calves, all the way down to the soles of her feet, her body was sore.

When Gunner and Sam heard their handler stir, they raised their heads to look in her direction, but never left their position coiled up in their beds. Sam whined and laid his head back down but continued to watch Sarah. Gunner thumped his tail in a slow, steady rhythm as he waited to see what his handler's plans entailed. There was an air of unbalance, distrust that could be felt and seen in the dogs' eyes as they studied Sarah's movements. She looked at them, puzzled. *Maybe they're just tired from all the search work over the past few days. I know I am. Maybe they're a little sore as well.*

"Hey guys, what's up? Finally decided to sleep in your beds for once?" Sarah spoke to the dogs as she sat up. Gunner got up first and made his way to Sarah. Sam followed Gunner's actions. This was his normal MO, as Sam was the more tentative and sensitive animal. Gunner was bolder, forward and blunt; he liked to face his challenges head on.

The dogs seemed to be testing the waters to see what kind of mood Sarah was in this morning. They both stretched a few times and yawned. Sarah could read her dogs and this behavior bothered her. They seemed unsettled, unsure. *We're all tired; maybe I'm just over-analyzing the situation. Overreacting,* she thought.

Sarah stood up. Gunner leaned against her legs and she bent down to pet him. She also reached out to Sam and he came just close enough for her to touch him, allowing her to scratch his neck. This seemed to release the tension in the air, at least a little. The dogs did not lift their heads to her, but kept them low, only turning their eyes up to meet hers. Their tails were low as well, wagging in a slow fashion.

Sarah shoved her feet into her slippers and grabbed her robe. Sam and Gunner jumped up, softly nipping at her nose and then turned to run down the hall in front of her, play biting at each other. "No!" Sarah yelled loud to correct them for their bold move. It was if they were releasing nervous energy. *That was out of character for both of them.*

"Settle, guys," Sarah called as she plodded behind them through the kitchen to the back door. "Wait." The dogs sat in a calm manner and waited for Sarah. Once the door was open, Sarah commanded, "Free," and both dogs took off through the opening and down the steps. They raced to different trees and lifted their legs as they lifted their noses to catch any scents wafting through the yard. *Guys!* Sarah laughed as she rolled her eyes.

She left the kitchen door open to allow the breeze to come through the stale house. Her screen door was old. It showed its age, rotting and in disrepair. The mesh had small holes where it had begun to dry rot and the dogs had banged into it numerous times with their snouts and paws making additional tears and gaps. She looked at the door and knew that she needed to attend to it soon. *Ha! Guess I need to put that on my honey-do list.* Sarah smiled sarcastically at the thought of having a honey-do list when it was really a Sarah-do list.

Turning to the cabinets above the counter, she opened the door to pull her coffee carafe out. "Hunh?" It wasn't where she normally stored it. *That's weird.* She started opening other cabinets until she made the discovery and found the carafe stuffed in her pantry between cereal boxes and pastas. *I really must be tired.* Puzzled, she was lost as to why she would have stored the carafe in her pantry, but brushed it off as being overly tired.

Sarah placed the container on the coffee maker and set about making her stiff and strong brew. She knew she needed something stronger than usual to clear her clouded mind, more than coffee alone. She opened the cabinet above the stove and grabbed a bottle of ibuprofen. Twisting the cap off, she poured two gel caps onto the countertop then put the medicine back on the shelf. Sarah washed the pills down with a glass of water. She thought the medication would help her sore limbs and perhaps her mental focus as well. *Torn in two. Always in conflict,* she thought as she tried to figure out what needed to get done that day. She unconsciously rubbed a small scar behind her left elbow as she stared into space.

The dogs had finished and returned to the back door. They whined and padded back and forth until she opened the screen to let them in. They stood in the kitchen looking at her and continued to whine. *Oh yeah, breakfast!* Sarah wasn't firing on all cylinders this morning. *Geez! Why am I so tired? It's not like I didn't sleep several hours last night and this morning.* She pulled the dogs' bowls from their crates in the dining room and returned to the kitchen to make their breakfast. Once finished she put the bowls back in their crates and the dogs ran in behind their food bowls. Sarah locked them in while they ate. "There you go, guys, enjoy."

With coffee brewing, and the dogs taken care of, she returned to the kitchen to figure out what to make for breakfast. She pulled eggs, bacon and biscuits from the refrigerator and set to work making a hearty breakfast. When her plate was ready, Sarah grabbed an extra-large mug of coffee and sat down at her dining table by the crated dogs.

Gunner and Sam lifted their noses to identify what was on her plate, but continued to be quieter than usual. She fired up her PC so she could check email as she ate. *Oh crap,* she reached into the pocket of her robe to find her phone. She had been up for almost an hour and just realized she hadn't checked messages or texts. *I guess it can wait for now. I'll look for it after I eat. No big deal, I can come first for once.*

After Sarah cleared her plate, washed the dishes and cleaned up the kitchen, she released Gunner and Sam from their crates. They still seemed subdued for unknown reasons. Sarah was a little put off regarding their quiet moods. She still thought they were just tired from two days of back to back search work. "Whatsamatter, guys?" Sarah sat down in the middle of the floor to check the puncture wound on Gunner's paw. It looked clean and he didn't respond as if in pain when she pushed around the small hole in his pad. She started to scratch Gunner's neck and he laid down for her to rub his belly.

Sam inched over so she could pet and love on him as well. He looked at her intently, licking her chin in a slow, thick manner like a mother dog would lick her puppy to reassure him after a life lesson of hard knocks. "Why are you so serious?" Sarah asked the dog. He kept his ears a little lower and turned back as she spoke to him. A submissive gesture some people would think, but Sarah read it as tentative and worried. *I wonder what's on his mind? What I wouldn't give to know what goes on inside their little brains.*

"Okay, time to get something done," Sarah told the dogs as she dragged her tired body from the floor. She had errands to run and bills to pay. Her breakfast, strong coffee and ibuprofen were beginning to kick in and give her a little energy boost. Sarah found her phone where she'd left it, sitting on the table by the front door. The phone was dead, its battery spent. She set it in the charging station for the moment and would check it later. It would be nice to hear from Dave, but the only person she really cared about missing a call from was Kellee.

Kellee knew Sarah wouldn't be available today to train or for any call-outs. Sarah had told her before they left the wilderness search last night that she and the dogs needed a rest day so she would be out of service, or OOS as her team called it, on Saturday so she and the dogs could catch up on some sleep and recoup from back to back stressful searches.

Sarah grabbed clothes from her room and headed to the bathroom to change, brush her teeth and put on her hair. She could feel scrapes and nicks on her arms. She wanted to apply antibiotic cream. She attributed the scratches to the sticker bushes her search team had to trudge through during the search yesterday. She didn't remember seeing those scratches last night when she had taken her shower before bed. But she had been on autopilot and didn't remember much about the previous evening.

The dogs didn't follow. They stayed in the dining area stretched out on the large throw rug under the table. *They must really be tuckered out from the last few days,* she contemplated, trying not to worry about their behavior anymore.

Sarah brushed her teeth then dropped her robe on the floor. She started to examine her skin for splinters, cuts and abrasions. It wouldn't be the first time. Bug bites, bruises, nicks and grazes were the norm when you trained canines in the outdoors or deployed to a wilderness search. Sarah inspected her left upper arm where she had a few small marks from stickers that found their way through her uniform to pierce her skin. She began to check her right arm, bending around in the mirror to check the backs of her shoulders. Then she saw it. Her heart rate picked up and she started to hyperventilate. "No, no, no!" Tears sprung to her eyes.

On the bottom outside of her right forearm, near her elbow, there in small crude capital letters in between several other lines of scars, the word EVA had been cut into her skin. It had been written backwards and when viewed in the mirror, came across correctly. The letters were less than perfect and to someone else, they could've passed as a strange scrape or cut. But Sarah recognized the letters. She recognized the deliberateness of the action, the statement. It was a branding.

She now understood what was going on, but could not accept it. Everything was beginning to fall into place. The tiredness she had been suffering from. The items she'd found around her house that were out of place. And the period of times lately she couldn't account for. She hadn't experienced blackouts since she'd left her foster family. The blackouts that had returned like the ones she experienced years prior. Sarah had left everything behind when she'd walked out of the foster family's house for the last time including her. Eva.

Sarah collapsed to the floor sobbing. Gunner and Sam came to the bathroom door and stood there looking at her, puzzled at first. Now she knew why the dogs had been acting so strange around her that morning.

But she didn't want to admit it. She didn't want to believe what was going on. She didn't know who to turn to or what to do. She dropped to the tiled surface. The dogs came to her side, panting, worried, but empathetic as they tried to relieve their handler of her stress. They stood protective by her. *This will ruin everything I've worked so hard for,* she thought as she lay despondent on the cool bathroom floor.

CHAPTER 32

Dave

Sitting in his patrol car early Sunday morning, Dave was torn between waiting for Sarah to call him back or driving over to her house. He had tried to call her several times without success. His last attempts went directly to voicemail. She had never invited him to her home—or anyone else he knew of for that matter. She was a very private person. He questioned whether he should respect that. *Maybe she's still sleeping,* he pondered. *She's had a couple long, physical days. Or maybe she had enough of me for one weekend. Could she be hiding something?*

The investigative nature in him continued to question information he found which linked Sarah to both of the dead search subjects. *Why didn't she say she knew both victims? Could she somehow be tied to all of this? Could she be in danger?*

Dave had checked with the state lab last evening after he had gotten to the office for updates. They were still waiting for the DNA results to come back. Hopefully they would have results, if not this morning, at least by sometime today. It was possible to get two-day results if they were hustled to the front of the line. He knew the samples had been driven directly to the lab and the FBI was putting the pressure on. But even then, if the DNA results were in, they would still need to be entered into the databases and go through proper protocol.

His cell phone pinged with a text. He pulled it from his pants pocket. It was a notification from his contact at the lab stating the DNA samples were now currently being processed but that's all he knew for the moment. *Perfect.* Now that the agencies believed they had a possible serial killer on the loose and the FBI was getting involved, it gave more leverage to get the results tested and findings as soon as possible. Heavy-handed pressure always got results. His contact promised to text him with the results as soon as they were able.

Still holding his cell phone, Dave decided he couldn't wait and pressed the lab contact's name. It brought up the phone number and connected him directly. There was other information he was after at the moment that his contact could help him with.

"Hey," Dave started, "can you pull up the autopsy reports from the ME's office and see if there is any information from them yet?"

"Sure thing, just give me a minute."

Dave waited patiently as he listened to his contact tap on his keyboard, clicking through the links to get into the requested reports.

"Anything?" Dave asked.

"Okay, here we go. Looks like they have most of the autopsy finished on the first victim—Brickner—the older man who they pulled from the lake. Only toxicology hasn't come back and that might take weeks."

"So what are the findings?"

"Well, hang on a sec. Let me read through a bit."

Dave sat silently on the line, jaw clenched in anticipation. Waiting. Impatiently. He stretched his legs. He changed his position. Mentally pacing while trying to remain seated. He tried to be polite but he was having a difficult time. He wanted answers now.

"Okay," the contact began again, "contusions to the forehead, back of the head and temple. Bruising on the upper torso as well."

"Like he was hit with something?" Dave replied.

"Well, yeah. Either that or he fell and hit his head in the boat. But they didn't find any blood within the boat and it appears that he was hit at least three times. The only blood they found was connected to the extra body part in the plastic baggy—but that didn't belong to him. Comments from the ME say it appears to be contusions from some sort of a wide source."

"Wide source?"

"Yeah, like possibly a paddle from a boat. They're ruling it a homicide. ME's report states 'blunt force trauma,' says he was hit several times in the head with great force." He re-read the information for Dave's benefit. "That he was also alive when he entered the water. Most likely, he was unconscious per the information stated on the report."

"Any word on the second subject?"

"Well, their report is not complete, but they are stating that the organ found on the boat belongs to the second victim—due to several observations including size of incision on subject matching up with size of what was found and more." The lab contact gasped as he read on. "Oh my god!"

"What? What else?"

"The ME is stating that the victim was apparently still alive when his penis and testicles were removed. His throat was cut from ear to ear with what could have been something thin and sharp such as a piece of piano wire. He had apparently finished bleeding out when his organ was cut from his body, dying most likely within seconds of both wounds."

"Ouch," was all Dave could say as he sat in his cruiser and absentmindedly squeezed his legs together. What people did to each other never ceased to amaze him. *The truth is always stranger than fiction.*

"Great, thanks for the update. Any word if the DNA has come back?" Dave continued to push for more details.

His contact was beginning to lose patience. He had given him all the information he had.

"Too early in the morning, like I already told you." He started to sound exasperated on the other end of the line.

"I owe you, appreciate it, but I really need to know this information."

"Well, wait a minute. I'm going to email you what I have so far regarding the ME's reports and then I'll check to see if the DNA info has come in."

"Okay, sounds like a plan." Dave flipped through his paperwork and kept an ear tuned into his police scanner in case he got a call.

"Well this is interesting," the contact started, "seems like whatever results that were found in the DNA lab is labeled confidential and the file is locked. I can't access it at my level of security."

"Hunh, that's strange."

"Well, I can't access them," he repeated. "You'll have to speak with the supervisor in charge of the lab to find out what's going on."

"Awesome, you've been a big help. Appreciate it. Call me if you find out anything new."

"Will do."

Dave hung up. *The drowned subject was definitely murdered,* he contemplated. *Aside from both being connected to the foster home, I wonder how these two are tied in this together? How? Someone had to be on the lake in the early morning hours, before the light of dawn to take him out. But who? And why? Does Sarah have anything to do with this?* He couldn't help but feel as though she was somehow tied to the murders.

Why would the records regarding the DNA be secured? There's more to this case than I'm privileged to, apparently.

Later today, he would be meeting with an agent from the FBI. He wanted to make sure he had all of his reports and information as complete as possible. Turning one of the copied court reports over, he jotted down a few more notes on the back regarding specific aspects he wanted to check into. He hoped he could get ahold of Sarah before he met with the agent, though. Give her the chance to explain herself prior to him turning over all of the material he had found last night. Maybe it would at least help Dave to understand. He wanted Sarah not to be involved in any of this mess... he hoped there was a good explanation.

Dispatch came across his radio. Dave pushed his paperwork across to the passenger seat. "Trooper 17, we have a possible 2502 and 3301. Stand by for location."

"Standing by," Dave replied to dispatch.

"Okay, 17, location in Penn Township, Hanover, 372 Howard Lane."

It took Dave a moment to digest the address. When he connected the information dispatch was reading over the radio, he was dumbfounded, puzzled. "372 Howard Lane? Are you sure?" Dave repeated.

"That's correct," dispatch reported. "Fire under control, body found by firemen. Death is suspicious as well as the fire."

"Copy, on my way, ETA five minutes."

"Ten-four, Trooper 17 in-route to 372 Howard Lane, arrival time 0938."

The location of the fire and possible murder victim was the drowned vic's address. The foster parent's home. The same address the subject of the wilderness search had lived at as a teenager. *Another dead body?* It was also the same address where Sarah had lived as a foster child—which Dave had uncovered in his research last night. Dave was finding it harder and harder to believe the circumstances could be just a coincidence. *Another victim?*

He placed a call to his lieutenant. He needed to fill her in on some of the odd occurrences surrounding the murders... but he left Sarah's name out of it. Something he might have to answer for later. *Something that might cost him quite a bit later.*

Chapter 33

Dave

"Hang on, Bella. Going to be lighting up, running hot," Dave said referring to switching on the SUV's alarms and lights.

Dave heard her change position in her dog box behind him. She knew how to brace herself for the ride. They had only been together for a few months and already had a private language between them. They understood each other. Dave had heeded much of the advice he had gotten from Sarah regarding dogs and dog language.

Dave buckled his seatbelt. Turning his sirens and flashing lights on, he took off out of the parking lot, spitting gravel and dirt from his rear tires. Traffic immediately stopped or pulled to the right to let him by. Bella began to howl. Every time Dave hit the sirens, she would cut loose with a deep, forlorn, heart-wrenching wail. It tickled Dave and made him smile. Normally he would laugh or comment to Bella on her off-key vocal abilities. But today his mind was still trying to take in the circumstances. He had been dispatched to the foster family's address that belonged to the drowned subject, and the wilderness search subject... *and* where Sarah had spent most of her younger years.

Not needing to use the navigational system, Dave was able to pilot his vehicle mostly from memory. Between knowing some of the area and looking at the neighborhood layout on a satellite map last evening, he knew most of the street arrangements. Working on his research last night, he had brought the address up on the computer, giving him an overhead view of the neighborhood and surrounding locality.

The distance between the community where the foster home was located to Sarah's current house was in close proximity to

Codorus State Park and Lake Marburg. *Sarah never mentioned that she had ever lived close to the park when she was younger. Another red flag?* He knew where she lived now was close enough to walk to the lake if you were in good physical shape and really wanted to. *But that doesn't mean anything. Does it?* He contemplated. *She never mentioned this information? Maybe it's just a coincidence.* But he knew better. His intuition was telling him she was entangled with the whole situation, but that was all it was telling him. Somehow Sarah was tied to the people from the foster home in more ways than she led on. *Somehow she's involved.* He just knew it. *But how?*

Whizzing past several Sunday morning church goers, he paid close attention. Many drivers were older and reacted slower to the blaring sirens. They didn't move over as quickly. Other drivers just stopped directly in front of him. "Move, dammit!" Dave shouted to no one in particular as the frustration and confusion continued to play out in his head. He couldn't clear his mind. He was fixated on trying to figure out how Sarah fit into the puzzle.

Paying attention to the main roads and street signs, he made his way across the county toward the address on Howard Lane. He had been back in this area for domestic calls, but it had been quite a while ago. He recalled details from the map regarding exactly how the section was laid out. From a few streets away, he could already see police and fire activity and drove toward it.

Pulling up on a curb a few houses away from the burned house, Dave stopped abruptly. He parked the SUV partway on the street and partway on the cracked sidewalk. He heard the bloodhound scramble in her crate.

"Sorry, Bella," he apologized to the dog.

Lowering the windows he made sure there would be good air flow inside the vehicle. He turned to look back at the dog crate to make sure Bella was okay. Once he was satisfied that all looked right, Dave stepped out of the patrol unit and locked the doors. He stood on the curb for a moment beside his vehicle. The street was jammed with firetruck apparatus and firefighters. With the area teaming with activity and commotion in all directions, it looked like a major cluster. A few officers from the local township PD were on hand to control traffic and the growing crowd of bystanders. Everyone wanted a front row seat so they could gawk at the attraction.

Dave looked around. He knew from prior calls that this wasn't a good neighborhood. Besides the domestic violence calls, the area was known for drugs, petty crimes and shootings. Most of the houses were decrepit and in complete disrepair. He tried to imagine Sarah growing up in a place like this. What she would've had to put up with, what she might've experienced or been exposed to... living here... in these conditions. *Maybe this was why she kept her past close and didn't share. Something she's not proud of, I'm sure. But it wasn't her choice by any means.*

Miscellaneous trash and old newspapers littered the streets. Lawns were non-existent. Bald and patchy spots greeted the front of most of the homes. Some residents parked their vehicles where the grass should've been. Not a care given for appearance or sanitation.

Dave observed the burned-out house. Small whiffs of smoke still emitted from the home. It was obvious the fire had only recently been put out. He walked up to the first firetruck he encountered. It was parked at a 45-degree angle directly in front of the affected house. Firefighters worked to drain, roll-up and replace hoses and other equipment into compartments along the side of the enormous truck. The engine still running, it vibrated the ground and anything around it.

Dave could see the fire chief standing in the front yard of the still smoldering structure. He was in an animated conversation on his cell phone. Spires of white smoke rose where the fire had been most intense. Dave patiently waited for the chief to finish and took in the complete scene as he stood there. The yard was mainly mud around the burned out structure from the fire being doused. The main beams and support walls of the home still stood, but the house was destroyed from the inside out and would most likely be condemned.

"Oh, hey there, Trooper Graves," the fire chief yelled to him as he shoved his phone into a holster. The truck's diesel engine made it difficult to hear over the noise. Dave waved to him to let him know he heard him and headed over to where the chief stood.

"I've been waiting on you guys. We got ourselves a deceased subject in the house here," the fire chief said in his heavy western Pennsylvania English. "She's only medium rare, not crispy. Someone got to her before the smoke and fire. There wasn't much fire in the area of the house where she was found. The fire had just started to spread out in that portion of the home."

Dave just looked at the fire chief with a vacant expression. He didn't appreciate the dark humor. He knew that every agency dealt with death in their individual way, but he found the fire chief's comments to be crude. "I was told your agency believes it's a murder? Can you give me some details surrounding the suspicious fire and the subject you found?"

"Well, the calls started to come in to dispatch about forty-five minutes ago. The next door neighbor was the first to call it in. She didn't know if anyone was home at the time. The woman who lives here doesn't have a car of her own or drive. Her husband left a few days ago with his pickup truck towing his boat really early in the morning and she hadn't seen him since. The neighbor woman's a real nosey one. Ya know the kind. Sometimes good to have around, they notice everything. She said the house was full of dark smoke and it went up in flames real quick like. Usually you will see that with an accelerant. We found a few areas where the floorboards are pretty well burned in a pattern as well." He continued to describe what they found within the house once the firefighters had made entry.

"Was there anything else specifically that was found that might make the fire seem suspicious?"

The fire chief raised his hand to Dave and turned to one of his teams. He spouted off a few instructions to the crew. "Sorry, couple rookies that I need to keep straight. Oh yeah, we also found an empty gas container at the bottom of the back steps. It looks like it was just thrown out the door—like it wasn't set down nowhere near where a gas container would normally be stored."

"Okay." Dave had his notepad out. He was scribbling notes as the fire chief detailed what they had found and what they knew about the scene. It was too hot yet to enter the house while it was still smoldering. He would have to wait a while prior to gaining access. It would have to cool down before he could view the body and look at the questionable findings. So Dave was in no hurry and took his time interviewing the fire chief.

"Well, we get here on scene and make entrance to the house by way of the front door. Flames had burned through the living room and front bedrooms quick. The whole front of the house is pretty well charred, while the back of the house is burned, but still pretty much intact. Another indication that someone used an accelerant thinking they could pour it in just one room and it would take care of the whole house. No, no, doesn't work that way."

"So where was the body found and why do you think it's a homicide?"

"Well, as my firefighters moved through the house checking for anyone who may still be in the there, they found this old woman. She was sitting at the kitchen table. Just sitting there upright leaning back in the chair. Even though it was smoky and difficult to see, when they went to check her pulse, their head lamps shown across her neck. There was no mistaking. Her throat had been slit. Her head was leaning way back over the chair and her throat was wide open. They left her in place since she was already dead."

"You sure?" Dave was alarmed. He tried to swallow but his throat had gone dry. He pulled his phone from his pocket to see if Sarah had called. There were no missed calls on his phone. He took a deep breath. Suddenly, he was very worried about her. *Where was she? Why hasn't she answered my calls or called me back? Maybe I should have someone ride by there.* He was losing his focus.

"Oh, I'm sure. As soon as the smoke cleared and it was safe to go in, I checked the body myself. My guys know what they're looking at. This isn't their first rodeo." The chief had taken slight offense to Dave. "When I was able to go in and look her over, I found more than just the throat wound. She has half a dozen or more areas on her body where she looks like she was stabbed—mostly in the chest area, the left side near the heart to be more 'pecific. Looks like somebody was pretty damn angry with her or had a debt to repay."

Dave was trying to maintain his composure. *Stay professional.* He needed to get in the building and view the body but the house was still too hot. It was too dangerous for him to enter the structure yet. It would have to wait a few hours at least. But he had an idea.

"Can you make sure to run crime scene tape and secure the house and yard as soon as you can? And stay in charge of the body? There's something I need to do." Dave pocketed his notepad and pen after he wrote down the fire chief's name and contact information.

"Oh sure. I have to stay on for a while anyway," the fire chief rolled his eyes sarcastically as he looked around at all of the activity he was already in charge of, "so I can help out in any way you need. Just let me know."

Dave turned and headed back down the street to his SUV and Bella, confident the fire chief would keep the scene under control. He dodged pieces of broken glass, empty beer cans and other miscellaneous discarded items as he made his way back to his vehicle. He noted where the glass shards were. Once he arrived back to his SUV and Bella, he sat down in the front seat and called dispatch to report what had been found.

"I haven't viewed the deceased subject yet. Have to wait at least a few hours for the structure to cool down and the fire chief to deem it safe for entry of outside personnel. Fire appears suspicious, arson, looks like an accelerant was possibly used. Scene is secured."

In response to the information Dave reported, his superiors decided to call in the arson investigator and his accelerant sniffing canine when they became available. Presently, the arson handler and dog were on another call several hours away. It didn't matter, the house was still too hot for the arson dog to sniff around inside, or anyone other than the fire team to enter. Only the firefighters had the appropriate gear to enter the house at the moment.

Dave continued to speak with dispatch. "Can you check to see if the DNA results have been made available yet? I'm sure the FBI has put the pressure on to get those done." Dave thought of trying his lab contact again, but decided better of it. He had bugged him enough earlier. He knew the guy would call or text if he could get his hands on any pertinent information.

"Okay, I'll have someone check and get back to you if we can get the results."

"In the meantime while I'm waiting on the arson handler, I'm going to pull Bella out and check around the house with her. Call me on my phone if you need me."

"Okay, copy." Dispatch finished the radio transmission.

"Hey, sweet pea," Dave spoke to Bella, "we're gonna go check some things out." He spoke to her as he grabbed his canine vest from the back seat and filled the pockets with dog treats. Bella watched Dave through the slats in her dog box. She started to howl when he put on his vest and picked up her leash and long line. She whipped her tail against the metal box with excitement.

Dave walked around to the back of the truck. He pulled the hatch up then dropped the SUV's tailgate. He was greeted by a happy Bella. She loved to go to work. It was more than just getting out with her handler, it was mentally engaging for her to use her nose and work a problem. Something she got rewarded for, it was satisfying to the dog.

Dave was working off a hunch. He and Bella had never trained for a scenario like this, but he'd heard of arson canines working scenes similar to this one. *It couldn't hurt,* he thought as he pulled Bella's vest over her head and secured her badge to the front, foregoing her Kevlar vest this time. Maybe she could pick something up, like a clue or a track.

Once he had Bella together, he allowed her to jump down from the vehicle. He removed the leash from her collar and snapped the long line to the back of her working vest. He stood there for a moment and surveyed the entire scene. The opposite side of the street directly in front of the smoldering house was full of people. There were small groups of bystanders all the way down to the end of the lane where a police vehicle sat with lights flashing, effectively blocking any vehicle traffic. The house itself still had firefighters entering and exiting with hoses. Firetrucks with their diesel engines still humming spewed spent fuel from their exhaust systems. The fire chief had run crime scene tape on both sides of the house.

To Dave, running a bloodhound in a situation like this would be challenging. So many obstacles and distractions to get through between sights, smells and activity. But he believed it was worth a try while he had down time. He hoped he wouldn't get in trouble for running her or compromise the situation for the arson canine in anyway, but he was working off a gut feeling. He believed in his dog and thought they could handle any type of situation together.

"Come on, Bella. Let's see if we can pick up any tracks from this house." Dave headed toward the crime scene with an open mind and optimistic outlook.

CHAPTER 34

Eva

Manipulation. Secrets. Skills Eva had learned early in life. If she didn't like you, beware. If you were on her good side, there were no worries. Sarah had always managed to stay on the right side of Eva, even though Sarah didn't realize it or make an effort to try. The two had met in their early teens when they were in foster care. Sarah needed someone to look out for her and Eva filled that void. Sarah, however, filled a void for Eva which could never be articulated. There was something unique there, inside of Sarah that Eva yearned for but could never have. Sarah had an inner illumination people were drawn to... that some people were envious of. You could see it in Sarah's fluid green eyes.

For a while Eva and Sarah had become inseparable. Sarah had exceptional ways of looking on the positive side of every situation—regardless of her background, life experiences and the abuse she had endured. She always seemed bright from within. There was a light or spark of hope that someday, somehow, their situation would get better. She knew there must be better people out in the world somewhere. Sarah was the only person that Eva couldn't or wouldn't manipulate. But Eva still had secrets she kept from Sarah. It's just that Sarah kept nothing from Eva. Sarah didn't operate like that.

When Sarah had become pregnant, Eva helped her conceal it for as long as she could. Eva would do anything to protect Sarah and the baby. But once the foster parents found out, they kept Sarah out of school until the baby was born. They kept her hidden even though Sarah barely showed. They were able to utilize the cyber learning system—school by computer—so Sarah could be kept behind closed doors until the baby was born. The night the baby girl came into this world, she was swept away by the midwife who had come to deliver it. The child was never registered, never spoken about. It was as if Sarah's baby girl had never existed. Eva knew that Sarah still longed to find out where her daughter was, to find out what had happened to her, knew that she never stopped thinking about her. Sarah's biggest wish was to someday find her daughter. *What a pipe dream! Like you could trace someone who never existed.*

Eva stood staring, mesmerized by the way events were unfolding. Captivated. A satisfied smile spread across her pouty lips. She had been the driving force behind all of the news surrounding the Codorus area. It was like she had control over the lives of more than just the people she immediately encountered. Her actions set in motion repercussions she alone had orchestrated. That was more fascinating to her then the actual event which started it all. She liked to manipulate people around her and watch their reactions. Manipulation was the dynamic energy behind why she existed.

Eva had returned to the Codorus Township area to answer a yell for help. It felt like Sarah had finally needed her again. She liked that feeling. Eva knew this had been her life's mission all along. She hated being neglected for so many years, while Sarah had "more important" people in her life, but was still grateful for the occasion to be with her. To watch over her.

Eva stood among the gathering bystanders as they watched firefighters working as a team to control the blaze. Entranced by the unspoken language, the bond they shared. Like ants working together silently in a world surrounded by disastrous disturbances. They each had a separate job to do as they pulled up in their trucks, jumping off before the engines came to a complete halt and grabbing their gear and equipment. Each individual's job was counted on by another team member. There was balance, camaraderie and focus working toward a single goal.

She watched the onlookers' expressions, observed their reaction to the destruction of the fire. Eva was caught up more by her fascination with the people standing around her than the actual event itself. The way everyone gathered to witness the destruction of the home, a power so immense, it could destroy the house completely. *Annihilate the house and everything with it. Including the memories. Burn them!* She wondered if the people standing around her knew what had gone on inside that house? *If they had, they never did anything about it! They're just as much to blame for allowing what went on in there.* The abuse, the pain and despair that it contained?

The police pushed the crowd back as it grew larger and more active. *Where had everyone come from? There can't be this many people in this neighborhood?* As the spectators were pushed back, they were forced to stand closer and band together tighter. They jockeyed to the front of the throng for a clearer viewing. No one seemed to notice Eva as she stood among them, near the front of the pack. She had blood smeared on her clothes and arms. Her black hair looked askew, haphazardly falling to one side. Her arms hung limp and her left hand was cupped, holding something hidden within.

Tiring, Eva tried to hold her ground at the front. The crowd pushed and swayed as the police officers continued to keep order while the firefighters worked. The blaze had been contained after several units arrived at the scene. It was under control finally, firefighters working to completely extinguish her handiwork.

Eva started to feel trapped. Too close for comfort. Her nerves were raw. Fatigued. She had begun to unravel. It hadn't been easy timing her work to mesh with Sarah's schedule. But she wanted to stay transparent and not bring alarm to Sarah. She didn't want to cause any more emotional damage than what Sarah had already experienced in her life. Eva was just paying back the people who had caused so much hurt both physically and emotionally to her friend. These sick, twisted pathetic excuses for human beings needed to pay for what they had done. But Eva was beginning to collapse under the strain of preserving the charade.

CHAPTER 35

Dave

Dave led Bella up the street past the police cars and a few of the firetrucks. He took care to make sure she didn't inhale diesel fumes by keeping a wide berth as the pair passed the engines. The commotion directly around the house was beginning to slow down. He spoke to the fire chief first to let him know what he was going to attempt to do. The chief had nodded, thinking it was worth a try and led him around back to where the empty gas container was lying. The plastic red container was on its side at the bottom of the steps that led from the kitchen stoop down to a patio and the yard.

"Has anyone touched or handled the container?" Dave inquired.

"No, I told each crew to steer clear of it. Several firefighters have been around here working on the house—so their *tracks* are all over—but no one should have touched the container."

"Okay, perfect. I'm going to run Bella around the house first and then come back to the container."

"Sounds great. Let me know if you need anything else." The fire chief tipped his hard hat and headed back to the front of the house.

Dave took Bella around the yard first, encircling the entire house, taking care to stay as far from the still smoldering building as possible. Dave didn't want to harm Bella in any way or allow her to breathe in smoke which might block her receptors and cause her to lose her scenting ability temporarily. Bella took her time, taking in all the tracks and scents left from the firefighters. She filed each odor in her memory bank and continued to work.

"This way, Bella," Dave guided her around the front of the lot. Turning the corner to the side yard they wound their way to the back once again. Nothing so far had seemed to interest Bella. Even though the scene was starting to calm down, there were still distractions and disturbances. News media had rolled up and were filming the still smoldering house to show on their news program. None of it seemed to bother Bella. Nor was she interested in any of it. She only cared about the scents on the ground and tracking them.

"Okay, girl, let's go check this out." Dave pointed toward the empty gas container and sent Bella in that direction. Bella immediately became interested, spending time at the container and directly around it. Her posture changed. She took her time singling out each scent the area held. Dave stood by, holding onto her long line with a loose grip. He had seen the muscling on her body tighten and her tail become straighter, a sign he understood to mean she had closed in on a scent that she could track.

Bella circled the container and area a few more times, checking, sniffing the patchy grass. The dog locked in on a scent she found interesting on the container's handle, then she checked the tracks again. Her body language changed. She stopped for a moment. Her body stiffened, tail standing in the air. *Bingo!* Dave could tell she had a track she wanted to follow. Bella looked back at him with a quick glance that asked if he was ready. He understood. "Go, girl!" he praised her and Bella took off following a track through the yard.

Bella tracked in a direct line from the backyard of the burned house to the rotted out fence line. She turned right and headed out the side gate leading to the street in front of the house. She worked her way down the street moving from one side of the road to the other. Bella stopped a few times, ran a circle around Dave as she lost the track, wrapping him in her long line. She would circle back, work the area as she cast about sniffing, locate the specific track again and continue to move forward.

"Good job, Bella," Dave continued to feed her praise. He had no idea what she might find or who she was tracking. He was curious to see where she would lead him. He hoped it wouldn't be a waste of time. He would think of any reason he could to bring Bella out of the truck and search with her. Dave was addicted to working with his canine partner.

As she moved down the street toward the crowd, Dave subconsciously unsnapped the cover of his holster exposing the butt end of his SIG handgun. Something he always did when he encountered the public in an event like this, especially in a high crime area. First rule of thumb was to "protect number one," protect yourself. He'd be no good to anyone if something happened to him.

Bella headed toward a sea of legs. She approached the crowd and lifted her head. Then she went back to sniffing the asphalt and sidewalk where the bystanders stood watching. Closing in on the crowd, most of them backed away, giving Bella a wide berth. The dog continued to work tracks and sniff at whatever shoes were closest, trying to discern the scent she tracked.

Several people had crossed over the path, destroying the integrity and contaminating it with other tracks. *Patience. I need to be patient and let her work this out.* Dave remembered their training sessions. Patience was one of the hardest lessons when learning to work with a dog. They go at their own pace, not yours.

Bella was excited and pulled on her line. So many scents to discern. But she found the original track again, the one she had started to follow from the beginning, from where the gas container lay. It was overrun by other footprints and she had to focus. She put all her energies into staying with the one scent. Bella slowed her forward movement to only a few inches at a time.

The people in the crowd continued to move away as the dog worked closer to them. Most were weary of big dogs, and the people in this neighborhood were equally weary of the police. They had no problem moving away from an officer and his canine. Some even worried the dog might bite, that all police canines were aggressive. Ignorant public assumed all dogs bite. Just because all dogs have the capacity to bite, doesn't mean they do.

As she continued to work within the crowd, the people moved back even further. Slowly, more bystanders peeled away. They wanted nothing to do with the dog or the trooper tethered to the other end. Bella was a large animal and most people were somewhat fearful. Others were genuinely respectful of a police canine and the possibility of what damage they could inflict. Even though Bella was a bloodhound and not a German Shepherd or Belgian Malinois, some folks still thought dogs could do terrible physical damage to a person.

Bella locked in tighter to the scent she had been following. She headed toward a young woman who never parted with the rest of the crowd. The woman didn't notice the trooper and Bella as they worked closer to her. The woman looked like she was entranced, still gazing at the house which had been on fire.

Bella almost knocked the lady over as she approached and sat down in front of her. Bella looked back at Dave who was still holding the end of her line, then looked up at the woman's face. The line was about thirty feet long. Dave looked from Bella to the woman. Dave had relaxed his grip on Bella's long line now that she was sitting—her indication she had found the object of her scent search.

The lady looked familiar, but Dave couldn't place her at first. Disheveled. Dark red stains covered her clothing and skin, resembling dried blood. Her hair sat weirdly askew on her head. *It almost looks crooked?* he thought. She looked dirty and unsettled as well.

As Bella continued to sit beside the woman, she bumped into her, sniffing at her with her large nose. The woman finally looked down. Fear replaced her blank, glazed-over look immediately. She backed up, still staring at Bella. Bella jerked the long line from Dave's relaxed grasp and pulled hard in a swift move to stay with the subject of her track.

The woman's mouth fell open. She started to scream. She raised her hands and arms above her head. One hand held a bloody knife. A second later she made a motion toward the dog with that hand. Dave yelled, "Drop the knife," but it was like she couldn't hear. Next he yelled for Bella, but Bella stayed with the subject.

Fearing for his partner, Dave went into protection mode. The crowd had completely dispersed around the woman and bloodhound. His police training took over. Another officer was in danger. In one practiced move he drew his gun from the holster, took aim and fired before the knife could penetrate Bella's hide. His gun went off, a thunderous explosion even with all the firetrucks and chaos surrounding him.

It was in that moment, lunging toward Bella to make sure she was okay, still staring intently at the disheveled woman that he realized who he and Bella had been tracking. He watched her fall in slow motion, slumping to the ground, in tandem with his heart.

CHAPTER 36

Dave

The woman's dark hair slipped from her scalp, exposing wisps of hair against an otherwise bald pate. Her expression gave way from fearful panic when she'd reacted to the dog, to a glazed look of total shock and puzzlement.

She sank to the concrete sidewalk. To Dave, she now more distinguishably looked like the person he knew. Recognizing the few hairs she had for eyebrows, the splash of freckles across the bridge of her nose. Dave grasped for any clue that it wasn't who he knew it was. His mind was in overdrive. *It can't be her,* he pleaded in agonized silence.

His gaze traveled down her torso, back up along the line of her arm where she had crumbled to the ground, to the back of her bare neck. Then he saw the paw-print tattoos.

Dave's mind reeled with the confirmation.

"Sarah?" he asked, almost to himself. Barely audible, Dave tried again to call her name. He sprinted to her side.

A local police officer who had been directing traffic ran to Dave's side to offer help. Dave barked orders to get the ambulance which was already on-site for the firefighters.

Dave stood mesmerized in the midst of the chaos for a hesitant second. It appeared he needed a moment to process the scene and figure out priorities. Going into automatic, he yelled for the paramedics to get their ass in gear as they pulled the ambulance up to where Sarah lay. Dave dropped to his knees beside her.

Two males jumped from the back of the unit as the vehicle came to an abrupt stop. Dave continued to shout orders to them as they descended upon Sarah.

Bella sat in the middle of the pandemonium. She continued to keep her vigil near her tracked subject and wasn't budging.

"Hey, can you grab my canine and take her back to my SUV?" Dave shouted to a local officer who was standing beside the paramedics keeping the bystanders controlled.

"Sure can," the officer replied as he stepped toward the dog and picked up her long line.

"Come on, pup," the officer called to Bella. He started to walk away with a quick step only to get jerked back as Bella stood her ground.

The officer looked at Dave, unsure how to proceed with a large bloodhound who refused to leave the chaotic scene.

It finally dawned on Dave. He pulled a hotdog from his vest and handed it to the other officer. "Here, give her this and tell her 'all done.' She should follow you then."

"We're losing her!" One of the paramedics stated. "Blood pressure's dropping. We need to get her stabilized before we can move her."

Dave still on his knees, continued to help the paramedics with Sarah as they lifted her onto the litter. The men persisted in their efforts to work on her, keeping her alive.

"I'm afraid we don't have much time. We need to make a decision here." The driver of the ambulance looked at Dave.

"There's no question. Call for life flight now!" Dave shouted. His face reddened, sweat dripped from his brow. His breathing came quicker. He was in shock believing he might lose her. *This might be it.*

Dave stood up and realized Bella was still in her indication position and had only given up enough of her turf so the paramedics could work on Sarah. He looked to the officer who held the end of her line and was answered only by the shrug of the man's shoulders.

"Life flight's on the way. We'll finish packaging her up and ready her for the flight. Do you know the victim's name?" one of the paramedics asked Dave.

Dave looked at him with a blank stare. It took all of his energy to make the words form on his lips. "Her name is Sarah. Sarah Gavin. She's a 911 dispatcher from York County."

"Really? What the hell was she doing here?" the paramedic trailed off, not caring if he received an answer or not.

"Not sure," was all Dave could muster.

The officer holding the end of Bella's line lifted it toward Dave, motioning for him to come get his dog.

Dave took the line and pulled out another hot dog for Bella. "All done, girl," he told her and released her from her pose. Bella swallowed the offering in one quick motion. On her time and decision, she stood to follow after Dave. She didn't play into the noise and commotion that surrounded her. Her temperament allowed her to stay calm and unaffected.

He walked her several feet from where the paramedics continued to ready Sarah. Knowing he'd done everything he could for Sarah and that she was in good hands, he still had a difficult time standing down from the situation. He watched as the paramedics loaded her into the ambulance so they could meet the life flight helicopter a block over in a cleared area. He looked to the sky, already hearing the powerful engines of the STAT Medevac. *Thank god they weren't already out on a call.*

Dave headed back to his SUV with Bella in the lead. It finally dawned on him that the whole incident had been caught on camera. The media had been filming for the evening news when Dave had begun to work Bella. He didn't realize at the time that they had covered him working his canine.

The media shouldn't have even been allowed on scene until the whole area had been investigated. The fire chief, nor firefighters had given out information regarding the body, but the media had their ways of pulling information from events. *I wonder how they got their information? From who? Maybe a bystander caught wind of what was in the house.*

Dave figured the media had to know something more was up with this fire than the norm and had fought their way into the scene. They would try to glean as much information as possible so they could be the first to deliver the delicious details to the public. Bystanders had filmed what they could from their smartphones as well. There were videos and pictures. Dave knew the fire and the shooting had both been well documented.

Dave loaded Bella up. He was on autopilot as he went through the motions of caring for his working partner. He was in disbelief of what had just transpired. He replayed the scene repeatedly in his mind. *What the hell just happened? Why? Will I be able to live with the consequences if she doesn't make it?*

But only Dave knew he'd locked more than his target sight on Sarah.

CHAPTER 37

Sarah

The bullet tore into Sarah's side sending immense pain to every part of her body. Instant shock took charge. She didn't know where she was or what she was doing. *What the hell is going on? Where the hell am I?* Sarah dropped to the ground gasping for air. The scene played out in her head in slow motion as she watched everything around her fade from sight. Her head dropped hard onto the corner of the concrete curb butting up against the sidewalk.

Bella and Dave were above her asking questions she couldn't answer. She couldn't make her lips work. It hurt so bad. She lost control of her motor functions. She thought this was it, that she was dying and didn't understand why or what was going on. Sarah lay on a broken and gray concrete sidewalk that was now covered in blood. A constant high-pitched ring plagued her ears. There were several people standing around her. People she didn't know. *Why does it hurt so bad?*

She reached to her side. Her stomach area and hip were burning. A white hot sensation spread across her abdomen. It felt like the whole world had slowed to a stop. Panic set in. She tilted her unfocused gaze from the bystanders to herself. Looking down, she could tell blood was pumping out of her body. She knew that could only be bad but her brain was having a difficult time processing what had happened. Instinctively Sarah tried to put her hands over her wound, but the blood continued to drain out. She couldn't stop it. She tried to stand, but her legs failed her. God, her head hurt so bad. She was dizzy.

Firefighters and paramedics were over top of her. They pushed the crowd away from where Sarah lay broken and bleeding. She tried to look up to see Dave. He took her hand. She tried to stay with it. He was talking to her, saying something she couldn't understand. Confused and lightheaded, she began to recede and eventually just let go.

Sarah didn't remember much regarding the incident. Waking up briefly in distress when she made it to the hospital, she tried to push herself up but fell back onto the stretcher unconscious. She was weak from the amount of blood loss and the excruciating pain. Everything was a blur. She tried to fight for some kind of control but lost. She thought she had fallen into a dark tunnel spinning out of control. Sarah drifted toward the light... toward the end of the dark tunnel. She let her mind release and shut down. She was in a state of shock. The physical pain had caused too much agony to endure. She let everything go and just floated.

Sarah could hear the medical team conferring, yelling orders across the room, across her body. She still didn't understand what was going on. Doctors and nurses swarmed over her from every direction. She overheard bits and pieces of information but couldn't reply to attempts made by the staff to communicate with her. "She's in shock," was one of the only comprehensible statements.

Occasionally one of the medical team would hover over her, look her in the face as they worked and called her name loudly a few times. But she couldn't connect, couldn't respond. Sarah just stared straight ahead. She could hear them calling her name as if they were far away, distant. Her primal instinct knew that her body was badly broken, but she felt an inner peace at the same time. Even though there had been much pain from her injuries, she was in a calm, tranquil state of mind. A feeling that she'd never experienced before.

"Sarah," a nurse almost yelled into her face. "You're in the hospital. We're here to help you. Stay with us."

It would be easier to just let it all go. Do I even want to come back to this painful existence that is my life?

CHAPTER 38

Dave

It all happened so fast. Faster than Dave wanted to remember. He would eventually have to recount the events later to an investigator. *WTF? How did this happen?* Dave wasn't sure why he hadn't aimed for the head or heart. Maybe it was that she was a woman... or that she was only wielding a knife. Did he subconsciously already know it was Sarah? He had been torn between shooting a victim and protecting his partner, Bella. She was a trooper as well. She wore a badge and warranted the same protection as the rest of the troopers.

Dave couldn't get Sarah's look of surprise out of his head. He kept replaying the scene over and over trying to make sense of it. It was as if Sarah had been possessed. She didn't even seem to know where she was or what she had been doing when he shot her. He felt she had only realized her surroundings when the pain pulled her out of the trance. The way her facial expression changed as she fell, he didn't understand. In that short moment, she had looked like the Sarah he knew. Dave hadn't hesitated to protect Bella. *But at what cost?*

He had stayed behind to fill out police reports and turn the scene over to his lieutenant when she arrived on scene. Dave called Kellee to let her know what had happened. He wanted someone at the hospital either way. If Sarah succumbed to her wound or if she came to, he didn't want her to be alone. Dave knew she had no one else in this world, no family nor close friends outside of work and her canine search and rescue organization.

Kellee assured Dave she would go to the hospital immediately to find out how Sarah was doing. She also volunteered to go by and pick up Gunner and Sam to make sure they were okay. Kellee would take them home with her to care for them.

Dave realized that he would automatically be put on leave until the conflict was resolved. He had discharged his weapon. An investigation would ensue until the conflict was examined and he was cleared. Though Bella was involved and was ultimately the reason behind the gunfire episode, she had no reason to leave the force. She would most likely be assigned to another handler temporarily. That would be harder on Dave than the forced leave of absence. It broke his heart to think he would have to let his girl go away, but he knew it was only short-term. She would be back with him in no time.

Dave tried to put Bella out of his mind and concentrate on only Sarah. *Weird*, he thought. Sarah had shown genuine fear of Bella. He had seen true fear in her eyes. *But why? She has two large German Shepherds. As big as Bella.* He stood beside his vehicle, lost, bewildered. *That makes no sense. I don't understand what's going on with her. God I hope she pulls through. I need answers.*

CHAPTER 39

Dave

When Dave showed up several hours later from the scene, he'd used his status as a Pennsylvania State Trooper to bully his way in to see Sarah. It was a conflict of interest because he had been the one who had shot her. But that didn't matter to him, he couldn't stay away.

Kellee had arrived first and tried to fill Dave in with what little information she had—which wasn't much.

"She's just out of surgery and is stable. Critical, but stable. She will need another surgery to repair her hip. They will keep her in the ICU ward for a few days for observation." Kellee looked into the distance, away from Dave's intense gaze.

When the pair had made it to the hospital where Sarah had been transported, they both tried to sign on as a responsible party for her. At first the hospital administration wouldn't even allow them to visit, due to all of the HIPAA privacy laws in place. Sarah was of age to make her own decisions... but in her current condition, couldn't. The doctors and nurses had to be the ones who took it upon themselves to save her life and take the necessary steps involved. Dave and Kellee could only stand by and hope for the best. Kellee had been left in the waiting room until one of the nurses finally realized no family was coming.

Kellee had dropped everything and driven straight to the hospital when she'd received Dave's call. He could hear the utter despair in Kellee's voice as he'd recounted the morning's events.

He had been fairly new to the state police unit when Kellee's daughter's case—Lindsey's abduction and murder—had made local headlines. He remembered it well. Dave knew that Sarah somehow filled a void for Kellee. Dave also knew they both shared a special bond. He was aware Kellee had been there when Sarah needed mothering. Kellee had needed someone to nurture and care for, too.

Kellee confided in Dave as they stood vigil over Sarah, each taking their short turn to visit as allowed in the ICU unit. "You know I watched her blossom into a beautiful person. Into the person she knew she could always be," Kellee said between dry sobs. "She's worked so hard to get to this point in her life. Her future was so promising." Dave touched Kellee's shoulder to let her know he understood.

"This isn't the end. It can't be," Dave replied.

One of the floor nurses that was assigned to Sarah explained to Dave and Kellee that the doctors had made the decision to put Sarah into a chemically-induced coma. They felt it would be her best option for a fuller recovery. The bullet had torn through one of her kidneys, a major artery and partially through her left pelvic area, damaging her hip where it had stopped and lodged. She had a Grade 3 concussion. She had lost so much blood; she had almost no blood pressure when she'd arrived in emergency. The nurse recounted her team of doctors said that Sarah was one very lucky individual. She had come as close to death as a person could but still make a turnaround and start to recover.

Dave listened intently as the nurse gave out sparse information explaining the seriousness of Sarah's situation.

"A specialized team of nephrology doctors were able to remove the damaged kidney. They had a difficult time getting the other kidney to properly function but eventually they got it to almost its full capacity. Her left hip is very badly damaged. She will be facing a long road of rehab to get back on her feet. It will be touch and go for a few days to see how she responds to the surgeries and medications."

Dave thanked the ICU nurse. He turned to look at Sarah through the walled glass that separated her from the nurses station. *You just need more time to let your body and soul heal.*

Dave could tell that Kellee wanted information on what had happened at the scene. He knew she wanted him to explain, but he wasn't ready to talk to her about it yet. He wanted to talk to Sarah first whenever she woke up. He felt he owed that to her.

Kellee told Dave there had been red flags for a few years, but she had always discounted them because of Sarah's foster upbringing. She had always been a little quirky from that. Occasionally, Kellee would see a side of Sarah emerge that she had no idea where it had come from. It was only every now and again... and it was fleeting. But it was there.

The last time Kellee said she'd seen Sarah's personality quirk was just a few days ago while they had been in the boat. "Sarah's facial expression and response were totally uncalled for. Completely out of character for Sarah." But Kellee had let it go as she normally did. Before that she hadn't witnessed the character change in years, she explained to Dave.

There was a trooper stationed outside of the ICU. Now that Sarah was considered a prime suspect in the killings, the agencies involved were keeping a close eye on any activity that surrounded her. The bureau wanted to question Sarah as soon as her coma was reversed. So far she had only been circumstantially linked to the stabbing of her foster mother and the burning of the house—between the blood on her clothes and knife. There were no eye witnesses.

She had also been circumstantially linked to her foster father and foster brother through several items found in the garage of her home. But again, there were no eye witnesses and the agencies were still trying to link DNA evidence which they had been unsuccessful in so far.

The state would assign a public defender to her. *Likely someone just out of law school or a long time loser who wouldn't give their best to represent her,* crossed Dave's mind. She was going to need someone far more experienced, a lawyer who had something to prove to get a lighter sentence for her. Maybe a new hotshot needing to make a name for themselves. Dave wasn't sure she would stand up as mentally stable either. He had been sure it wasn't Sarah standing there in the crowd. He had been sure it wasn't Sarah whom he shot protecting Bella. Maybe she would be found incompetent to stand trial. Dave knew he would be on trial as well when he would be called as a witness in the case.

Dave had challenged the trooper who was sitting outside of the ICU ward. Sarah was not supposed to be allowed any visitors. The trooper obliged by allowing Dave and Kellee to enter the room, thinking it didn't really matter because she was in a coma. "Probably not going to make it anyway," he grumbled.

She was still listed in critical condition. And if she did survive, no one could predict if she would suffer damage to her brain.

Dave knew that Kellee had a busy schedule and wouldn't be able to stay very long. Once she found out Sarah was still critical, but stable—and would most likely remain that way for a few days—Kellee headed home to take care of her dogs and Sarah's.

Kellee's hands would be full trying to care for several energetic German Shepherds. Other team members would help Kellee over the next several weeks—possibly months. They would make sure Sam and Gunner received everything they needed from daily care to continued search and rescue training. It would help the dogs deal with their handler being missing from their lives.

Dave remained behind. Sarah was a mystery but he was fascinated by her. He felt compelled to stay by her side and take care of her. To stand up and fight on her behalf. He didn't understand it himself, but he felt like she was worth a fight. He felt there was much more to Sarah. She deserved a chance to explain everything that had transpired over the last several days. Maybe he was in love with her. *Love?* He questioned himself.

He wouldn't have anything else to do anyway. He knew the protocol. The agency would most likely put him on paid leave until the shooting investigation was complete. That's how it normally worked when an officer was involved in a shooting.

The FBI had completely taken over the complicated case. Bella would be in the hands of another trooper. He made the decision to stay beside Sarah as long as he was allowed. He wanted to be there when she woke up and to be there to see where her future would go. Maybe where *their* future would go. He was optimistic.

***

Dave headed home sometime in the early morning hours after Sarah's initial surgeries and the first round of questioning from his superior who had found him in the hospital lobby. He still needed to take care of Bella who had been in her dog box the whole time sitting in the hospital parking lot.

Pulling into his driveway, he slid the SUV into park and sat there resting his tired head in his hands. He felt as if a vice was squeezing his heart and his head simultaneously. The officer who had taken his statement while at the hospital informed him that he was automatically suspended and another trooper would be by this morning for Bella. Dave had handed over his service weapon. *In just a few hours I'll be losing her.* Bella remained quiet in her box. *No one had asked Bella what she wanted to do,* Dave thought. But it's *only temporary,* he kept telling himself.

Dave stepped out of the vehicle, swung around to the back, lifted the back window and dropped the tailgate. "Hey there, girl." Bella's long tail started to thump against the side of her crate. He opened the dog box allowing Bella to jump out onto the driveway.

"Come on, sweetie," Dave called to her as he headed across the yard to the front door. Bella followed, stopping briefly to relieve herself and then followed him into the house. "Well Bella, not sure how to tell you this, but Carl will be here shortly to pick you up." Dave continued with his one-sided conversation. "It's only for a little while."

He found a duffle bag and began to pack up a few of Bella's items. Bella didn't seem that concerned. She made her rounds through the house, quenched her thirst and lay down stretching out by the sliding glass door that led to the back yard. The floor was cool and refreshing for the dog.

Once finished packing up her toys, dog bed, blankets and food, Dave sat down on the floor beside his dog and leaned up against the wall. “This is all temporary, this situation is only temporary,” Dave stated out loud more for himself than for the dog. Bella never moved her head but looked up at him with her deep, soulful brown eyes and slapped her tail against the floor. She seemed to understand his pain, but she also seemed to be tolerant of the challenges faced in life, accepting whatever came their way.

Dave came to terms with what needed to be done. He sat peacefully there on the floor as he waited for his co-worker to arrive.

Chapter 40

Dave

The following week found Dave slumped over in a chair beside Sarah's hospital bed. He was tired and had fallen into a light sleep, resting his head on the edge of her mattress. The stark empty atmosphere was beginning to weigh on him. He had kept up a personal vigil sitting next to Sarah for several days. He spoke to her, letting her know she wasn't alone and there were people who were concerned about her. He told her he deeply cared for her and would be there for her under any condition.

He had convinced himself the person he saw the day of the fire hadn't been Sarah—not the Sarah he and everyone else knew and cared about. Dave decided he would stand by her no matter what direction her path lay. Unsure of her future, possibly his as well, Dave knew that he more than just cared for Sarah. It was deeper than that. *I think I love her.* Could he really be in love with her? He knew he needed to be close to her, wanted to be at her side when she awoke from the coma.

He had thought long and hard about Sarah and her situation. About what she had possibly done, but he knew that wasn't her. He knew deep down it was someone else who carried out the horrendous acts she would eventually be put on trial for.

But he was hopeful as well. He had thought about her past. Between her background—what she had endured in the foster home over many years and overcome—she might just have a case.

Kellee stopped in almost every day to check on Sarah. They went over any new changes in her condition. Dave felt like Kellee was coming in to check on him as well. She brought him snacks and gave him daily updates on how Sam and Gunner were doing.

She had her hands full now that they were staying with her and Meika. It made for a full house... and a house full of dog hair.

Over the past week, Sarah had shown improvement. The medical team had upgraded her to serious from critical after the third day. By day five, her condition was still serious, but stable. Her remaining kidney was functioning at a normal rate. The doctors took her off the *thiopental* pump. Now it was a waiting game to see if and when Sarah would emerge from her deep slumber.

The MRI's computerized results showed she had suffered a wicked concussion when she fell to the concrete sidewalk. She had several bleeds on her brain but they were healing. The EEG showed her brain activity to be functioning and normal.

But it would take time as she emerged from her coma to know for sure how much, if any, permanent damage she may have suffered mentally or physically. It would still be a wait-and-see game.

"Sarah, we're here for you. I know you're in there. You just need to wake up now." Dave stayed by her side speaking to her, giving her encouragement. Time would tell whether the new Sarah would be anything like the old Sarah. *But hopefully not the Sarah I saw the day of the fire.*

CHAPTER 41

Dave

Locally, news of the murders and the shooting spread like wildfire through the small community. Dave switched through the local stations. It was non-stop coverage. The national stations had picked it up as well. Nancy Grace, a popular crime show host and analyst had even picked up parts of the coverage. The story was dragged out for everything it was worth—and then some.

Southcentral Pennsylvania's residents weren't used to being in the spotlight, especially for a serial killing. Normally, York County's small townships and boroughs were quiet, laid back. Its residents kept to themselves. Everyone stuck to their groups or small cliques. They felt safe, secure in their tight-knit neighborhood and surrounding communities. That band of closeness tightened further as they tried to weather the adverse attention. Friends and neighbors, family members checked on each other more often.

Agents from the FBI had descended upon the townships that encompassed Codorus State Park and Sarah's home. Their territory included the lake, the forest within the state park, Sarah's home and work place, as well as the foster care parents' burned out home. Once the agents combed over all three crime scenes, they split into teams. One covered Sarah's house, another began collecting information about the foster care home, while a third gathered autopsy reports, records and background information on the murdered subjects and scenes.

Dave had been brought back to help work the case. He had been found within his active duty rights and cleared of any wrong doing regarding the protection of his canine partner. Lieutenant

Langenberg brought him back in on administrative duty though, instead of active field duty. He still wasn't allowed to carry a gun. It was mandatory since the shooting was tied to other murder investigations.

She wanted his help on the case. Dave was all for it. It would keep him in the loop, privy to any information gathered on the cases. *It could also jeopardize my job*, he thought. Working a case where Sarah was the main suspect—once his relationship to her became known—would no doubt compromise his position. He decided not to let on just how close he was to Sarah. The lieutenant knew they spoke but thought it was purely professional.

Dave sat at his desk at headquarters. He had pulled the most up-to-date reports he could find in the system. Information on the murder victims had been processed in the labs and posted. Evidence from the crime scenes was limited, but technicians were able to find clues that helped tell the story of the subjects' demise. Each murder appeared to be targeted and well planned.

A major break was discovered by the head ranger. When Ranger Owen learned the drowned subject had head and torso injuries prior to entering the water, he took it upon himself to check out the kayak rack which stood along the opposite shoreline of Lake Marburg. Under close scrutiny of the secured equipment, he found a paddle that wasn't locked in place.

It looked like someone had pried it out from behind the cables but whenever the perpetrator replaced it in the rack, it was returned to its slot without trying to get it back underneath the cable. He alerted the FBI. Under closer scrutiny by the lab, they found DNA from the drowned victim along the wide end of the paddle. They were also able to pull partial palm prints from its handle. The paddle fit the injury patterns on the drowned victim's head and torso.

Other, more pressing information was found when they tested the victim's DNA. Information that would shed light on an older murder mystery. A cold case that had caused years of torment since it had gone unsolved.

Dave had been made aware of the details by the lieutenant. She informed him he would be needed that afternoon for a board meeting—and to be prepared. When their discoveries were revealed to him, he could only pretend to understand how his acquaintances would react. Although the information would bring closure, it was sure to open up old sufferings as well.

* * *

Bill and Kellee Durham were called to Pennsylvania State Police Headquarters in Harrisburg for a special meeting. They were to meet at the top floor where several conference rooms were situated. Neither was sure what was going, but both believed it had something to do with the "Codorus Killings," as the media had dubbed them.

"Hi, Dave. Didn't expect to see you today," Kellee stated as she and Bill were buzzed through the secure north entrance. Dave was standing just inside the corridor. Lt. Langenberg had instructed him to wait and accompany them to the meeting. Dave knew Kellee expected him to still be on administrative leave. She probably thought he would be at the hospital with Sarah.

"Do you have any idea what this is all about?" Bill questioned Kellee as they made their way into the elevator on the first floor. Bill looked at Dave, eyeing him for an answer as well. Overly polite to one another, the air between the two was stiff, awkward as Kellee and Bill tried to make small talk. Dave watched them exchange words almost as a courtesy to each other while the elevator rose.

"Not completely," Kellee responded, "but I'm sure it has something to do with the three murders. After all, I'm tied to finding the first two bodies, and also to Sarah. Between circumstantial evidence from the start and now DNA, Sarah is tied to each murder." Kellee turned and watched the numbers light up as they climbed each floor. "Not exactly sure why you were called, other than you're the state's attorney and you did view the subject found in the forest." In just over a whisper as the elevator doors opened, Kellee commented, "And you're tied to me. Dave?"

"The lieutenant has some information to disclose to both of you." Dave put their questions off. They would have answers soon enough.

As the trio reached their destination and the elevator doors slid open, Lieutenant Langenberg was there, standing on the landing waiting for them.

"Good morning, Kellee. Nice to see you again, Bill." The lieutenant shook both of their hands.

"Ditto, always good to see you as well," Kellee replied.

"Nice to see you, lieutenant," Bill bowed his head and smiled.

"The agency has some news to share with both of you. We chose to do this privately before we made the matter public. It will only be a short time before it's somehow leaked and I'd prefer to brief you before we give a press conference," the lieutenant explained.

Kellee and Bill looked at each other in mild alarm. Bill raised his shoulders in puzzled response. Each must have realized the other had no idea why they had been called to headquarters. Dave watched as the pair looked at each other for some recognition of why they had been called there, to this meeting. He wished he could've somehow let Kellee know since they had developed a closer bond, but the lieutenant had made it clear to him not to disclose any information prior to the meeting

"Follow me," the lieutenant instructed and turned on her heel. She headed down the hall past walls lined with images of Pennsylvania State Troopers who had fallen in the line of duty. The overhead fluorescent lighting cast unflattering shadows on the plaques and figures. It gave an ominous feeling to the faces of the dead staring from within their decorated and framed commemorations.

"Jesus Christ!" the lieutenant mumbled as they passed a darkened window looking out onto the east side of the parking lot.

Dave angled himself to catch a glimpse out the window. That entrance was straight off the main highway which ran by headquarters, and two local media stations' trucks were pulling into the lot. The lieutenant cursed as cameramen jumped out as soon as the vans pulled to a stop.

"Somewhere between here," the lieutenant pointed to the floor of headquarters, "and there," she turned her finger to the media outside, "we have a leak. Something we'll have to look into ASAP. This has happened too many times over the last several weeks for it to be a coincidence."

"When was the information supposed to be made public?" Dave asked softly so only she could hear.

"Not until after this meeting. I wanted to make sure the Durhams had it first," she nodded to Dave and Kellee. "Someone must have already leaked the information out there. This is unbelievable." She shook her head in disgust.

"In here," the lieutenant pointed. Stopping in front of two large doors, she pulled one of them open and secured it with her foot. She motioned Kellee and Bill toward the large conference table where several people were already seated.

"Good morning, Mr. Durham, Mrs. Durham." An attendee that knew Bill from the lab greeted them. There were a few others present from his past as well that he had worked with on court cases. Dave knew most everyone seated, he also knew that Kellee most likely wasn't familiar with anyone there.

Dave and the lieutenant followed them in. "Go ahead and have a seat. We only have a few minutes to go over this information and then we have to prep for the press conference. Word has gotten out."

Once Kellee and Bill took their seats, they went around the table and proper introductions were made. The lieutenant pulled out a ragged file from her briefcase.

Bill's eyes lit up, his jaw clenched down tightly. *Apparently he recognizes his daughter's case number,* Dave thought as he continued to watch Bill's body language for a reaction to the file in front of him. *Why shouldn't he? I'm sure it will forever be burned into his memory.*

"Why do you have that?" Bill asked. "What does this have to do with our daughter?"

"Well, we have some very important information regarding your daughter Lindsey's case." The lieutenant sat back in her chair. She looked up from the large manila file on the table and eyed Bill and Kellee. "There has been a dramatic new development in the information surrounding Lindsey's murder. I tried my best to get you both in here as quick as I could to break it to you before it became public knowledge. But with so many eyes and ears around this place, apparently it was hard to keep it under a lid."

"What news?" Kellee spoke up, her voice soft and light. She sounded like her heart was in her throat.

Dave felt empathy for the couple. He sat beside them. He watched Kellee flinch at the sound of her deceased daughter's name. He knew it never got any easier to deal with the pain of a lost loved one, especially one lost to such a senseless act.

"Pretty big news. We still have some tests to re-run, but we believe we have solved Lindsey's murder."

"*What?*" Bill jumped up, face contorted, visibly excited and upset at the same time. Even though the murder had happened nine years ago, it was evident to everyone in the room the parents' pain was still fresh. Sitting within reach of their hearts, they still bore it on a daily basis.

The state worker Bill had known from the lab stood up to offer him support. "So sorry, Bill," the lab worker said as he looked down at the conference room table. No one knew exactly how to support a parent who had lost a child, especially a child who was violated and brutally murdered. The air became heavy. Dave could feel the tension mounting in the small conference room.

Bill nodded his head toward the man and sat down hard in his chair. "I'm sorry, this has just caught me off guard."

"No problem," the lieutenant continued without showing emotion. "Originally, when Lindsey's body was found, the ME was able to take semen samples from the body and clothing. They were good samples and were preserved well. The DNA from those samples were entered into the system at the time but never produced a match." The lieutenant maintained her staunch, professional posture and tone. "Until now."

She drew in a breath, "Over the last five years, we have updated our system and entered several older records from many databases into the FBI's CODIS system, including the information we obtained from Lindsey's killer." The lieutenant paused for a moment allowing Kellee and Bill to digest what she was trying to say.

Bill will understand the terminology and technical jargon, but will Kellee? Dave also knew that Bill had been taken off several cases when Lindsey was murdered. Rumor had it, Bill's judgment and focus became clouded and he couldn't deal with it.

"Moving on. The murders from last weekend... we were able to get both victims' DNA information within a few days and enter it into CODIS. The FBI found the match almost immediately, but withheld the information from us for a few days until they decided how to proceed."

"What information?" Kellee was growing impatient. "Are they somehow related to Lindsey's killer?"

"Yes." Silence followed for a moment. "The DNA from Dwight Harrison, the subject you helped find that was mutilated in the forest is a 99.9% match to the DNA found on Lindsey." Kellee let out a gasp as Bill turned to look at her. The lieutenant paused. Dave watched as she regarded Bill and Kellee's reactions. "We ran it twice and had two different lab technicians check it."

Tears slowly slid down Kellee's face and she began to weep softly. She hid her face in her hands. Bill's eyes glistened with tears. He stood up, then bent down and embraced Kellee. She leaned into him and started to cry harder. Everyone in the room was moved with the heavy emotional outpouring.

"You're sure?" Bill asked the lieutenant as well as the technicians who sat around the table. They nodded in response.

"Harrison would have been eighteen. He was still in school, a senior at the time of the murder." Dave pushed a file toward Bill as he spoke. "Their paths could have crossed on a daily basis with the middle school and high school on the same campus, and some shared common classrooms. Harrison has a record a mile long that started when he was in seventh grade, but nothing serious enough to warrant collecting his DNA to keep on record. Domestic abuse, spousal abuse from the last few years that he was never indicted for is the heaviest record in his arrest history. The agency could never get the wife to press charges against him... so there was never a court case."

The lieutenant slid another file across the table to where Bill stood beside his ex-wife. It was Harrison's juvie file. On the front was a picture of Dwight Harrison as a teenager. Bill stared at the photo for a long moment before opening the folder. He flipped through copies of a few police reports, countless court documents and other records from the subject.

The information within was plain to see that he had been a leech on life, someone not worth the time of day, Dave thought as he watched Bill leaf through the file he had put together.

"I know this is moving fast, but we would want both of you to stay on for the press conference."

"But we just found out. We've got nothing prepared as far as a statement regarding the information or how we're feeling about all of this," Bill retorted.

"That's fine. We don't want either one of you making a statement at this time. We just want you standing beside the Major as he breaks the news. Do you think you two can handle that?"

Bill looked down at Kellee. She was trying to wipe away the mascara that had run from under her eyes. She nodded.

"Are you sure?" he asked.

Kellee sat taller in her seat and replied, "I want to stay."

"Yes, we will both stay and support the announcement." Bill took Kellee's hand in his and stood guard beside her as the small gathering broke apart, headed in different directions to ready for the press conference.

Dave wondered how Kellee would handle hearing the details again as they were read to the public. A nagging thought crossed his mind, a thought he hoped would prove irrelevant. *Had Sarah known about this?*

CHAPTER 42

Sarah

Over the course of several days, Sarah began to ease out of her chemically-induced coma. Tubes and wires ran in every direction feeding her medications, keeping track of her vitals, hydrating her. The IV attached to her hand restricted some of her movement. Her left side and leg were throbbing with discomfort. She felt like she was trying to claw her way out of a coffin deep in the ground. Her breath was short, restricted. It burned if she tried to breathe too deep. It felt like her side was being pierced with a branding iron. Her throat was scorched and dry.

The brightness from the fluorescent bulbs stung her eyes when she tried to open them. She remained disoriented and confused about her situation. But there was one thing that was clear to her—she didn't feel like she was in conflict with herself anymore. Her mental anxieties seemed to have vanished.

She covered her eyes with her free hand, opening them only slightly as she tried to adjust to the light. Sarah felt almost at peace except for the pain. At first she couldn't figure out what was different, but it was the feeling of solitude, reconciliation. She was no longer in contradiction with herself. It was a surreal moment when she realized what was different within her mind. Eva was gone. She had perished in whatever trauma Sarah endured.

"Hey, there." Dave shifted in the hospital recliner when he saw Sarah move. The heavy plastic covering protested under his weight as he changed position.

Sarah could hear Dave by her side. With her eyes still partially closed, she tried to turn her head in his direction. She winced. The movement sent shards of pain throughout her body.

"Don't move. I'm right here." Dave laid his hand softly on her exposed arm. Visible scars stood out like measures on a staff. The reason she always wore long-sleeve shirts. Normally Sarah flinched when anyone touched her, but she didn't this time.

Sarah squinted as she opened her eyes to barely a slit. She tried to focus on her room and then Dave. Panic crossed her face. "Gunner? Sam?" she tried to choke out.

"They're both okay. Kellee has them." He watched her calm down.

"Water?" she whispered.

"Sure, I think. Let me see if I can scrounge some up."

Dave left to tell the nurses that Sarah was awake and coherent and to find her some water. Sarah looked around her surroundings. She figured out where she was. The event which led her here was like a dream. She remembered bits and pieces but wasn't sure what was real and what wasn't. She had no idea of the time lapse.

She looked down at all the wires leading to her body and back to machines which stood beside her and hooked into the wall. Her left leg was held rigid, in some sort of traction device. She leaned slightly forward and touched the bandaging on her stomach area. It stretched from the front of her abdomen and wrapped around to her lower back. A violent tremor shot through her head and caused her to forcibly close her eyes again and lay back.

Dave returned with a styrofoam cup filled with ice chips and water. A bendable straw sprouted from the enclosed top. A nurse was hot on his heels as he came through the door. She observed Sarah's vital signs on the monitor, took her blood pressure, looked at her dressings and checked the position of her leg.

"All looks good here," the nurse stated.

Dave offered the water to Sarah slowly, bringing it to her lips. Sarah took a few sips and swallowed hard. It brought instant relief to her parched throat, but took all of her energy to perform the basic task. She pushed the cup away.

"How are you?" the nurse asked Sarah.

"Hunh? Not sure yet, tired," Sarah replied.

"Do you know where you are?"

"I think, I think so. A hos-hospital?" Sarah stumbled with the words.

"Yes, yes you are. Do you know why you are here?"

"Something happened to me? Something bad?"

"Yes, you were shot. The bullet penetrated your abdomen and shattered your left pelvic bone. You lost a kidney. Try and rest for now. But I'll summon the doctor on call. He'll be able to explain it all to you when you're ready."

"I was shot? How?" Sarah became alarmed. Her breathing quickened. She was still trying to understand her situation.

"You need to relax for now. The agents will want to question you as soon as possible. I won't be able to hold them off very long."

"Agents? I don't understand." Sarah opened her eyes a little wider allowing a bit more light in. "I don't know what's going on." The rate on the heart monitor shot up.

"Calm down. Someone will be in to explain it to you more in depth. Try and rest for now." The nurse left it at that. Sarah could hear the woman in the hall having a hushed conversation with a few others standing near her doorway. She knew it concerned her and whatever had transpired that put her in the hospital.

"Dave?" Sarah turned and looked toward where he was standing. She needed answers. "I need to know what's going on! Why am I here? Nothing's making sense."

She could hear him let out a deep breath. He sounded exasperated, almost defeated.

"Sarah, this puts me in a compromising position. I want you to know everything that is going on, and I want to help you also. I can get in some very deep trouble for filling you in on everything that has transpired. But I am also here for you. Do you understand that?"

Sarah tried to follow him with her eyes as he paced back and forth beside her bed as he spoke. It made her head spin, she closed her eyes again for a moment to steady herself.

Reopening her eyes, she tried once again to focus on Dave's movements. "I need answers. I'm so confused? I'm not really understanding what is happening? My head hurts so bad!" Sarah emitted her plea, she sounded hurt and perplexed.

Dave stopped and stood beside Sarah with his hands jammed deep into his front jeans pockets. He looked at her then glanced down at the floor.

Sarah's eyes tracked him. "What is it?" She had a feeling Dave needed to tell her something significant as she studied his body language.

"I have to tell you what happened, how you ended up here... why you ended up here," he said as he scanned the room.

"I'm here, Dave. I'm listening," Sarah said in a raspy whisper.

"It was me who shot you, Sarah," Dave stated with direct intention. He made it clear what had transpired.

"What? Why?" She was trying to register what Dave was telling her. *What could I have possibly done that caused such a thing?*

"This isn't easy for me, Sarah."

Sarah tried to be patient as Dave worked to find the right words.

"We were in a situation. You raised a knife at Bella. But it really wasn't you, it was somehow someone else. You were wearing a black wig..." Dave trailed off. It had brought up the issue of Sarah and her alopecia.

Sarah raised her hand to her head. She felt for her semi-bald head, but she felt more than her normal patchy wisps. Sarah was alarmed that she was so exposed. She could feel a smoothness that wasn't just skin. There was a very short layer of thick padding on her head.

"Yes, your hair is growing in. Look at your arms."

She focused for a moment on her forearms. There was bright red, almost orange hair peeking through her sparsely freckled skin. A smile crossed her face.

Dave smiled back.

"Okay, getting back to why you're here. We don't have much time before the doctors show up, and possibly the agents." Dave hesitated for a short moment. "I didn't know it was you at first. You were standing in a crowd. Bella tracked up to you from a recently burned home. She scared you."

"Scared? Me?" Sarah's expression showed bafflement. Her pinched brows raised questionably. "What do you mean I was scared? Frightened of Bella? Are you sure?"

"Like I said, it wasn't you."

He continued on. "I know this sounds crazy. But it was like you were someone else. The short, black wig, the way you were dressed, it just didn't make sense. When Bella closed in on you, you raised a knife at her. I thought Bella was in danger and shot you to protect her. I'm sorry, Sarah. I'm really sorry."

"I think I know why, but I'm not sure. My head is so cloudy," Sarah stated. She stared at the graying hospital ceiling and gathered her thoughts. *How can I explain something I don't completely understand myself?*

"What are you talking about, Sarah?"

"I think it was Eva. Someone I met when I was a teenager in foster care. There were black-outs, periods of time I couldn't account for. Especially during darker times at the hands of the foster family. Sometimes others would call me Eva after these black-outs and I didn't understand."

"Like another personality?" Dave asked. A look of confusion crossed his face.

"I'm not sure. I never understood what was going on," Sarah answered. She was trying to understand it all as well. She was so foggy headed.

"You're circumstantially linked to the Codorus murders, Sarah. I need to tell you this. You need to know what is going to happen. What the protocol will be."

"How?"

"You are their prime suspect. They may have more than circumstantial evidence. There's DNA that might link you to each crime scene. You need to be prepared when the bureau agents come to question you."

"None of this makes sense."

"I know how it sounds. But you need to tell them everything. If you don't remember, if there was anything strange going on with you, they need to know."

"I thought I was losing my mind. Things around the house were misplaced. Gunner and Sam acted weird sometimes... they were wary of me. Like they were waiting to see what mood I would be in each time I woke up. I was having periods of time that I couldn't account for."

"The agents are going to push you for as much information as they can. You're going to need a good lawyer, Sarah. A real good lawyer." Dave stood up and looked out the window. The situation looked like it was wearing on him. "But you need to heal first. You need to concentrate on getting well. This is all just a *setback*. I want to be here for you if you'll let me."

"I just don't understand." Sarah's voice wavered. She was near tears. Her throat was burning, making her voice raspy. Closing her eyes, she turned away from Dave. She was tired.

"There's something else I want to ask you, and I hope you don't think I'm prying. I really just want to help you. *Need* to help you, Sarah. There was a piece of paper that had been in your other hand when I got to you at the scene. It was crumpled up. It fell from your hand when it happened, um, ...well, you know..."

Sarah turned her head to face Dave again. It was clear that she needed to rest.

"Hunh? Paper?"

"This piece of paper had the word 'Charlottesville' scribbled on it. Do you know what that would mean? Any idea?"

Sarah became visibly upset. She closed her eyes again and started to cry. Dave leaned down close to Sarah and took her hand. She accepted him into her space, the closeness. She allowed him to console her.

"What is it, Sarah? I need to know so I can help you with this. You don't need to do this alone anymore. I care about you, Sarah, way more than I think you can comprehend right now. You need to let me help you. I need you to let me help you with this."

In a response that was barely a whisper, Sarah mouthed a few words. Words she never thought she would be able to say to anyone. Dave couldn't make out what she had said and leaned down close to her.

"I don't understand what you're saying, Sarah. Tell me again."

"There was a baby." The tears flowed uncontrollably. Between sobs and broken words, Sarah managed to explain to Dave. "She was taken from me right away. I never even got to hold her. They stole her. No one knows about her."

"When did this happen? How long ago? Who?"

"I was fifteen. The people who took the other younger kids from our home." Sarah had regained some of her composure. She reminded herself that she could trust Dave. What else did she have to lose at this point? How much farther to rock bottom could she get? "I don't know much more than the people came from the Blue Ridge area of Virginia. I'm not sure, but I think she was trying to find out where they had taken her. I think she was trying to pinpoint and help me find her. She was trying to find exactly where my child might be and who the people were that took her. And the others..." Sarah trailed off.

"*She* who, Sarah?" Dave asked, caught off guard.

"Eva."

Dave looked at Sarah for a moment, his brow wrinkled in confusion. It took a minute, but then realization crossed his face. "Is she... um..." his voice trailed off, struggling to find just the right words. "Is she *gone* now?"

ACKNOWLEDGMENTS

Eva has been trying to get her and Sarah's story onto paper for over a decade. After a false start a few years ago, I was lucky enough to meet Demi Stevens from Year of the Book. If it hadn't been for her one lone email from York County Library System, that almost made its way to the trash bin without being read, I doubt their story would have ever emerged in print.

Although they are both fictional characters, I have been carrying them around in my head far too long. Thankful beyond words, I am truly lucky to be part of Demi's group, Year of the Book, and her literary world. She has been a dream to work with. Thank you, Demi!

Words cannot express my gratitude to my husband, Matt Hillegas, for pushing me to write and believing that my story was worth telling. Special thanks go to my children, Garrett Hillegas, for designing my cover, and Laura Hillegas, for the encouraging words to continue when writing fodder failed to find me. I am very grateful for my wonderful family.

Special appreciation to my readers who took their personal time to read through my manuscript and give me feedback. Thank you to Pam Caya, Kellee Millheim, Emilia Milheim, Barbara Hillegas, Linda Fitchett, Matt Hillegas, Steph Kratzer, and Linda Murphy.

Special thanks and appreciation goes to Lisa Kakavas from Mason Dixon Rescue Dogs for reading through my initial drafts as well as the final round.

Thank you to the search and rescue canine community that I have been a part of since the early nineties. Much of the background was drawn from training experiences over the years.

If search and rescue piques your interest, or you would just like to know more about what goes into becoming a first responder, please check out the following organization:

Ardainc.org

Trotsar.org

Nasar.org

Coming Soon:

Setback

The Canine Handler, Book II

Sarah Gavin has to let go of her independent nature as she tries to sort out her life. She finds herself on trial for three brutal murders, and must rely on help from an unlikely source... a police officer who cares for her deeply. What will happen with her working partners? Will she lose Gunner and Sam? How will the trial unfold? What will become of Sarah and Dave?

61066357R00159

Made in the USA
Charleston, SC
13 September 2016